Dreamshaper

by

J.W. Crawford

Black Rose Writing

www.blackrosewriting.com

ISBN: 978-0-9819742-8-6

PUBLISHED BY BLACK ROSE WRITING

www.blackrosewriting.com

Printed in the United States of America

Dreamshaper is printed in 12-point Georgia

Dreamshaper is dedicated to my family and friends, and everyone who believed in me.

This book never would have happened without all of you. A dream without effort is just false hope, and your guidance and faith helped me craft this book into what it is.

PROLOGUE

Sometime beyond the toll of midnight, 10-year old Orson Bailey sat upright in his bed, stirred by the sound of something sniffing at his bedroom door.

Orson pulled his blankets up over the bridge of his nose, leaving enough room for him to see the fuzzy shape of the door. He hated being dependent on his glasses and the thought of reaching a hand from the safety of his blanket to grab them was about as appealing as taking a syrup bath before lying on an anthill. Still, it was either take a chance or remain blind to whatever was prowling outside the door, so he quickly snatched his glasses and pushed them onto his nose, nearly poking out his eye in the process.

A long inhale of breath sounded just outside his door, followed by a slow purring hiss that ended with an odd clucking that reminded Orson of a tongue licking the roof of its mouth for that last unreachable trace of peanut butter. A sour smell slithered into his room and Orson scrunched his nose further beneath the blanket. It smelled like someone had left a package of meat out long enough to spoil. Orson fought to suppress a gag. The last thing he wanted to do was *Urp*—as his mother had so tactfully named his vomiting episodes—and alert the thing outside that *he* was inside.

The glow of the moon through his window left a long sliver of light in the shape of an arrow on his floor, pointing ominously at the door to his room. The thing outside scratched at the door with what sounded like long, sharp fingernails.

Orson shivered, ducking the rest of the way under his blanket. This was all very wrong, he knew, there were no such things as monsters. There were no shadows that bumped in the night, no bogeymen waiting in closets and definitely no strange creatures scratching on the outside of bedroom doors. Those were all stories made up by parents to scare children into behaving. Everybody knew that.

Everybody except the thing scratching on the other side of *his* bedroom door.

The scratching sound stopped and Orson risked a quick peek over his blanket. The hairs on his arms all stood at attention when the doorknob rattled and turned. The door opened and something long and dark poked in, slightly silhouetted against the light from the window. A pair of dark lips peeled back, revealing rows of dangerous, spiked teeth. A thin stream of drool leaked out and spattered to the floor. The rotten meat smell was stronger now and Orson choked uncontrollably, slapping a hand over his mouth in horror.

With a loud bang, the door to Orson's room hammered inward, knocked so hard that the hinges came loose and it crashed to the floor. Orson barely had time to register his newly broken door as the prowling monster stepped into his room. Wide-eyed in disbelief, Orson found himself staring into the beady red eyes of what appeared to be a living, breathing dinosaur.

It stood upright on two powerful legs that rippled with muscle underneath the dark mottled scales that covered its entire body and glistened in the moonlight. Scratching irritably at each other, a pair of tiny arms poked out comically from its chest.

"I can sssmell your fear, boy," the huge lizard hissed, drawing out each letter 's' with a deep exhale of breath between its sharp teeth. Orson whimpered fearfully; if everyone knew that there weren't supposed to be monsters scratching at bedroom doors, they *certainly* knew that those monsters wouldn't be able to speak. This particular monster —*Orson's* monster—seemed intent on breaking all of the rules.

He tried to duck back under his blanket but it was torn away from him, leaving him exposed in his pajamas on the bed. The dinosaur spit out the blanket and looked at Orson coolly.

"Surely you wouldn't cower ssso shamefully," it hissed. "Not the Chosen One, he who would sssstand againsssst usss!"

Orson crawled back on his bed until he hit the wall. "Leave me alone," he tried to say, but the words came out as little more than a squeak. He hadn't the slightest idea what it was talking about. The only thing he understood was that something horrible was happening and if he didn't do something soon it was going to get much worse.

"No, I don't think ssso." The lizard dropped back into a low crouch. "But enough talk! Your time isss over, before it beginsss!"

With an ear-numbing screech the lizard launched into the air, flying towards Orson with its tiny claws outstretched and its mouth wide open. Orson raised his hands helplessly over his face and screamed.

"*NO! LEAVE ME ALONE!*"

He waited for the feel of those sharp, biting teeth. Waiting, because there was nothing else he could do. It would be on him in a second.

Except that second never came.

"What isss thisss trickery?" the hissing voice bellowed and Orson opened his eyes. The monster's snout was inches from his face, the yellow teeth coated in thick, oozing saliva. The rotten stench of air puffing from its snout was overwhelming and Orson's stomach gurgled in sick protest. He was starting to dislike that feeling very much.

"What have you done to me, boy?" it squealed and Orson realized that it hadn't just stopped, but was *frozen* in place. The lizard's entire body hung in midair with its tail sticking straight out behind it. Only its eyes and tongue moved, shifting back and forth anxiously as it struggled against the invisible bonds keeping it from its prey. The forked tongue flicked out, long enough to graze Orson's cheek and leave behind a sticky wet streak.

For a moment all Orson could do was stare, terrified beyond anything he had ever felt before. His mouth worked without sound as he tried to make some sense of all of this. It took a long moment for him to realize that he was wasting his chance to escape. That thought quickly got him moving. Sliding along the wall, careful not to touch the lizard's skin, he dropped from his bed and bolted out of the room.

The moment he stepped through his broken doorway, everything began to change. His breath caught in his throat as the very air around him swelled in a whirlpool of colour. Looking into it made his head start to spin and he closed his eyes against the dizziness, wishing it would all just stop. Now was definitely *not* the time for this to happen, not with a gigantic lizard hanging around his bedroom.

When he opened his eyes again, the whirlpool of colour was gone. Orson saw that he was no longer standing inside his house. The hallway outside his room was gone, replaced by a long corridor with red and black walls that were completely barren of any decoration or windows. Cobwebs hung loosely from the roof; webs so thick and large that Orson wondered what terrible creature had spun them and feared that whatever it was may still be nearby. One strand broke free and drifted across his forehead and he slapped it away in fearful disgust.

Orson turned to look at the doorway to his room, now floating impossibly in midair like a painting held aloft by invisible strings. Behind it, the same odd red and black hallway stretched on, but through the door he could still see his bedroom, complete with it the lizard still floating above his bed. Orson wondered how long it would be stuck there. Its tail twitched. That was all the incentive Orson needed to get running.

As he rounded the corner, something thumped heavily behind him and the lizard's raspy voice called out angrily. "There isss no point in running, boy!"

Orson ran as fast as his legs would carry him. He looked around frantically as he ran, searching for a door or window, even a crack in the wall large enough for him to slip his skinny body into. There was nothing. He started to panic.

He rounded another corner. Behind him he could hear the lizard quickly closing the gap between them. He had maybe a few seconds left and there was nowhere to go. Running as fast as his legs would carry him, he nearly ran straight past the small metal door that materialized out of nowhere in the center of the wall straight ahead.

Skidding to a halt, Orson grabbed the handle and pulled the door open, staring into what appeared to be some sort of laundry chute. Risking a quick glance back to see how close the lizard was he yelped as it came whipping around the corner, lunging after him with hungry excitement.

Turning to the dark chute that led to who-knew-where, Orson swallowed hard and flung himself inside.

The chute angled steeply downward for several feet before pitching Orson out into the open air. He dropped several feet before landing on his back in something soft and wet. The slimy mound was probably the only thing that saved him from being hurt, but that didn't stop him from grimacing in disgust as he pulled himself free of the ghastly sludge.

From his back he could see back up the chute, enough to see that the lizard wasn't looking down at him. It was probably already moving on, trying to find its way down to the room with the muck pile. Orson guessed that it wouldn't need much time. Dark, smelly and gross, this place seemed like the sort that a giant lizard would know well.

There was only one door leading out of the room. Orson stepped up to it and pulled on the handle. It wouldn't budge. "Locked, great," he groaned. "What am I supposed to do now?" He yanked on the door again and it didn't crack an inch.

"This has to be a dream," he said to himself. "I have to wake up! Wake up, Orson, wake up!" He continued to chant, his voice broken and frantic. Heavy footsteps pounded outside the room. Somewhere outside the room another door slammed open. Orson backed as far from the door as possible, barely noticing when his feet sunk once more into the slimy mound.

Something big hammered against the door.

"I know you're in there, boy," the lizard's hissing voice growled. It slammed into the door a second time and the wood began to splinter. On the third blow the door burst inward with an explosion of wood shards. Leering in at him over the wreck of wood, the monster snarled at him.

"Now you're mine!" it squealed, stepping into the room. Sliding back into a crouch, it pounced forward, arms outstretched, reaching out to grab Orson before he could escape again.

"NO!" Orson screamed. "WAKE-UP!"

Dreamshaper

Orson jerked awake in his bed, breathing hard and heavy as he swallowed the panic in the back of his throat. His mouth was dry and his heart pounded as he stared unknowingly at the walls around him. It took a moment before he realized that he was back at home, safe in his own room.

"It was only a dream," he told himself, his breathing slowing and growing easier. "Just a dream. There's no monster."

He reached for his glasses and found only an empty space on the nightstand where they should have been. "I must have knocked them off when I was dreaming."

Feeling hot, he wiped a hand across his brow, not surprised to find it beaded with sweat. His throat was parched and a terrible thirst nagged at him. He must have tossed and turned something awful.

Slipping his feet into the pair of fuzzy slippers beside his bed, he walked to the door and turned the knob. As the door swung open he stepped out and directly into a great wall of fur, solid enough to knock him onto his backside. Orson watched as the wall bent slightly to fit through the doorway. When it was inside, it stood over him and peered down with yellow eyes that glowed in the dark of the room.

When the thing spoke, its voice was like a clap of thunder to Orson's ears. "Orson Bailey! I've finally found you!"

"NO!" Orson screamed again as a great furry hand moved towards him. *"GO AWAY!"*

Dreamshaper

Orson sat up in his bed again, fully awake this time, or at least he hoped he was. He reached hesitantly for his glasses and found them on the nightstand where they should be. Sitting tangled beneath his blanket in the unnerving silence of the room, he tried to make some sense of what had just happened.

He must not have awakened the first time, when the lizard was about to catch him. Somehow he had stayed in the dream and that other monster had been waiting outside his room, ready to catch him.

What if he still was not awake? What if there was something else out there, waiting in the hallways? For that matter, was it even *his* hallway outside the door, or that strange red and black place with the enormous cobwebs and the laundry chute that ended in a disgusting pile of slop? Everything seemed normal enough, but as his mother often said, looks could be deceiving.

Sinking deeper beneath his blankets, he buried himself up to his eyes and stared at the door. He spent the last waning hours of the night that way, waiting for his alarm to buzz and tell him that morning had come at last.

⌐ ONE ⌐

"Wait!" Orson Bailey burst out from the front door of the small, three-bedroom bungalow he shared with his sister and mother, his arms flailing as he tried to flag down the school bus. "Wait for me!"

His feet betrayed him on the second step leading down from his front door and he tripped, rolling down the last few steps and landing facedown on the sidewalk. His backpack exploded, littering the ground with papers, pencils and a brown bag lunch. The honking horn of the yellow school bus laughed as it pulled away from his house and disappeared around the corner at the end of the block.

"Great. Charlie's gonna love this one," Orson grumbled, running a hand through a mop of impossibly tangled red hair as he pulled himself off the ground.

Charlie, the ornery driver of the Mardell school bus, liked nothing more than catching a kid asleep at the switch and leaving them stranded, and seemed to like catching Orson more than anyone else. Orson could already imagine the smug smile that would undoubtedly be on Charlie's ugly mug when they met again at the end of the day.

Picking his glasses out of the grass, Orson pushed them back over his nose. The frame was slightly bent and sat crookedly on his face until he twisted them back. The frame had been twisted and bent so many times by now, it was a wonder it hadn't snapped in at least a dozen places.

Already cursed with an unnatural lack of size and girth

11

compared to the average Grade Fiver, Orson was also lucky enough to have inherited his father's "weak eyes," as the optometrist had put it. For the last two years he had been forced to wear a pair of ugly, round-framed glasses every waking minute of the day. It was no wonder he was the prime choice of bullies everywhere. It would be so much easier to just toss the glasses out with the trash or out his bedroom window to let them smash on the sidewalk below. Seeing was overrated anyway. To top it all off, he was also blessed with an unruly mop of red hair and boring brown eyes; taunts of "firetop" and "carrothead" had followed him since kindergarten.

With a heavy sigh, Orson started collecting the debris from his backpack when his mother stepped out onto the front stoop, cradling his baby sister in her arms. Sarah was mewling and chirping annoyingly like always. She wasn't even a year old yet and Orson already hated her. All her little baby noises grated on his nerves, and Orson knew he had at least another eight months of these burps and spits to deal with before she would finally start talking like a real person. Eight months; eight long and undoubtedly tortuous months.

"Again, honey?" his mom sighed. "Alright, pick up your things and I'll give you a ride to school. You really should start waking up earlier in the morning, Orson. You were in such a rush you barely touched your breakfast."

"I wasn't hungry," Orson grumbled, shoving the last of the papers into his ruined bag and stepping past his mom back inside the house. As he passed, he turned and stuck his tongue out at Sarah who responded in kind, adding a disgusting stream of drool in the process that dripped onto his mother's arm. She barely noticed as she frowned sternly at her son.

"Don't tease your sister."

Orson heard the tired irritation in his mother's voice and bit his tongue. He supposed it wasn't her fault that Sarah had turned out so annoying. Truthfully, he thought his mother was doing a spectacular job raising two children alone after their father had just up and disappeared one day. It just so happened that one of those children had turned out to be little more than a squeaking and leaking fleshbag.

Five minutes later they were sitting in the front seat of his mother's beat up Dodge, puttering along on the road towards Mardell Elementary School. Sarah's daycare was on the way and they dropped her off, Mrs. Bailey grumbling about being late for work the entire time. Ignoring her, Orson fingered the house key hanging around his neck. His mom had made it a habit for him to wear the key around his neck at all times, so he wouldn't lose it. Apparently she didn't realize that only losers wore their keys around their necks.

When they pulled up in front of Mardell, the last few stragglers were making their way inside. Orson popped the car door open and started to clamber out when his mother caught his arm. "Try not to get into any trouble today, okay? Just try to get along with your friends."

"What friends?" he said sourly, shrugging away an attempted kiss on the cheek and slithering out the door. He knew his mom would be watching but didn't turn around. Tugging open the door to the school slightly more dramatically then he had intended, he finally looked over his shoulder just in time to see the Dodge pulling away.

Mr. Pratt was standing outside of his classroom, staring at his watch. A wiry little man with almost no hair left on his glaring crown, he was dressed in the same plaid sweater he always seemed to wear.

"Three...two...one...cutting it close again, aren't we, Mr. Bailey?" Mr. Pratt said as he pulled the door shut loudly behind Orson. "Jimmy told me about your little mishap outside of your house this morning, so I took the liberty of marking you as late already."

Of course Jimmy did, Orson thought wryly. That was good old Jimmy Scrags for you, always looking out for his fellow classmates.

Jimmy Scrags, Big J to his friends, was the resident school bully, running the playground with a sausage fist that fit perfectly with his sausage body and marshmallow head. Jimmy had repeated fourth grade twice before the teachers had finally gotten tired of seeing him and passed him up to grade five, at least that was the rumor, and Orson thought it would explain how much bigger he was than everyone else in class. The rest of the Fivers were ants compared to Big J, and he was the boot waiting to squash anyone foolish enough to cross him. Even the grade 6 students gave him and his gang of misfits a wide berth around the school.

Orson could feel Jimmy's eyes on him as he took his seat and reached into his bag for his notebook and a pencil, grabbing uselessly at a few ripped pieces of paper that fluttered to the floor. He kept his eyes turned away from the bully, but Jimmy called over to him anyway.

"That was a nice trip this morning, Strings," Big J said with a laugh. He waved his hands like he was flying through the air and a few of the other students laughed loudly. Their laughter died when Mr. Pratt turned his glare on them.

"Mind keeping your mouth closed so we can start, Mr. Scrags?" Jimmy closed his mouth and fixed Orson with a quick heated stare as though it were his fault he had been reprimanded. Orson swallowed hard. His fault or not, he probably hadn't heard the end of it from Jimmy. The bully wasn't one to let things go easily, and a punch in the guts from Big J would be the perfect ending for an increasingly miserable day.

Orson pulled a familiar piece of paper from the pocket of his jeans and unfolded it. It was a cartoon he had drawn himself of a man geared up in full army attire, a camouflaged bandanna tied tightly around his head as he glared down at a pile of darkly silhouetted shapes with a daring smile on his face. The title above the picture was written in fantastic bold-faced words: *Sergeant Sharpe*.

Sarge had been Orson's hero since he had first stumbled upon a Sergeant Sharpe comic book in the back of a bookstore downtown. He saw the cover, bought the comic on a whim and hadn't missed an issue since. Most of his measly weekly allowance went towards the next comic. Orson didn't mind the expense. With no real friends to pal around with, there wasn't anything else worth spending his money on anyway.

Orson usually turned to the Sarge on days that seemed determined to hold him down. Today he would need all the help he could get, that much was already clear.

Orson snapped out of his thoughts as someone brushed past his shoulder, walking to the front of the classroom. It was Mike Spencer, and he was carrying a few pages of something up to Mr. Pratt. Orson realized with a start that Mike wasn't the only one; the entire class was rustling to find last night's homework to hand in.

"Mr. Bailey," Mr. Pratt said as he collected the work. "I asked for the stories you were to have completed as homework. You *did* write your story, of course."

Orson slapped his hand to his head with a groan, forgetting about his glasses and pushing them painfully against his face. He had forgotten all about the story after Sarah had spilled her baby mush on the draft he had started during dinner. He had meant to redo the work after they finished eating but got caught up flipping through his stack of Sergeant Sharpe comic books.

He cursed his baby sister under his breath; just another piece of the misery pie she was always feeding him. In fact, she was to blame for a lot of his grief lately. She was always burbling and spilling all over his things. Whenever he got mad at her, his mother would give *him* trouble for teasing her. Orson frowned, thinking of how much easier his life would be if she would just disappear.

"Your story?" Mr. Pratt asked again, holding out an expectant hand. From the look on his teacher's face, Orson thought that the hand was the only part of Mr. Pratt that was actually expecting anything other than excuses.

"Mr. Pratt, I can explain..."

15

Mr. Pratt sighed and shook his head. "That's twice this week, Orson. Is this starting to become a habit?"

"I'm sorry, sir." Orson dropped his eyes to the floor.

"Not as sorry as you'll be if I don't have that story on my desk first thing tomorrow morning, Mr. Bailey. *Before* the opening bell, or it's a zero, do you understand?"

Orson nodded and Mr. Pratt collected the last of the papers, piling them in a disheveled heap on his desk. Sitting down heavily in his seat, Orson leaned his head on his hand.

This was *definitely* going to be one of those days.

⌐ TWO ⌐

Orson spent the morning recess on the backside of the small hill just east of the school playground with a notebook open on his lap, the pencil crayon in his hand scribbling furiously.

Recess was both a blessing and a curse, providing a much needed pause from what had been a terrible morning, but also freeing up Jimmy to come looking for him in retaliation for the morning's trouble. When the recess bell rang, Orson had been the first one out the door, ignoring his locker as he ran outside. When Jimmy couldn't find him in the playground he would check the soccer fields and baseball diamonds, but he wouldn't think to look behind the hill. Jimmy never thought to look behind the hill, something Orson had gratefully discovered earlier in the year. He may be mean and nasty, but Big J was also very lazy. If it required work, Jimmy wouldn't bother for long.

Orson's hand was starting to cramp up underneath the hard doodling and he paused, taking a moment to look at what he was creating. He doodled a lot in his notebooks, spending more time creating vast worlds of imaginative and often ridiculous pictures than he did actually taking down any notes.

Two beady red eyes stared back up at him from his notebook, slightly hidden beneath the dark, scaled brow of some giant lizard or dinosaur. The lizard's mouth hung open hungrily and its two tiny claws were stretched out in front of it. There was no mistaking the monster from his dream last night.

Looking at the picture, Orson could actually hear those jaws snapping closed and for a moment thought he could even smell the fetid rotten breath of the dinosaur-like thing as it tried to bite him. The thought made him shiver. It was the most realistic picture he had ever drawn, but that hardly mattered at the moment.

"Why did I draw this?" he asked as though someone were actually around to answer him. The last thing he needed today was a reminder of the nightmare that had kept him up half the night. His memory of that terribly vivid dream was still stuck in his mind with startling clarity.

A nagging voice in the back of his head yelled at him to tear the page from the notebook and rip the picture into a thousand pieces. Something about having created a physical memory of the monster from his dream sent a cool trickle down his back and he shivered. For a moment he held the page between his fingers, fully intent on listening to the voice and tearing the picture into a dozen useless pieces.

Instead, just as his fingers started to twist and crinkle the paper, he stopped and pulled it free from the notebook, tearing it neatly along the coil. For some reason the thought of tearing up the picture felt wrong, as wrong as the idea of the lizard itself and he folded it neatly before sticking it in his pocket. He may not like what the picture projected, but it made him feel slightly better that it should be stuck in the same confined pocket as the Sarge.

The bell rang and Orson hurried to pack up his pencils and notebook. Jimmy had gone into the school early to use the washroom and was already in his desk when Orson walked into the classroom. The bully sneered at Orson, who looked down at his desk where he found a small, hastily written note:

Luky u werent outsid, strings. I'll c u later.

Orson didn't need to guess who the author of the note was. The scratchy, misspelled words reeked of Jimmy Scrags, as did the implied threat. Sooner or later, probably lunch time or after school, Jimmy would find Orson. It was only a matter of time. Orson crumpled the paper up and tossed it back over his shoulder in a false show of bravado. A moment later he felt the paper hit the back of his head as the kid sitting in the desk behind him told him to watch what he was doing. Jimmy laughed cruelly.

As Mr. Pratt began the next lesson, the fatigue of a lost night's sleep hit Orson hard. It hadn't been the first night this week he had had trouble sleeping, and the lack of rest finally seemed to be catching up with him. Of course, listening to Mr. Pratt droning monotonously on about this week's bonus math problem didn't help either.

Dipping his fingers into his pocket, he tried pulling out the picture of Sergeant Sharpe. Instead, his fingers found the folded picture with the red-eyed dinosaur. He studied the picture tiredly, his eyes growing heavier with each curve of the lizard's body. The edges of the paper began to blur, and his efforts to make them clear again were quickly lost in the fight to simply stay awake.

Giving in, Orson let his chin fall to his chest and drifted off shallowly into the world of dreams.

⌐ THREE ⌐

Orson jerked up in his seat, gasping for air. His heart was pounding impossibly loud against his ribs and his forehead was slick with sweat.

Something was wrong. The room around him was one big blur, and it took Orson a moment to realize he wasn't wearing his glasses. Squinting, he felt along the top of his desk and below, finding the glasses on the floor underneath his seat. Sliding them back over his ears, he breathed a quick sigh of relief that they weren't bent any more than they had been before his little catnap. Even with his glasses, however, he still felt a thick strangeness that was far outside his normal apprehension in class.

Everything looked proper; all of the kids were sitting in their desks and Mr. Pratt was standing up at the chalkboard, a piece of chalk in his hand. Orson looked past the chalk in his teacher's hand and frowned as he tried to read the words Mr. Pratt was writing, or rather the words that *should* have been there. Instead of clear letters, the writing on the board was fuzzy, as though it were completely separate from everything else and hidden behind a dirty pane of glass.

Orson pulled his glasses off and wiped them on his shirt. When he replaced them, nothing had changed.

He looked back at Mr. Pratt, and saw another sign that he was in trouble. Mr. Pratt was still up at the board, holding his chalk in the exact same place he had been a moment ago. At first, Orson thought Mr. Pratt was just thinking about what to write next, but after a few moments the teacher still hadn't moved. He didn't even appear to be breathing.

"Mr. Pratt?" Orson asked quietly, not sure if he really wanted to get his teacher's attention but becoming increasingly unnerved by the way Mr. Pratt was standing so completely still and motionless as though he was frozen to the spot. If the teacher heard he didn't react.

Orson looked around the room and saw that Mr. Pratt wasn't the only one who had become stuck in place. All of the other students were frozen as well, some with their pencils pointed down towards the paper on their desks, others in mid chatter. Jimmy Scrags was sitting in his desk with a scowl on his face, his pencil neatly snapped in two, one half between the sausage fingers of each hand. He was looking right at Orson, and from the expression on his face, Orson quickly interpreted the meaning behind the broken pencil.

The girl right behind Jimmy had her textbook open and standing on end to hide the fact that she was—or *had* been, before freezing up—trying to stuff a piece of chocolate cake from her lunch into her mouth. Smears of chocolate spread from her lips to her cheeks and down her chin.

"What happened?" Orson asked nervously, switching his gaze from one student to the next. "What's wrong with all of you?"

The lonely echo of his voice was the only answer he received. He looked around the room and noticed only one empty desk, the one belonging to Natalie Morrison, a brown-haired girl who had never gone out of her way to bother Orson, but never really seemed to even know he existed, either. Had she been there at the start of the day? Orson struggled to think if she had been absent but couldn't remember and frowned.

A movement caught the corner of his eye, and Orson turned back to the board at the front of the room and gasped.

The fuzzy letters on the chalkboard had come alive, shifting around on the board and picking up speed, blending into one another before separating again into letters that were as clear as day. There were eleven letters in all, and as Orson watched they moved together into two jumbled piles:

MDERA and *PSEHRA*.

Letters weren't supposed to just move on their own, Orson thought nervously as he studied the words, unable to decipher their meaning. Letters simply didn't move around on a board with nobody to move them. That left only one explanation; he had to be dreaming. And like last night, this dream had a decidedly *alive* feeling to it.

He bit his lip, hoping the painful sensation would wake him up before Mr. Pratt had a chance to see him asleep at his desk. His lip throbbed between his teeth but he didn't come awake as he had hoped. The classroom around him remained frozen, with one empty desk beside him. Frowning again, he rubbed his lip thoughtfully as he looked back at the nonsense words on the board.

Mdera and *psehra*, were those supposed to mean something? Orson stared at the letters in confusion, frowning as he tried to work out their meaning, when he understood what they must be. "Anagram," he muttered angrily and shook his head. "I *hate* anagrams."

The class had started looking at anagrams last week and so far Orson had proved horrible at the task of unscrambling the random word puzzles. Now, gazing at what appeared to be two jumbled words on the board, he couldn't help feeling a slight pang of frustration before he even started trying to work them out. He thought about ignoring them for a moment, but he had never seen letters move on a board without any help before. Sighing, he pulled out a piece of paper and a pencil from his desk.

He spent the next several minutes arranging and rearranging the letters, scratching out his work and starting all over again. At first he tried to look for clues in both of the jumbled words, and when that didn't seem to lead anywhere he turned his focus to one at a time.

After several minutes, two words appeared on the page underneath a dozen failed attempts. He stared down at the words for a long time, trying to understand what they might mean. Picking up a piece of chalk, he tried to write his solutions directly underneath the already present jumbles but the chalk left no mark. Growling, he pressed the chalk harder. Nothing happened until he accidentally brushed the tip against one of the letters already there. The letter itself moved beneath the chalk, sliding along the board until Orson lifted his hand away from the board, staring in dumbfounded confusion.

Pressing the chalk tentatively against another letter, he shifted it down below the anagram and the letter moved with his hand, stopping when he pulled the chalk away.

"Now, that's *definitely* not right," he said before touching the chalk to another letter.

He moved the letters around with the chalk until the message on the board matched the one he had created on his paper. The words *ARMED* and *SHERPA* looked back at him.

"Armed Sherpa," he grunted. "What's that supposed to mean?"

From what he remembered from Social Studies, a Sherpa was someone who helped carry a mountain climber's gear. So what did one have to do with his dream, and why was it armed? What did *armed* mean, anyway? In police talk, it meant someone was holding a weapon. Maybe a Sherpa was carrying something, a knife or a gun, but that had nothing to do with Orson. Writing the words down on a piece of fresh paper, he folded it and shoved it into his pocket, not remembering that this was a dream and it would be gone the moment he woke up.

Outside the classroom, muffled footsteps walked past the room, breaking his train of thought.

"Hello?" he called out quietly. The footsteps were farther now and showed no sign of stopping. Whatever was outside, it was going to be gone if he didn't move quickly.

Still he hesitated, unsure whether he should go out there, but the idea of being stuck in here with his frozen classmates and moving words was starting to creep him out so he left his desk to make for the door.

When he reached the doorway, he peeked out carefully into the hallway. All of the lights were on and at the far end of the hallway he caught a quick glimpse of someone turning the corner by the school library. Stepping out of the classroom, Orson walked down towards the library at the far end.

When he reached the corner, he looked around the edge and saw someone standing in front of the gymnasium. It was a girl with a brown ponytail, and she was staring at the gym doors.

"Natalie?" Orson said, approaching slowly so as not to startle her. "Is that you?"

Natalie turned to look at Orson. She was frowning and tugging at her ponytail.

"Orson? What are *you* doing here?"

Now it was Orson's turn to frown. She must have seen what had happened in the room, all of the frozen kids, and now that she found someone who *could* move, the only thing she could ask was *what are you doing here?* Still, he told himself, this isn't *really* Natalie; she was still in the classroom, no doubt laughing at him as he drooled in his desk, fast asleep. This was only a *dream* Natalie.

"I've never dreamed about you before," Natalie explained as though reading his thoughts and Orson's mouth dropped open.

"Dreamed of me? This is *my* dream, Natalie," he informed her and she shook her head.

"Sorry, but I think you're a little confused, Strings. I must have fallen asleep at my desk. You know how boring Mr. Pratt's lessons can be."

"Don't call me that," he growled.

"What?"

"Don't call me Strings. I hate that name."

Natalie shrugged *whatever* but let the issue slide. "Were you in the classroom? Did you see everyone?"

"They were all frozen," Orson answered, still irritated by the way Natalie had spoken to him but relieved that he wasn't alone, even if it was all a dream. "What do you think those words on the board meant?"

"What words? There was nothing on the board, at least not when I was in there."

"There were fuzzy letters, when I was there," Orson said importantly. "But they cleared up while I was watching and turned into an anagram. I think I solved it."

Natalie looked at him like he was crazy. "What did it say?"

"Armed Sherpa, I think." He pulled out the piece of paper he had written the words on and showed it to her. "What do you think it means?"

Natalie shrugged again. "You're the one that saw it, not me. You sure that's what it said?"

Orson put the paper back in his pocket. "I'm pretty good at anagrams," he lied. "It was the only combination that made any sense."

Natalie looked like she was about to say something back but she was interrupted before she could speak by a noise from inside the gymnasium. Orson looked past Natalie's shoulder at the double doors. "Is someone in there?"

Natalie shrugged. "I was just wondering that myself when you showed up. I thought I heard something, but the doors were closed. I was about to take a peek."

One of the doors suddenly creaked open a little and both of the kids took a step back. All of the lights were off in the gym, making it too dark to see what might be lurking in the shadows beyond the doorway. Natalie shifted slightly and Orson realized with some embarrassment that he had taken a tight grip on her sleeve. He let go and smiled sheepishly, but Natalie didn't notice as she stared at the thing stepping out of the shadows.

25

Orson heard Natalie's sharp inhale of breath as a huge form emerged from the darkness. For one brief moment he expected the dinosaur-thing to come lunging out, teeth bared and claws out, but the creature that materialized was covered in thick, coarse hair rather than cold, mottled scales. What little relief he felt at not seeing the lizard was replaced in spades when he saw this new monster.

Rather than a pointed face with beady red eyes, this monster had the head of an enormous wolf crowning a furry but otherwise human looking body; a seven-foot tall body full of sinewy muscle that bulged and flexed with each movement. The wolf-man's ears perked up and its tongue lolled out of its mouth in a horrible, sharp-toothed grin as it looked down at the two children.

Orson recognized it instantly as the other monster from his dream last night, the one that had been waiting at his bedroom door when he had thought he had woken up the first time.

"Orson Bailey!" the wolf-man said in a booming voice that echoed down the hallway. "I've found you again!" It took a step towards Orson and he grabbed hold of Natalie's shirt again.

"Orson..." Natalie said breathlessly. She stepped back, pulling Orson with her. "What is *that?*"

The wolf-man took another step closer and in his attempt to back away, Orson's feet caught on one another and he toppled to the floor, pulling Natalie with him. The wolf loomed above them, looking down with golden yellow eyes. Reaching down, it opened a great clawed hand towards them.

"No!" Orson screamed, swatting desperately at the furry hand. "Leave me alone!"

"Orson," the wolf said. "I'm not here to hurt you."

"Get away from us!" Natalie yelled much more forcefully, waving a fist up at the wolf. It stared down at the girl curiously, as though she were something completely unexpected, but retracted its hand nonetheless.

26

"You don't understand," it said, cocking its head comically to one side.

"You heard her, leave us alone!" Orson screamed. "Get away from us!"

The expression on the wolf's face changed from curiosity to something else, an unreadable look that made Orson even more nervous. The wolf licked its long snout, seemingly unsure what to do next, and the children used that moment to hop back up to their feet and move a few steps further away, until their backs pressed up against the hallway wall. With nowhere else to go, they watched helplessly as the wolf stalked forward.

"Listen to me, please," it said, but Orson didn't hear it as he continued yelling.

"Get out of here! This is my dream and *you're not welcome!*"

The wolf-man stopped its advance. "Please, if you'll just listen..."

"*No!* I said you're not welcome here! GO AWAY!"

The air around the three of them vibrated beneath his words. Like the letters on the board, the walls around them began to blur; the colour drained out of them as they lifted off the floor. The colours swirled around them and the wolf threw back its head and howled, a sorrowful sound that reached them even as the wolf was swallowed into the swirling colours and evaporating walls.

"Orson, what's happening?" Natalie asked, but her words were lost along with the rest of the school as the dream exploded around them and Orson jerked awake in his seat.

⌞ FOUR ⌟

Orson and Natalie's eyes met across the gap between their desks. Natalie's mouth hung open and she looked as though she wanted to say something but didn't know what words to choose. One thing was perfectly clear: if Natalie was looking at him like that, she remembered. It was impossible, but she remembered.

"Mr. Bailey!" If the class had been quiet before, the sound of Mr. Pratt's voice killed it completely. "Perhaps if you were more concerned with getting enough sleep at home, you would be better able to stay awake in class. Or perhaps find the energy to complete your assignments *on time.*"

Orson swallowed hard. On his first day in grade five, he had been told the legend of Mr. Pratt's vein. It was said that whenever Mr. Pratt was angry his voice would drop, his eyes would pop almost completely out of their sockets, and the vein on the left temple of his face would throb so hard that you could actually *see* it pulsating from across the room. It was a legend that had proved true several times over this semester.

The vein was throbbing so hard just then that it was turning purple.

"Yessir," Orson mumbled, fiddling nervously with his pencil.

"Detention," the word dripped out of Mr. Pratt's mouth. "You can make up the time you've wasted *napping.* And since you've felt comfortable joining him in his midday siesta, Ms. Morrison, you may keep him company after school as well."

"But Mr. Pratt..." she protested but was silenced with a glare. Sinking down into her chair, she shot Orson a look that he couldn't read; anger perhaps? She had no right to be angry with him, though. There was no way she could actually think any of this had been his fault.

Orson shrugged his shoulders, not knowing what else to do. Rubbing his eyes, he straightened his glasses. His mother was not going to be very happy when she heard about this. Another detention, which meant he would have to take the late bus home. At least he wouldn't have to deal with Charlie. He had been dreading *that* meeting since stumbling out of his house this morning.

The impending detention loomed darkly as the rest of the day dragged on. When the final bell rang, Orson sat dejected in his desk beside Natalie as all of his classmates piled out into the hallway. Jimmy poked his head in through the door quickly to offer a deeply heartfelt and unsympathetic laugh, but a single look from Mr. Pratt sent him scurrying.

Even though there were only three of them left, the room was incredibly tense, and Orson wanted nothing more than to crawl into his desk and hide amidst the piles of loose paper and pencils. There was a knock on the door and things went from bad to worse. Poking her head into the room, Principal Blondin shook her head at the two students.

"Orson and Natalie? We don't normally see you two in detention."

Natalie didn't even glance over at the principal. Mrs. Blondin didn't say anything more, instead looking back to Mr. Pratt and asking him to step into the hallway for a moment. In his head, Orson could see the two of them sharing a good laugh over this. Detention *was* the best form of torture, and torture must be an absolute riot in the staff room.

Natalie hadn't said a word since the start of detention.

It left an uncomfortable silence between them, and Orson wished she would just say something. *Anything.* If she was angry with him—which Orson thought *completely* unfair in these circumstances—she should just get it out and be done with it. One more person hating him wouldn't matter much in the grand scheme of his already lonely existence. Sitting here wondering what she was thinking only made an already uncomfortable detention even worse.

When she did talk, waiting until the door closed behind Mr. Pratt, her voice wasn't angry at all but confused.

"That was...weird," she said, turning to look at him. Though he wouldn't admit it, Orson was relieved she wasn't yelling at him, or punching him, or whatever it was girls did when they were mad.

"Yeah, you could say that," he said.

"I mean, that...that actually happened, right? We were both there. Together. The two of us."

"I think so."

Natalie went silent again for a moment. Orson took the time to write down the words that he had unscrambled from the chalkboard onto a piece of paper. *Armed Sherpa* made no more sense now than it had in the dream, but he would have another look at it later, when he was in the peaceful confines of his own room.

"That thing, how did it know your name?" Natalie asked him as he slipped the paper into his pocket.

"What are you talking about?"

"The wolf-man-*thing*. It knew your name. Why?"

Orson shook his head. "I saw it once before in a dream I had, but I didn't think it would be a good idea to get too friendly. I...well, I *disappeared* before it could grab me."

Natalie frowned but seemed to accept his explanation, at least momentarily. Orson supposed she had to, seeing as how they both just *disappeared* from another dream. "Wow," she breathed. "That was pretty intense."

Orson used a finger to clean out his ear. Had she really just said that? "I don't know if that's what I'd call it."

"Do you think other people have seen that? I saw a movie once, when my parents weren't home, about a monster that hunted people in their dreams, but I don't remember what it was called. Something about nightmares."

"What happened if they got caught?"

Natalie shrugged. "They died, at least most of them. The creep wore a dirty old sweater and had these wicked claws on its hand that he used to..."

"I don't need details, thanks." Orson grimaced.

"How many times has this happened to you?" Natalie was getting more excited as they spoke, an enthusiasm lost on Orson. The more they talked about it, the more freaked out he felt.

"Well, I've seen the wolf-thing once before, with a big dinosaur, but this is the first time I've shared a dream with anyone. Hopefully the last, too."

"The last?" Natalie said a little too loudly. She had turned around completely and was staring in wide-eyed disbelief at her after-school companion. "Are you crazy? You've just made the discovery of a lifetime, and you want it to go away?"

Orson looked towards the door almost wishfully for Mr. Pratt to come back inside so they could stop talking about it. "The last thing I need is some monster with clawed hands hunting me down in my dreams. In this movie you saw, when they died in the dream, did they...you know..."

"Die in real life? Of course. Wouldn't be much of a scary movie if they didn't. Besides, I heard that if you die in a dream than you're supposed to die in real life. Mom says it's just an urban legend, whatever that means. Hey, you look kinda pale, Orson. Are you feeling alright?"

"If you call scared for my life, yeah, I'm fine. Fantastic. I may never sleep again, but who needs sleep?" Orson couldn't keep the testiness out of his voice. He wanted this conversation to end, and quickly.

"Chill out," Natalie said, tugging on her hair. "This isn't a movie, and that thing didn't look anything like the monster I saw. It was bigger, but there was something about it...Probably wasn't even real, anyway."

"Well it seemed pretty real to me," Orson said, a little more briskly than he had intended. Natalie was about to say something else when the door opened and Mr. Pratt came back into the classroom, eyeing his two prisoners suspiciously. Satisfied that the two of them weren't misbehaving, he went to his own desk and started looking through some papers.

Natalie slumped back in her seat, but not before giving Orson a knowing little wink. He frowned back at her, but she had already looked away.

⌐ FIVE ⌐

That night, for the second time in less than eight hours, Orson found himself walking down the empty halls of Mardell School in the midst of a dream. The last thing he remembered was lying in bed with a pile of Sergeant Sharpe comics, buried deep in his blankets and recovering from an impressive tongue-lashing of epic proportions. Needless to say, his mother had not been impressed with his detention and had sent him straight to his room after dinner, where he must have fallen asleep while reading.

The moment he touched down in the hallway of the school he knew he was dreaming. He was starting to become an expert at telling the difference between dream and reality; it probably helped that except for him the school was completely empty. Still, each dream seemed to gain a stronger sense of consciousness, almost like it was a world all on its own, and for some reason he couldn't quite understand, that notion scared Orson. It scared him badly.

The fluorescent lights flickered above him. As he walked underneath them, he thought glumly that he would have preferred his mother's scolding to this place. Her tongue didn't have claws, scales, or fur. At least all the lights were on in the school. In horror movies, the lights were always turned off to give that dread feeling of horrible anticipation. He had a quick but lurid vision of walking down the halls of Mardell with all of the lights off, nothing but shadows around him...

The light above him abruptly exploded in a shower of blue electric sparks. Orson cried out and covered his head in his arms. One by one, as though they had read his thoughts of only a moment ago, the lights throughout the hallway burst, each one popping loudly as it blew out. Within moments he was enveloped in a shroud of darkness too dense to even see his fingers wiggling in front of his face.

Except for the electric humming of the broken light fixtures and wires above his head, the air in the hallway was thick and still.

"Great, just great," he moaned miserably in the darkness. It was just a coincidence, that's all. The lights hadn't been reading his mind; that was impossible.

As impossible as sharing a dream with Natalie? a voice asked shrewdly in the back of his head. "Oh shut up," he told the voice and it went away.

Still, it had a point. Was it really a coincidence, or *had* something been listening to his thoughts? And was that something stalking him in the darkness? Stranger things had certainly happened lately.

Orson's breath stuck in his throat as he waited for something to happen. He thought about the movie Natalie had mentioned—the one about the man with finger claws who haunted people's dreams—and imagined feeling those claws against his skin. Swallowing hard, he forced the image down. It was just a movie, nothing more. There were no clawed men in here waiting for him.

The only things here with claws were dinosaurs and wolves.

Orson shivered suddenly and violently. From somewhere in the darkness, he was sure he could feel something watching him.

Up ahead a square of light that had managed to survive the electric bursts floated in the darkness. It was at least fifty feet away, and it would be easy to trip over something in this darkness or run into a wall, so Orson forced himself to not go sprinting recklessly forward. That may be what they expected of him; run scatterbrained into a trap, where the wolf or the lizard or both would be waiting with open arms, razor teeth and hungry stomachs.

Of course, they could be stalking him in the darkness, and he wouldn't be able to see them until it was too late. At least if he made it to the light he might be able to see what was here with him, but did he really *want* to know? Maybe he would be better off blind to whatever was going to happen.

Caught between darkness and light, Orson gulped again and took a tentative step forwards, trying to remember what obstacles he might encounter. He knew that there should be a garbage bin halfway down the hall on the left, and a water fountain a few feet past that. There was something else as well, but in his unease he couldn't remember what until his knee barked roughly against it and he nearly fell face first to the floor. Catching himself against the wall, he growled at the small table and chair that sat outside Ms. Collier's classroom. Ms. Collier was Mr. Pratt's neighbor in Mardell, and often had misbehaving students sitting at the table in the hall for everyone to see.

His knee throbbing annoyingly, Orson crept along slowly, always waiting for something to grab him from the shadows. He could feel the eyes following him every step of the way, following every movement. The hairs on the back of his neck stood on end in answer to the nagging voice inside his head begging him to turn around. The idea of being stuck in the suffocating darkness drove him on, inch by agonizing inch.

As he drew closer, Orson saw that the light was shining out from the library window. Through it he could see the ends of a couple of bookshelves. He had never been particularly fond of the library, with all its encyclopedias, atlases and dictionaries, but it was something familiar and that was enough. Feeling his way to the door, he slipped quietly inside, guiding the door softly closed behind him.

As he turned to face the rows of bookshelves, he was

hit almost immediately by a foul and sickeningly familiar smell. The library reeked of rotting meat, and he realized at once that he had made a terrible mistake. Reaching for the door handle, he was ready to bolt from the room when he heard a voice from deep inside the library.

"You'd better not be lying to me, boy," a raspy and serpentine voice hissed from behind the last row of books. Just hearing the giant lizard's voice brought a tremor of fear. He began to turn the door handle when a second, even more familiar voice froze him.

"I'm not!" Jimmy Scrags implored in a high, shaky voice. "I promise! Just don't hurt me!"

Orson was so surprised to hear such obvious fear in Jimmy's voice that he didn't realize his hand was slipping away from the door handle until it was too late. The handle returned to its favored position with a soft click that sounded like a car backfiring to Orson's ears. He cringed, praying the sound was only loud in his head, that nobody else had heard...

"Shhhhh," he heard the lizard hiss over Jimmy's blubbering and knew it had heard. "Quiet, boy!" The words were followed by a *swish* sound, like something whipping through the air. There was a resounding *crack*, and Jimmy fell silent.

He heard the lizard sniffing, tasting the air with its reptilian nostrils. Orson froze, not wanting to make any sounds. Maybe it would just think a book had fallen, or that there hadn't been a sound at all, that there was nobody else here...

"Thisss may be your lucky day, boy," the lizard hissed. "It ssseemsss my *prey* hasss come to me."

The pounding of heavy footsteps shook the floor and Orson knew he was in a heap of trouble. Looking around quickly, he saw a large trolley filled with books and took cover behind it just as the lizard emerged from behind the last bookshelf. It sniffed at the air, and Orson covered his mouth with a trembling hand, choking down a whimper.

Jimmy whimpered for him, and Orson felt some relief that the other boy was all right. Bully or not, nobody deserved to be at the mercy of this thing. Of course, such generous notions wouldn't save either of them if they didn't find a way to escape quickly. The dark hallway and its concealing shadows suddenly didn't seem so bad.

Something whistled through the air, and Orson didn't even have time to cry out as the trolley was obliterated with one lashing swing of the lizard's great tail. Books flew everywhere and Orson fell back as a piece of broken wood struck him on the cheek. His skin burned and he wondered how badly he was cut.

"Clever boy," the lizard hissed. "Did you really think you could hide from me?"

It stepped closer, crouching low on its two enormous legs. One of its huge feet came down on one of the trolley's broken wheels. The wheel rolled under the huge foot and the lizard crashed clumsily onto its side, roaring in annoyance.

Orson used the distraction to scamper away and take refuge behind a large leather chair directly underneath the library window. He had barely pulled his feet in behind him before the lizard was back on its feet again. After a few heavy footsteps, the room turned eerily quiet.

Jimmy whimpered again, and Orson wondered if the lizard had gone back to finish Big J off. He hated to leave Jimmy to his own resources–Jimmy wasn't the brightest marker in the box, after all–but if there was any chance to escape, it was now or never. He prepared himself to move when something splattered on the floor beside him.

A low purr rolled over him and a warm, sticky drop dribbled onto his forehead, sliding down his face and into his shirt. The pungent smell of rotten meat hit him again and he thought he was going to throw up. He craned his head to look up at the lizard, who was leaning over the back of the chair, its mottled lips curled back in a grim snarl.

"I can sssmell your fear, boy," it hissed, spraying him with another rain of saliva. "And now you're mine." It opened its mouth and reached for Orson.

The water fountain from the hallway crashed through the window with tremendous force, hurtling solidly into the lizard and knocking it away from the chair. Orson covered his head against the shower of shattered glass that rained down around him. First electricity, now glass. Maybe someone would like to pour some gasoline over his head to finish the cycle.

"Stay away from him, Sithyrus," the huge wolf growled as he climbed through the broken window and stood over Orson, hackles raised and golden eyes blazing furiously.

"Ssstupid dog," the lizard hissed back in winded gasps, pulling itself back to its feet. "Do you really think you can sssave him?"

The wolf's knuckles popped menacingly as he curled his clawed hands into fists. "Why don't you come and find out."

The lizard roared, feigning a lunge before twisting at the last second and whipping its tail. Orson had seen what that tail could do to a trolley and didn't want to see what it would do to flesh. The wolf was ready, however, and as the tail hit him in the chest he caught it between his two massive hands. In one fluid motion he spun and heaved, using the tail's momentum to fling the lizard heavily into a bookshelf. The shelf collapsed with an explosion of books.

Madame Blanchette would be really mad if she saw this, Orson thought of the school librarian. Luckily this was all a dream, so she wouldn't ever see it unless *she* happened upon one of his dreams like Jimmy and Natalie. Stranger things had certainly happened lately.

Pulling itself to its feet again, the lizard snarled at the wolf, who had stayed rooted in front of Orson.

"Thisss isssn't finished, fleabag!" With a last hiss, the lizard flew at the wolf and dodged to one side, past the wolf's furry hands and through the broken window into the darkness of the hallway beyond.

The wolf watched the lizard vanish, peering into the

darkness for a few moments. Satisfied that it wasn't coming back, he turned and looked down at Orson, who lay shivering on the floor amidst piles of splintered wood and broken glass.

"My name is Lupus," he offered Orson a great paw, "and I have been searching for you."

⌊ SIX ⌋

"That was close," Lupus said, looking down at Orson. "Are you alright, Orson Bailey?"

Orson scurried backwards away from the hand until he was right underneath the broken window. Glass crunched underneath him, biting into his hands, but he was too afraid to care. The cut on his cheek stung, and he could still smell the disgusting drool on his face and chest. Dream or not, he knew it would take a dozen baths before he felt clean of that stench.

"I wouldn't sit there," Lupus spoke again. "Sithyrus could come back."

Orson risked a glance up at the open window and knew the wolf was right. If it *were* waiting out in the hallway, he would be an easy target if he stayed where he was. He looked between the window and the wolf, not sure which would be the better bet.

"That's what that...*thing*...is?"

"Not what, *who*," the wolf said. "Its name is Sithyrus. If you like, you can stand behind there. I won't move from this spot, you have my word." Lupus pointed at Madame Blanchette's huge desk.

Orson eyed the wolf nervously, wondering just how good the word of a giant wolf-man really was. If he moved, the wolf could be on him in a second, chewing on his head or doing whatever it was wolf-men did to their victims. Of course, he wasn't any safer cowering against the wall underneath the broken window, sitting in a pile of broken glass. At least with the desk he would have something between the two of them.

Crawling away from the window, he didn't stand up until he was safely away from any grasping hands—or tail—that might try to grab him. As he reached the door, he momentarily pondered the idea of bolting out of the library, but the thought of Sithyrus in the hallway kept him honest. The wolf hadn't made any moves yet, standing patiently as Orson moved. At least in the library he could see what was happening. If he ran into the darkness of the hallway he would be completely blind to an attack.

A fat lot of good that reasoning did you before, dummy, the voice was back and he shooed it away.

Stepping behind the desk, he searched with his hands for a weapon—he didn't dare take his eyes off the wolf—until his fingers closed around a stapler. He felt more than a little silly holding a stapler, especially since the wolf probably wouldn't feel a staple through all that fur, but held it up nonetheless.

"Who are you?" he asked, trying to keep his voice level and failing miserably.

The wolf made no motions to come any closer. "As I told you, my name is Lupus, and I have been looking for you."

"What do you want from me?"

"That is slightly more complicated, but suffice it to say that I mean you no harm. I only wish to talk with you."

Talking was definitely better than eating. Orson relaxed slightly but didn't let his guard slip too much. It could still be a trick. "Talk about what?"

"I'll be blunt, if I may. I need your help, Orson. The Dreamlands need your help, to be more precise. Do you mind if I sit?"

Lupus waited until Orson shook his head before crossing his legs and sitting on the library floor. Orson watched him, wondering if this was just another ploy to ease his suspicions, though he was forced to admit that if the wolf *was* planning to attack him, it would be much harder to do it from the floor. He let the stapler fall to his side but kept a tight grip on it.

"Dreamlands? I have no idea what you're talking about."

Lupus sighed, a huge gust of breath sifting out of his snout. "The Dreamlands are in danger, Orson, and I have been sent to seek you out. It has been a long search, but at last I have found you. It was imperative that I had a chance to speak with you."

"I think you've made a mistake," Orson said, utterly confused. "I don't even know what the Dreamlands are."

"There's no mistake. The presence of Sithyrus is enough to convince me of that. The Nightmares would not have sent it after you if they were not certain you were the one. Had I not found you in time..."

Lupus trailed off, but Orson could read the thoughts behind the words. If the wolf hadn't arrived when he did, Sithyrus would be enjoying a healthy ten-year-old snack right now. Natalie's words sifted through his mind again and he winced. *A monster that hunts people in their dreams. They died, at least most of them. Wouldn't be much of a scary movie if they didn't.*

"The one? The one for what?" Orson protested. "How am I supposed to help you with...*what* am I supposed to help you with?"

"Our battle against the Nightmares, of course." If the wolf was joking, he was doing a good job of hiding his amusement. "Sithyrus is one of the Nightmares, the *definitive* Nightmare, I guess you could say, their greatest hunter. It is a wonder you escaped the first time it found you. Not many do."

"That makes me feel loads better," Orson grumbled.

"Orson, the Dremians have been at war with the Nightmares for thousands of years now, fighting with them for control of the Dreamlands. Up until now, we have been able to keep them at bay, but their strength has grown and we are in serious danger of crumbling. That's why I was sent to find you."

This was all too ridiculous to be true. Orson was embedded deep in a dream, actually worried about what would happen to him, and listening to a giant wolf tell him that some strange land needed his help. None of this was real, it couldn't possibly be. Soon, he would wake up and everything would be normal.

So why did the cut on his cheek sting so badly?

"I don't understand any of this. What are Dremens, or whatever it was you called them?"

Lupus shook his great head. "Forgive me, I've never been good at this sort of thing. I'm not much of an emissary, I'm afraid. The Dremians are the good creatures of the Dreamlands, the ones who fight to hold back the Nightmares."

"And they sent you to find me, a ten-year-old kid," Orson said, shaking his head. "To help you save the dream world."

"Dreamlands," Lupus corrected.

"Do you know how stupid that sounds?" Orson said sharply. "I'm about bite-sized for you, and you're telling me I'm supposed to somehow help in a battle against dinosaurs like that Sithy-whatsit?"

"Sithyrus, and yes, that's exactly what I'm trying to tell you. I know it may sound a little strange to you, but if you'll just hear me out..."

"A *little* strange? It sounds completely bonkers, bananas and looners! If I didn't know this was a dream..."

"Have you noticed a change in your dreams lately?"

Orson wasn't prepared for the question. Of course he had noticed a change in his dreams. Hadn't he just thought about how vivid they were getting before the lights in the hallway went out? "Well, there's been more bad dreams lately, but I don't see what that has to do with anything. I've always had nightmares. Everybody does."

"What about how they *feel*?"

Orson knew the answer the wolf was searching for. He had felt the difference in the dreams the last few days and understood that the vividness wasn't the biggest change. But they were still dreams, not reality. It was crazy to think anything else.

Ask Natalie how crazy it is, the voice in his head said. *Crazy like Christmas.*

Orson hated to admit it, but it made a good point. Frowning, he answered Lupus's question. "They feel more real. Like they're actually happening."

Lupus nodded his great furry head. "Because they *are* more real. More than you may realize. And the worst is yet to come. If you don't help us, you will soon find out how horrible reality can become."

Orson felt a chill sweep him with the wolf's words. The note of threat was clear, not a direct threat from the wolf to Orson, but a threat of something else entirely. It was crazy to think that this was any more than a dream, something he would soon wake up from, but Orson felt the fear nonetheless.

"Orson," Lupus continued, "you are stronger than you realize. That's the reason the Nightmares have sent Sithyrus. They're aware of the threat you pose and want to get to you before you realize who you truly are or what you're capable of. You scare them, and with good reason. Once you find out who you are, what you represent, and are properly trained, you may be the edge we need to stop the Nightmares once and for all. You have the power to save us all."

"You're wrong," Orson said. "So is that stupid dinosaur. I can't help you with anything. I can't even help myself against a bully and his meathead friends."

Orson had completely forgotten about Jimmy until now. He was sure Jimmy hadn't slipped out the door, he would have seen him. He was probably still hiding somewhere, if he was even still in the dream. Orson hoped he had woken up by now. He hated to think of what school would be like if Jimmy heard any of *this* particular conversation. Even if it was a dream, the bully might be stupid enough to take it out on Orson anyway.

"Orson, listen to me. There is no mistake. You have already shown us that you are the one we seek."

"How? How could I have possibly shown you I would be any help in this stupid war of yours?"

"By escaping Sithyrus when it first found you, and by how you escaped from me, twice now. Did you think that happened by chance?"

Orson had no answer. This was all simply too ridiculous to even consider and he couldn't believe he had listened this long. This was all a dream, nothing more, no matter how real it might feel. His dreams had always felt real until he woke up, and this would be no different. That chill he was feeling was only because he was letting the wolf's words get to him. When he woke up, everything would be back to normal, and soon these stupid dreams would end.

What about Natalie? Can you deny that as well?

Orson shook the voice away. That was just a weird coincidence, nothing more. Somehow, their brainwaves had gotten mixed up and they had ended up in the same dream. Orson had never heard of something like that happening before, but that didn't mean it *hadn't* happened before. None of that mattered right now, anyway. All that mattered was he had no idea what this wolf was talking about, and didn't *want* to know what he was talking about. All he wanted was to wake up in his room, wrapped up snugly in his blankets and done with these strange dreams.

"I want to go home," he said. "Do you understand me? I want you to go away."

Lupus looked suddenly disturbed. He started to rise from the floor. "Orson, please, listen to me. Hear me out..."

"No!" Orson cried out. He wanted out of this library, away from monsters and exploding lights and giant wolves and, most of all, nightmarish dinosaurs. He wanted to wake up, to be in his own bed, and to crawl into his mother's room and lie down with her, let her tell him none of this was real, like she used to do when he was just a toddler.

"Orson, if you would just come and see the Queen, she can explain," Lupus said with some urgency, standing up. "She can explain it better than I."

"Now there's a Queen, too?" Orson said, shaking his head. "This gets more unbelievable by the second! I just want to go home, and I want these dreams to stop! Just get out of my head and leave me be!"

"Orson," Lupus stepped forward, reaching out an imploring hand. It was a bad move. Orson jumped back, the stapler once again held up in front of him.

"You lied!" he yelled at the wolf. "You said you wouldn't move! You lied!"

Lupus immediately stepped back but it was too late. With that one step, every chance of gaining Orson's confidence had crumbled. Orson threw the stapler with everything he had, and Lupus batted it down effortlessly.

"Leave me alone," Orson said, angry and forceful. "I want to wake up!"

"Orson, I'm sorry. I didn't mean to..."

"Wake up! I want to wake up!"

Lupus looked scared now, a sight that Orson would have found remarkable had he not been lost in his own determination to get out of there.

"Leave me alone! *Leave...me...alone!*"

"Orson..." but Lupus's words were lost as the library blurred around them. With a flash of light, it disappeared and Orson snapped awake, tangled safely in the blankets of his bed. His cheek was throbbing slightly and as he brought his fingers up to touch it he felt a slight sting as though something had scratched him. With a mix of dread and terrified apprehension, Orson looked down at his pillow.

On his pillow cover, two wet drops of blood stared back up at him.

⌐ SEVEN ⌐

A thunderclap boomed outside. Orson looked listlessly out the window; bored and utterly disinterested in what Mr. Pratt was rambling about at the front of the room. He was exhausted; even though he had been asleep for more than eight hours, the dream last night must have made his sleep restless and light. He felt as though he hadn't slept for a week.

The small scratch on his cheek was still raw. It had been a shock when he woke up and found a few drops of blood on his pillow. The scratch was faint and much less vicious than he would have expected after being struck by a broken trolley, but the fact that there was anything there at all was enough to concern him deeply. The only explanation that made any sense was that he must have scratched himself in his sleep, and somehow that scratch had translated into his dreams.

It was the *only* explanation. He wouldn't accept anything else.

Looking to the desk nearest the window, he watched as Jimmy Scrags glared angrily into his scribbler. Orson didn't think the bully had ever looked so infuriated. Every few minutes, Orson would catch Jimmy watching him, but as soon as Jimmy saw Orson looking he would turn his eyes down to his paper again.

Orson didn't want to think about why Jimmy would be acting so strangely today, but couldn't shake the feeling that he already knew the answer.

The bell rang to end the class and on the way out the door Orson was treated to an especially vicious punch in the arm. Jimmy threw him roughly aside, pausing to fix him with a glare that made Orson uncomfortable for more reasons than the threat they implied. It was a look that said too much, one that wanted to validate everything Orson was trying to ignore.

When he had woken up this morning, Orson had prayed everything would be normal today, that Jimmy would treat him with the same cool arrogance that had become the everyday custom. Apparently nobody was listening to his prayers. At least that much was normal; nobody ever seemed to be listening.

How would Jimmy even know Orson had been there? Big J had been behind the bookshelves in the dream and hadn't come out from hiding, not unless he had peeked out from around the bookshelf when the lizard had left him alone.

Orson shook his head. "I must be going crazy," he muttered. He couldn't believe he was even contemplating this. Jimmy had not been in his dream; people simply didn't share dreams. Jimmy had been terrorizing him since his arrival at Mardell; it was reasonable to expect the bully to show up in a few bad dreams. Natalie was a strange exception, but Orson knew there had to be a reasonable explanation for that, a *scientific* explanation.

His fingers rose unconsciously towards his scratched cheek, and he pulled them away quickly.

As soon as he stepped into the locker room for gym class, Orson knew there was going to be trouble. Jimmy was already inside, barring the way to Orson's locker with his band of thugs to either side. The rest of the boys were standing at their lockers, but all of their eyes found Orson as he stepped around the corner.

"Think you're gonna live through gym today, Strings?" Jimmy said, leaning heavily against the door to Orson's locker. "It's dodgeball."

"Get out of the way, Jimmy," Orson said and immediately regretted it. All of the air was sucked out of the room as the rest of the boys pulled in deep breaths. Nobody talked to Big Jimmy Scrags that way, not unless they had a death wish. "Please," he added too late.

"Are you gonna make me?" Jimmy asked, a look of amused surprise on his own face. There was something else there, however, a look of uncertainty in the bully's eyes that Orson wondered if any of the others could see. Uncertainty or not, Orson still knew he was in trouble. "Hey guys, check it out. This little bean sprout is gonna beat me up!"

"You better watch out," one of Jimmy's cronies, a thick-necked buffoon named Barton Spinkerton, scoffed. "He looks pretty dangerous."

Barton was only slightly smaller than Jimmy and looked like he could have been the lost son of Frankenstein's monster. Jimmy's other chum, Frank Ciccone—an Italian boy with a thick accent and slight lisp—had called in sick to school today.

"Dangerous as a wet spaghetti noodle," Jimmy agreed and the other boys laughed. "Well, come on then, twerp, gimme your best shot."

"I just want my clothes, Jimmy. I'm not gonna fight you."

"Too late for that now, Strings. Can't stop what you already started." Jimmy stepped forward and pushed Orson roughly backwards. Orson slammed hard into a locker and fell to his knees. "Get up, Orson. You're tough, ain't ya? You can handle a little push, an *important* guy like you."

Orson shook his head, trying to clear the pain spots away. He looked up at Jimmy and frowned. Why had he said that? Orson wasn't *important*. Orson struggled to his feet, the back of his head hurting from the blow against the locker. Tears began to sting his eyes.

"Aw, did you hit your head a little too hard, Strings?" Jimmy said, grabbing Orson's shirt and dragging him forward. "Here, lemme help clear the loonies outta your head."

Big J pushed Orson back against the locker, this time holding him there and leaning in, squishing him against the hard metal. Orson gasped for breath, flailing helplessly with his arms, slapping at Jimmy's back. Jimmy laughed and stepped back, leaving Orson to fall to the floor again.

"You're not so important, are you, Strings?" Jimmy said and his cronies laughed. "In fact, I kinda feel sorry for you. Why don't you take your binder and just get outta my locker room? Here's your free pass."

Jimmy had picked up Orson's binder and was holding it out to him. Orson reached for it and Jimmy hurled it hard against the lockers. The binder exploded with papers.

Just like the books in the dream, the thought came from out of nowhere.

Jimmy took a swing at Orson, who couldn't duck out of the way fast enough. The bully's mammoth fist hit him hard in the forehead, sending him down to the floor again. The room went black for a moment.

Hands grabbed at his shoulders and Orson was hauled roughly to his feet. The front of his head hurt as bad as the back now. Jimmy was inches away from him; it had obviously been a long time since Big J had brushed his teeth. His breath reeked almost as bad as the lizard's.

The lizard, the voice in his head said urgently. *Use the lizard.*

It took a moment to understand what the voice was trying to tell him, but when he did catch on he didn't hesitate. This might be his only chance of getting away from any further punishment. Slipping his arm between himself and Jimmy, he managed to reach into his pocket, hoping he had worn the right pants today. His fingers closed around a folded piece of paper.

"Well, aren't you gonna hit me, chump?" Jimmy snarled, holding Orson by the collar of his shirt. "C'mon, take a swing."

Orson's head was still swimming, but he managed to pull the piece of paper from his pocket and hold it up to Jimmy as a last ditch effort. Jimmy sneered as he snatched it away. He let go of Orson, who tumbled awkwardly to the floor, gasping for air.

"What's this, a love note? You gonna give me a paper cut?"

Orson watched as Jimmy unfolded the paper, hoping he'd been right. If he was, he may have a chance to escape before any more damage was done, at least for today. If he was wrong, well, it couldn't get any worse. He could already feel the welt on his forehead swelling up where Jimmy had punched him. The only real fear Orson had of giving the paper to Jimmy was that if he *was* right, it would be hard to deny the truth.

It was a double-edged sword, but at least it might stop Jimmy's fists from swinging and that was enough for now. He would deal with anything else later. Besides, he was sure he was wrong, and Jimmy would simply crumple the paper up, laugh at Orson and finish giving him the beating he had started.

Orson watched from the floor as Jimmy opened the paper and looked at it. Jimmy stared at it for a long moment and his face turned pale and sickly. His hands started to shake and Orson thought the bully's eyes were going to burst from his head.

"You...library...how..." Big J mouthed. The paper fell from his hands, landing on the floor for everyone to see the picture of the lizard with red eyes that Orson had drawn behind the hill yesterday.

"What's wrong, Jimmy?" Barton was trying to get a look at the piece of paper. "What'd the little twerp give you?"

Jimmy looked around, his cheeks bright red and eyes wild, but Orson had taken the opportunity to get out while the getting was good.

⌊ EIGHT ⌋

Sleep was the last thing on Orson's mind as he lay under his blankets, doing everything in his power to stay awake. Dreams brought too many unwanted ideas these days, ideas Orson could do without. Despite his best efforts, however, every second brought more weight to his already heavy eyelids.

Grabbing the bottle of concentrated lemon juice he had stolen from the downstairs fridge, Orson finished off the last few drops, barely enough to make his lips curl back. Lemon juice was an old trick he had discovered a few years back, one best saved for weekends when a good late movie was on, but each sip only offered a few minutes. With an empty bottle in hand, his time was up.

Groaning, he let the bottle fall to the floor. His mother had almost caught him when he grabbed the lemon juice, so he couldn't risk another trip to the kitchen. Besides, other than a few cans of half-eaten soup and some milk there wasn't much else he could take, and he doubted cold broth would do anything other than make him ill.

Orson tried to think of another plan to stay awake. He had already gone through his stack of Sergeant Sharpe comics, some of them twice, and finished the three puzzles he had stacked away in his closet. He silently cursed his mom; a few weeks ago he had asked for a small television in his room, something to hook up his Playstation to, but she had pointedly refused. "I don't want you staying up forever playing those games," she had said. "Your marks in school are shady enough as it is."

"Bad marks seem like a pretty small thing right now," he grumbled to himself as he slouched down on his bed. He was out of ideas, and that was going to mean trouble if he didn't do something quick.

The less he thought about sleep, the easier it should be to avoid it, he finally decided. It sounded reasonable enough. He resolutely started thinking about anything other than sleep, math problems, Natalie, his old dog Odin, anything but sleep. He thought so hard about these that he didn't even notice when his eyes closed. When his arms started to tingle, the hairs standing on end, he realized that something had gone wrong.

A faint breeze carried the soft scent of pine, and Orson opened his eyes, staring up into the midnight stars and the shadowed branches of a pine tree.

"You have got to be kidding." He shook his head. "This isn't happening. I tried so hard!"

Sitting up, he threw back the covers of his bed, which instead of being in his room was now lying directly under the lone pine tree in the far corner of his backyard. The yard was quiet and all of the lights in the house were dark. He'd camped out a few times in the backyard before, but it had never been as disquieting as it was now.

Still wearing his pajamas, Orson slipped around the side of the house, pushing open the front gate and peeking out onto the driveway to make sure the coast was clear. Everything was quiet, but as he stepped out onto the driveway and looked across the street he felt a familiar lump blooming in his throat. A dark forest had replaced the usual houses that should have been there. Even from across the street he could hear the leaves of hundreds of trees rustling in the faint night breeze.

Standing alone in the dark was unnerving and Orson found himself wishing Natalie would show up. He may not like the idea that the two of them had actually shared a dream, but he would let that slide for a little familiar company right now, the kind of company that came without fur or scales.

"Natalie?" he tried calling gently, keeping his voice barely above a whisper. "Are you there?" Of course she wasn't. Why would she be all the way over by his house, even in a dream?

"Natalie?" he tried again anyway, a little louder this time. In his head, he visualized her showing up suddenly, popping up beside him like she had been there all along. He willed for it to happen, knowing how ridiculous that was, all the while keeping his eyes on the trees, ready to run for the front door of his house at the first sign of danger. What he would do if the door was locked was another matter; run for the gate, he supposed.

When nobody showed up, Natalie or other, Orson risked a quick glance over his shoulder at his house. Upstairs, his bedroom window was dark and he wondered what he would find if he went inside. Did his room even exist anymore, or would he find himself stuck in that weird hallway from a few nights ago?

"Orson?" the voice nearly made him jump right out of his skin. Whipping around, he saw Natalie approaching the driveway. She was dressed in a loose-fitting T-shirt and shorts, and looked confused but smiled as she waved. "Back again, huh?"

A huge wave of relief washed over him. "Natalie! But how did you...did you hear me?"

Natalie shrugged. "I don't know if *hear* is the right word. I was dreaming and felt something in my mind. I turned around, and this weird doorway had opened up, right in midair! It was just floating there, and I could see your house on the other side. I figured you might be here, so I stepped through. Nice pajamas, by the way."

Orson had forgotten he was still dressed in his pajamas and felt his cheeks burning as he tried to stammer a response. Natalie had completely lost interest in his pajamas, however, and was staring up at his house.

"Hey, is someone else here, too?"

She pointed back at the house and Orson turned around, forgetting all about his nighttime attire. There was a light shining from the window that belonged to Sarah's room.

"That's my sister's room, but that light wasn't on a minute ago and I never called her."

"Maybe she just showed up. You didn't call me in the first time, remember?"

"I guess not. Wait a minute, you agree that this is *my* dream? Last time you didn't seem to think so."

"That wolf called out your name, didn't it? When it saw me it looked like it was confused, like I didn't belong. I just put two and two together."

Her logic was simple but sound. "That makes sense, though I wish it didn't. I wish these *weren't* my dreams."

"What are you talking about? This is wicked! I wonder if anything like this has ever happened before?"

Natalie's eyes were sparkling with excitement, something Orson wished he could understand. She was so interested in exploring this strange new phenomenon, while he wanted nothing to do with it. Of course, she hadn't been chased by rotten-breathed dinosaurs like he had. Not yet, anyway.

"Well, somebody else can have it, because I don't want it."

"Maybe so, but you have it, so you're gonna have to deal with it. Now, what do you want to do next?"

And that was that; Orson's concerns dismissed just like that. He stared at her for a hard moment and she just stared back, nonplussed, until he gave in. "I don't know. What do you think we should do?"

"Your dream, your choice. Personally, I think that if it is your baby sister in there, we probably shouldn't leave her all by herself. I also don't trust those trees. It might be a good idea to get away from them. Did you check them out before I got here?"

Orson shook his head. "Of course not. They're creepy, and there's no way I'd go near them by myself."

"Well, that settles it then."

She started walking up the driveway, Orson a few steps behind. Her confidence was hardly contagious. His hands were shaking, and he felt about ready to throw up, yet Natalie was acting like this was just some amusement park haunted house. Still, he was glad she was there. He didn't think he could handle another one of these dreams alone.

The door to the house wasn't locked and Natalie walked right in, Orson hurrying to keep up, standing close enough to her that he felt a strand of her hair tickle his nose. To the right, the living room was quiet and undisturbed. Straight ahead, he could see the kitchen, and to the left the stairs leading up to the bedrooms.

"Where should we start?" he asked Natalie. The way she was looking up the stairs gave Orson a pretty clear indication of what he thought she would say.

"It looks pretty dark around here," she said, flicking the light switch by the front door. Nothing happened. "That can't be good."

"What?"

"Why isn't this light working like the one upstairs?"

"Maybe she's using a flashlight," Orson offered.

Natalie gave him a funny look. "Your sister's a baby, Orson. What would she be doing with a flashlight?"

"Good point," Orson said, feeling stupid.

"I guess we should check her out first, make sure she's okay. Although this is all a dream, so I suppose she can't really get hurt."

Orson's hand rose automatically to the scratch on his cheek, but he said nothing. Natalie started up the stairs, Orson close behind. A part of him thought he should be in the lead, it was his house, after all. But if she wanted to go first he wasn't about to complain.

At the top of the stairs they paused to listen. The far

end of the hallway was dark except for a small sliver of light that peeked out from underneath Sarah's door. No sound came from the room. Or his room, thankfully. Still, even through the shadows he could tell something was wrong.

They walked past his bedroom and Orson gasped when they found the door smashed in, just like it had been when he had been attacked by Sithyrus a few nights back. Natalie cast a look at him as they looked inside the ruined doorway.

"What happened here?"

Orson shrugged, his heart pounding fiercely in his chest. "I dunno," he lied, afraid that just talking about it would bring the lizard back again. That was, of course, if it had ever actually left. They moved past his room and towards Sarah's. Orson sniffed at the air, trying to taste any rotten flavour that might give away an unwanted guest. He thought he smelled something funny, almost rotten, but the smell was too old and faded to be sure.

When they were in front of the door, Natalie knocked lightly before Orson could stop her. "Sarah? Are you okay?"

There was no response from the other side, which made Orson simultaneously relieved and apprehensive. Natalie reached past him and grabbed the doorknob, but before she could turn it Orson gripped her arm tightly.

"What if it's a trick?" he said. "What if that wolf is there again, or something worse?"

"Only one way to find out." She turned the knob and carefully pushed the door open.

The dim light in the room was coming from the small mobile rotating slowly above Sarah's crib. The light from the mobile cast comic animal shapes on the wall, chasing each other around the room in a never-ending circle. A toy squeaked under Orson's foot as he stepped into the room. Looking down, he saw that it was one of her stuffed toys. Ironically, it just happened to be a dinosaur. He swallowed hard.

"Your sister actually falls asleep to this?" Natalie

whispered. "Kinda creepy."

"There's usually a little music box that plays with it. It's pretty hard to be scared with *It's a Small World* playing again and again."

"Have you ever been to Disneyland? Trust me, there's nothing good about that ride."

Orson shook his head, not quite sure what Natalie meant by that. This definitely didn't seem the time to talk about travel ideas, but before he could say as much Natalie was already crossing the room towards the crib.

"Your sister's not here." Orson joined her and looked down into the empty crib. The blankets were bunched up in one corner, which was odd. His mother always tidied up Sarah's bed when she wasn't asleep. Orson shook his head; he was walking in a dream and not really in his house. Of course things were going to be different. He lifted the blanket and an envelope fell out from its folds.

"What's that?" he asked as Natalie bent down and retrieved the envelope.

"Looks like a letter, and it's got your name on it."

Orson took it from her and saw his name written in red ink on the front. "That's weird."

"What does it say?" Natalie said, looking over his shoulder. Orson pulled the flap open and pulled out a folded paper. He opened it up and found a note scrawled on the page in dark ink.

I've tried to find you, but somehow you've managed to stay outside my reach. Now it's your turn. I have your sister. If you want to see her again, you will have to come and find her. Come and save your sister, little boy. We'll be waiting.

Beneath the note was a large letter *S*. Orson read it

again before looking up at Natalie. "That can't be possible," he breathed. His whole body was shaking, and he had gone pale, even in the dim revolving light.

"What can't be? What did the note say?"

Orson struggled to catch his breath. He stared down at the envelope and noticed another piece of paper sticking out, although he was sure it hadn't been there a moment ago. Pulling the paper out, he unfolded it. It was the picture he had drawn of Sithyrus. Orson passed the note to Natalie but stared down at the picture. He had no idea how it had gotten inside the envelope or in Sarah's room, but the message in the picture was clear.

"My sister," he said, his voice quiet and trembling. "Sithyrus has kidnapped Sarah."

⌐ NINE ⌐

Orson waited in the lobby of the hospital, watching his mother pacing back and forth impatiently. The doctors had been with Sarah for over an hour and hadn't said a word to their mother about her condition.

When he had woken up from his dream, Orson had immediately gone to check on Sarah. When he first went into her room he thought everything seemed all right. His sister was sleeping cozily under her blankets, clutching her favorite bear tightly to her chest. It wasn't until he noticed how shallow her breathing was that he had yelled for his mother.

Mrs. Bailey had spent twenty minutes trying to wake Sarah, but the baby wouldn't respond; Sarah wouldn't even open her eyes. When his mother called for an ambulance, Orson rushed back to his room to get dressed, not wanting to sit in a hospital in his pajamas, and had been surprised to find his picture of Sithyrus lying on the floor beside the toppled pile of Sergeant Sharpe comic books. He stared at the picture for a long moment. Looking at it sent a chill down his spine. He knew he had left it with Jimmy in the locker room, so how had it appeared in his room?

Orson knew this was all connected to his dream, despite not wanting to believe it. Parts of the dream were fading, but he still remembered the note that had been in Sarah's crib and, even more disconcerting, the picture of Sithyrus that had been stuffed in the envelope as well. There hadn't been time for him to brood over any of those thoughts in the mad rush to get his sister to the hospital, but now that they were stuck in the quiet lobby awaiting word, time was aplenty.

"This can't be happening," he said for what felt like the hundredth time. "It was just a dream." Jimmy must have slipped the picture back into his desk or one of his binders when he wasn't looking, and it had fallen out while he was looking through his comic books. Except that his comic books were nowhere near his school bag, so there was no way the picture could have fallen out from there and landed with the Sarge.

"What did you say, Orson?" His mother paused in her pacing. Orson hadn't told her of his dream, she had enough to worry about without having to deal with a son becoming obsessed with living dreams. People couldn't be stolen in dreams, she would tell him. Sarah was sick, that was all, and the doctors would find a way to help her.

"Nothing, Mom," he said. "I'm just talking to myself." Mrs. Bailey grunted and looked away.

The door opened and a man in a long white coat and a stethoscope around his neck entered the room, looking very grim and serious. The second the door closed behind him, Mrs. Bailey was in his face.

"Well? Is she okay? What's wrong with her?" Orson had never heard that kind of fear in his mother's voice before. It was very unnerving.

The doctor gently removed her hands from his coat and guided her to a chair. Taking a seat beside her, he talked to her in a gentle voice. Orson had to lean up against his mother to hear.

"Mrs. Bailey, I'm afraid we're not really sure what's wrong with your daughter."

Mrs. Bailey's face turned even whiter. *She looks old,* Orson thought uncomfortably.

"What do you mean, you're not sure?"

"I've never seen anything like this," he explained.

61

"Neither have the other doctors. We ran some tests on your daughter and everything seems normal. All her readings are strong; she seems to be functioning fine. Her brainwaves are good. A little stressed, but nothing that should be cause for any concern."

"My daughter is in the hospital, not waking up, the doctors don't know what's wrong with her, and there's no cause for concern?"

"I know how it sounds, Mrs. Bailey, but we're doing all we can. It's almost as if Sarah just doesn't want to wake up."

"Or can't," Orson added, too low for the adults to hear.

Mrs. Bailey dropped her face into her hands and Orson heard her choke back a sob. "What should we do?"

The doctor placed a hand on her shoulder and gave it a reassuring squeeze. "For now, we'll keep her here. We'll keep an eye on her, run a few more tests and make sure she's comfortable. If anything new happens we'll let you know immediately. That's the best we can do right now, I'm afraid."

The doctor looked sympathetically at Orson, offering a smile. Orson looked away. With nothing left to say, the doctor retreated from the room, leaving Orson alone with his mother.

"This isn't right," Orson said, taking his mother's hand. "They're doctors, they *have* to know what's wrong with her." On television, doctors always had the answers. *Give'em 12 cc's of mercafatinoplex*, they would say, or some kind of secret doctor's language that nobody else could understand, and everything would work itself out.

But this wasn't television, and Orson knew deep down what was wrong with his sister. It was something a doctor couldn't cure.

"What am I supposed to do?" he wondered out loud. His mother looked at him and offered a trembling half-smile.

"Just think good thoughts," she said, misunderstanding his question. "That's all we can do for now."

"Okay, Mom." He wanted so badly to tell her what had happened, but couldn't bear the thought of bringing her any more pain or confusion. Her face was tired and drawn, and the last thing she needed to hear was that *a dinosaur kidnapped Sarah, and wants me to come and find her in my dreams.* She would probably call the doctor back, and Orson would be poked and prodded and lying in a bed next to Sarah. Or put in a room with white walls and a door that locked from the outside. At least that's where they put crazy people in the movies.

Orson sighed and looked down at his feet. Yesterday he would have laughed at the idea of his sister being gone; nothing would have pleased him more than to be free from her annoying giggling and her ability to spill all over anything he brought to the dinner table. Now he would give anything to have all of that back.

"I'd like to go home now," he said quietly.

"Sure, honey," his mother replied. "I guess there's nothing else we can do here."

The bus ride to Mardell the next day was gloomy at best. Orson hadn't wanted to go to school and had argued fiercely to no avail. His mother didn't think it would do him any good to sit around the house.

"You've already missed one day and fallen behind," she said. "I don't want you struggling even more than you already are."

Orson thought it was a weak argument. Missed homework seemed hardly important when your sister was in the hospital. Besides, spending the day in Mardell would only remind him of the weird dreams, but that wasn't something he could tell his mother.

Instead of being at home where he should be, he sat

staring darkly out the bus window, ignoring the looks of the other students.   A few of them tried offering their sympathies, which Orson barely acknowledged with a grunt. He wasn't sure how everyone seemed to know, but would have bet his Sergeant Sharpe comics that Mr. Pratt had something to do with it. Or Natalie, but as brash as she sometimes was, Orson doubted she wanted to tell anyone she was sharing dreams with the class loser.

For those who tried to smile sadly at him, pat his shoulder, or even talk to him as though they were friends, Orson had no reply. These false sympathies from people who just yesterday would have spit on him if they had the chance only frustrated him more. The last thing he needed was the pity of people who could honestly care less if he was there or not.

The only person in the class that didn't seem to feel the need to be unnaturally nice was Jimmy Scrags. If Big J felt sorry about Sarah, he was doing a marvelous job masking it. If anything, Jimmy seemed even angrier today than he had been two days ago. Orson wondered if the bully was still seething over the incident in the locker room.

All Orson really wanted was to be left alone, and while most of his classmates seemed happy to oblige, their awkward looks were enough to make him uncomfortable. With their constant staring, he fought to keep his eyes down on his notebook as he doodled in frustration all over the page. When lunch came, he picked sparingly at his food. It was hard to find an appetite when his sister was sick in the hospital. In the end he tossed most of the food away and made his way outside.

Natalie was waiting for him behind the hill, munching on the last of her own lunch as Orson approached. Just seeing her sitting there, imposing herself on *his* private spot, was enough to draw his ire. How had she known about that spot to begin with? When he sat down beside her, she cast him a careful smile.

"Why are you here?" Orson asked pointedly.

"Hello to you, too," Natalie responded, but there was no anger in her voice. "I just wanted to say I'm sorry about your sister."

Orson grunted. He knew she meant well, as had the other kids, but even with Natalie and what they had been through together he still couldn't believe she actually meant it, at least not fully. Besides, he had an unpleasant feeling she was here for another reason entirely.

Natalie sat quietly for a moment, her face bunched up as though she was fighting with what to say next. When she finally spoke, her voice was soft and tight.

"Your sister's not really sick, is she?"

Orson shrugged. "The doctors don't know what's wrong with her."

"Did...do you think it has anything to do with the dream? It sounds crazy, but...I don't know." Natalie tugged on her ponytail. "This is unbelievable."

Orson nodded. "Yup," was all he could think of to say.

They sat in awkward silence for a few minutes. A brisk wind fluttered around them and when Natalie finally spoke again, Orson had wrapped himself tightly in his coat.

"So, what are you gonna do?" she asked him. Orson, who had spent many hours thinking about that exact question, gave her the only answer he had.

"I don't know."

"If this is real, and your sister really did get kidnapped in a dream, how are you going to get her back?"

"I don't know," Orson snapped. "What am I supposed to do? I'm just a kid! How am I supposed to fight dinosaurs and wolves?"

"Dinosaurs?"

"It's a long story." Orson shook his head again. "I just hope the doctors find some way to help her. Otherwise I just don't know what's going to happen."

The bell rang. They walked back towards the school, Orson wanting to be alone and Natalie hanging back with him anyway. Before stepping inside, Natalie pulled Orson aside for a quick moment and did the last thing he would ever have expected. She hugged him.

"If there's anything I can do, Orson, all you have to do is ask."

Orson nodded, dumbfounded and unable to speak, suddenly embarrassed of the cool way he had treated her since finding her on his hill. He watched in stunned silence as she walked inside the school, leaving him alone outside in the cool autumn air.

⌞ TEN ⌟

When Orson entered the world of dreams that night, it came as no surprise but still carried the anxious winds of impending danger. The door to his room was still missing and the floor was littered with shards of broken wood. From his bed he looked out through the open doorway and was relieved to see at least it was his hallway out there and not the weird red and black place, but that relief was short lived when he remembered that the strange hallway hadn't appeared until the moment he stepped out of his room.

That thought alone was enough to make him not want to be alone again. There was no sign of Sithyrus or Lupus, but that didn't mean they weren't close, and he didn't feel like facing either of them alone, not tonight. There was one person he thought he could call, but after the way he treated her at school he doubted she would be thrilled to see him. Of course, she *had* given him that surprise hug at school. Swallowing his pride, he called out her name.

"Natalie, are you there?"

She wasn't here. She was in her own house, asleep in her own bed, not worrying about scaled and furry monsters. Yet when she walked in through the open doorway he wasn't surprised. It felt right somehow, like she was supposed to be there.

"Orson?" Natalie said. "I didn't expect you to call me *this* soon."

"I'm sorry, I just...well...I thought you might want to

come around tonight. You seemed excited about the whole thing."

Natalie patted him on the shoulder. "Scared, huh? No need to apologize. I told you I'd help you out." She stopped and looked at him for a moment. "Nice pajamas, by the way. Is this how you always dress when you're meeting a girl?"

Orson looked down at his favorite Sergeant Sharpe pajamas. Again. Gesturing irritably for Natalie to turn around, he looked through his dresser and was relieved to see his normal clothes piled messily in the drawers. He quickly changed into something more presentable.

"So, when are we going to look for Sarah?" Natalie asked when he finished dressing.

"Excuse me?" Orson said. He hadn't been prepared for that question, even though it was the most logical explanation for them being there.

Natalie rolled her eyes. Orson imagined she did that often, but still felt a twang of annoyance. "Well, that *is* why you called me, right? To go and find your sister?"

"I guess so," he answered. "I hadn't really thought of it yet. I just showed up here, to be honest. It wasn't really by choice."

"Maybe not, but it's what we're going to have to think about now. So what do we do? Where do we start looking?"

Her matter-of-fact tone of voice was beginning to make Orson wonder why he had called her into his dream in the first place, but deep down he knew it was for that exact reason. She may be irritating, but she had a strength and confidence about her that he was sorely missing. In a strange way, he felt she sort of balanced out his own weaknesses. Not that he would actually admit that out loud, of course.

"How should I know? Things have always just sort of happened. They usually come to me, not the other way around. Where do you think we should start?"

Natalie considered for a moment. "Well, I'm pretty

sure that wherever they're keeping Sarah, it's not here in your room. Getting out of here would probably be the first step."

Orson nodded, but had no idea where they would go. "Where do we go, then?" he asked, and Natalie shrugged.

"The door would probably be a good place to start." She pointed at the hole where his door had once been. "Unless you plan on jumping out the window."

Orson ignored the little jab as he looked at the doorway. A tremor of nervous tension pulled at the hairs of his arms as he thought of what might be waiting out there. If they left the room through the door, would they end up in that same strange red and black hallway? Or somewhere even worse?

"Something wrong?" Natalie asked him with a puzzled frown.

"No," Orson said. "It's just, well, I've gone out the doorway before, and it didn't exactly lead me to a place I want to visit again." For some reason, his mind wandered to the muck he had landed in at the bottom of the laundry chute and he grimaced. "It was a pretty gross experience."

"When did that happen? Where did it lead?"

Orson told Natalie the full story of his first dream visit. She listened carefully as he spoke, nodding occasionally, other times frowning. It was the first time Orson had told anybody about the dream, and he felt a huge relief when he was finished, a burden shed from his back. And when he finished, she wasn't looking at him like he was crazy.

"It was also the first time I saw Lupus," he ended, remembering how the wolf had appeared at the door after he had thought he was awake.

"So you *have* seen the wolf before," Natalie said when he was done. "That's why it knew your name."

"Sorry, I should have told you, but things were just too weird. They still are too weird."

"You apologize too much, Ors," Natalie answered,

punching him playfully in the shoulder. "Well, I guess there's only one way to find out what's behind the door, and we can't stay in here. If this lizard or wolf come looking for us, we're trapped if we stay in here. The only other way out is the window, and that's a pretty high drop. Or by waking up."

Orson sighed. However much he hated the idea, Natalie was right. To just sit here where he had already been found would be risky. Still, the idea of leaving a familiar place was not a comfortable one.

"Alright," he said finally. "Just give me a minute to get ready."

He started looking around his room, searching for a weapon of some sort. Besides a few dropped clothes hangers and some scattered pieces of Lego there wasn't much that would help and he let out a groan. He had once had a baseball bat, one he had used with his father, but it was probably packed away in the attic somewhere. Fat lot of good that would do him, anyway. He swung a bat about as good as he played basketball, which was not very good at all, and would probably end up hurting himself with it rather than whatever he was swinging at. He knew Natalie was watching him, and peeked over his shoulder in time to see her stretch out a hand to lean against the full-length mirror nailed into his wall. She looked utterly bored. Orson ignored her and took one last look in the back of his closet.

Natalie let out a choked cry of surprise and Orson jerked back from the closet.

"Natalie, wha..."

His words caught in his throat. Natalie was gone.

"Natalie?"

No answer. The air in his throat seemed stuck.

"This isn't funny, Natalie," he said, hoping this was just her attempt at a joke. A *bad* joke. He had only looked away for a moment, hardly enough time for her to hide, and she would have had to run across the room to reach the open doorway from the mirror. She had cried out when she was in front of his mirror, and there wouldn't have been enough time for her to make it to the doorway before he had come back out of his closet.

Orson walked over to where she had been standing seconds before. The mirror on the wall was still in place, but there was no sign of Natalie. He looked at the mirror and saw his reflection staring back at him with the same worried expression. He almost turned away before he saw that something was different about the reflection.

"It's moving," he said, although *moving* was probably not the right word. His reflection seemed to be *rippling*, much like a puddle after you dropped a pebble into it. Reaching out a very tentative hand, he brushed his fingers up against the reflective glass...

...and pulled them back immediately as they started to sink into the mirror. Orson cried out in alarm, wiping his fingers on his pants even though they were completely dry. Shockingly cold, like he had dipped his hand into a bucket of ice water, but dry. Small circular waves spread out from where his fingers had sunk into the mirror.

He grabbed a sock that was lying by the foot of his bed. Balling it up, he tossed the sock at the mirror and watched as the mirror ate it. More ripples spread along what should have been solid glass.

The nagging voice was back in his head again, telling him to back away from the mirror, to crawl back into his bed and wait for this dream to end. Only this time, it wasn't Jimmy who was trapped by a strange monster, or in a strange world. It was Natalie, and she had come here because of him, *for* him. He couldn't just leave her.

He reached out a shaking hand, pushing his fingertips back through the mirror. The cold chill was almost painful and he pulled back again. Pacing around his room, he muttered to himself under his breath, angry that Natalie had been stupid enough to fall through the mirror, and angrier still at himself for not having the guts to go in after her. Of course, there was no way of knowing she had actually gone through the mirror. She could have gone somewhere else, but deep down he knew he was only searching for an easy way out. She was in there and he needed to go help her.

Breathing out a growl of frustration, he raised his hand and slowly pushed it towards the mirror again.

The cold seeped into his arm, but this time he held his ground. The feeling was unbearable for a few moments but gradually began to fade as his skin accustomed itself to the chill. He pushed his arm in deeper, wiggling his fingers. The deeper they went, the warmer the air around them grew until he realized they must have emerged out of the other end.

A thought made him pause. Maybe Natalie hadn't fallen through the mirror; maybe she had been *pulled* through. If that were the case, whatever had grabbed her was probably on the other side, staring at his wiggling fingers, reaching out to grab them. With his arm submerged in the mirror, he felt more vulnerable than he would have liked, and started to pull out. There was no way he could go through with this. He hated the idea of leaving Natalie in there alone, but what could he possibly do to help her? There had to be another way; maybe he could make a rope or something and dangle it through the mirror for her. If the thing on the other side, and by this point he was convinced there *was* a thing on the other side, grabbed the rope and tried to pull him in he could just let it go.

A decision made, he started pulling his arm back out of the mirror. He made it as far as his wrist when something grabbed hold on the other end.

He cried out, trying to yank his arm away from whatever had him—it felt like a hand—but another one took hold. With nothing to steady or brace himself against, he started sliding towards the mirror. His arm sunk deeper, up past his elbow, then to his shoulder.

Orson pulled harder, but the thing on the other side was relentless. Whatever it was must have superhuman strength, because no matter how hard he struggled, twisted or turned he couldn't pull away. Finally, the thing gave one final tug and Orson's feet left the ground as he hurtled forward into the icy liquid mirror.

Crawford

⌐ ELEVEN ⌐

Orson used to wonder what having a bath in a tub full of Jell-O would feel like, and suspected this was the closest he would ever come to that. He decided that if a Jell-O bathtub was anywhere near as disgusting as the warm goop he was passing through now, it would be an experience he would never need again. It lasted only a moment before he emerged into midair, five feet above the ground. The tight grip on his arm slackened, and something cried out as he landed on it with a hard "*oof!*"

"Do you mind?" Natalie said from her back as she tried to pull herself from underneath Orson. The sock Orson had thrown through first had somehow planted itself over her face and she pulled it off, spitting distastefully. "When was the last time you did your laundry?"

"What's the big idea?" Orson ignored her jibe as he climbed off of her. "I thought something was trying to grab me!"

Natalie giggled, already forgetting about the sock. "I saw you pull your hand back the first time it came through—which was weird, by the way, watching your hand floating in the air with nothing else attached to it—and figured you were freaking out. When I saw your arm come through again, I thought I'd help you out a bit."

"I wasn't *freaking out*," he answered hotly. "You could have given me a warning or something, you know."

"I tried, but I didn't think you heard me, and I didn't

think you would want to miss seeing this place."

Natalie waved her arms in a circle. For the first time since emerging from the mirror, Orson looked around the strange new world he had stumbled—or been unceremoniously *yanked*—into.

The land stretched out for miles in every direction, broken only at the far edge of his vision by the dark silhouettes of what appeared to be mountains. Orson had seen mountains before, plenty of times, but even from this distance he knew the ones he had seen were nothing compared to those lining the distant horizon of this unfamiliar land. As he stared out at these mountainous silhouettes he felt something like an electric jolt shoot through his body.

"What's wrong?" Natalie asked, following Orson's gaze out towards the mountains. "Did you see something?"

"Those mountains," he answered. "Did you feel that?"

Natalie squinted towards the distant range. "Feel what, the wind? It is a little breezy here."

Orson frowned and shook his head. "No, it's not the wind. Something else. Something...different."

"Different how?"

"Dark. They feel dark, and cold."

Natalie stared at Orson, a look of concern on her face. "How do you *feel* dark?"

Orson shook his head, unable to explain what it was he had felt from the mountains. Besides, the feeling was gone now and he wondered if it had actually been there to begin with.

"I dunno," he said. "It's probably just the leftovers of coming through that mirror."

Natalie shrugged. She was already looking past Orson towards the outstretched land. "Where do we go from here? It all looks the same to me."

"Not back to my bedroom, apparently," Orson said nervously, looking behind him at the spot from where they had fallen. The doorway was nowhere to be seen. That must be what Natalie had meant when she had said she could only see his hand floating in midair. He waved his hand, hoping it would find an invisible patch of the mirror goop that had brought them here, but it only passed through the air. He swallowed a lump down in his throat. "It looks like we're stuck in here."

"I'm sure we'll just wake up when it's time," Natalie said and Orson again wished he could share in her confidence. "Besides, we needed somewhere to start looking for Sarah, and I suppose this is as good a place as..."

The sky above them exploded, booming forcefully enough to knock them both off their feet. Lying on the grass, they could do little more than watch as the sky came alive with pockets of faded colours that swirled unchecked in random bursts, rainbows erupting in streams of constantly changing patterns.

Orson wanted to cover his eyes but couldn't, hypnotized as the sky opened and swallowed itself over and over again, slowly dwindling until the swirling colours thinned out into small tendrils and finally vanished all together, leaving the sky as calm as it had been moments before. The entire spectacle lasted only a few seconds, yet to Orson it felt much longer. When he closed his eyes he could still see the shifting colours beneath his eyelids. Those soon faded as well, leaving him wondering if it had actually happened to begin with. Speechless in the face of such an overwhelming display, the two of them lay there for a long moment before Orson finally found his voice again.

"What...was...that...?" he said, his words stammered by rapid and shallow breaths. Natalie rubbed a hand over her eyes in disbelief.

"I don't know," she said and a slow smile spread across her lips. "But it was awesome."

The word *awesome* hardly seemed powerful enough for what they had just seen. Orson remembered staying up late one night during a vacation to the mountains with his parents so they could watch the Northern Lights—*Aurora*

Borealis, his father had told him they were called—where the sky glimmered with a dim, green light for several minutes. He had been impressed at the time, but what he had just witnessed made the Northern Lights seem dull and boring.

"Now *that* I felt," Natalie said, standing up.

Orson nodded, realizing his mouth was still hanging open. He quickly clicked it shut. "I'm thinking maybe we should have stayed in my room."

Natalie gave him a funny look. "Are you serious? And miss all of *that*?"

"Whatever *that* was," he answered. "We don't even know if it was a good thing. Have you ever seen the sky blow up like that?"

"Maybe it is normal for this place. In case you forgot, we're not exactly home right now. Matter of fact, we might not even be on the same *planet* right now! This is still a dream, right?"

Orson had no answer. "I hope so, because I'm about ready to wake up now."

"You have absolutely no sense of adventure, Orson," Natalie said with a slight smile. She reached out to ruffle his hair but he stepped quickly away from her hand. "If we're stuck here, we may as well have a look around until we wake up. We just need to pick a direction."

Orson looked at her darkly for a moment, trying to comb back his knotted hair with his fingers and failing miserably. When her look of excitement didn't diminish after a few seconds, he sighed and cast a look back at the silhouetted peaks in the distance. "Anywhere but that way," he said, remembering that strange feeling when he had first looked upon the mountains. "A trail would be nice. I hate walking around aimlessly. It would be way too easy to get lost in this place, and I want to be able to get back here if we need to."

"Why? You said yourself we can't get back from here. I don't think it matters where we go."

"I'd still like to be able to get back here. Maybe the

door will come back, or we just missed it."

"I don't think so," Natalie said. "But it looks like you're in luck. Look behind us." Orson protested as Natalie grabbed his shoulders and spun him around, but the words were lost as he looked down at the path that began only a few steps away. Well, maybe not a path, exactly, the grass was beat down flat, like somebody had driven a miniature steamroller or something over it, but it was a definite trail nonetheless.

"That wasn't there before," he said, eyeing the new path suspiciously.

"We probably just missed it," she said. "Anyway, you said you wanted a path. Are you gonna complain about it now?"

Orson frowned at her and she stuck her tongue out playfully in return. That path hadn't been there before the sky show, he was sure of it. There had been nothing but grass in every direction. He opened his mouth to say something to Natalie again but she had already stepped onto the flattened grass. He bit his tongue, knowing that whatever he said would probably be answered sarcastically anyway. Maybe this path *was* here the entire time. He could have missed it; he had certainly missed a lot of things in his life before today.

In a weird way, Orson hoped he was right, that the path hadn't been there a moment ago. With the grass beaten down the way it was it would have to mean that something had been there before them, and that thought unnerved him. The last thing he wanted was to be following the trail of some unknown creature—or even worse, a *known* creature, possibly one with scales or fur.

Natalie had already started following the trail. Swallowing down the fresh lump in his throat, Orson hurried to catch up, not wanting to be left alone, and they began following the beaten trail.

There was no way to tell how much time had passed as they walked, but Orson suspected it had been at least an hour before they took a short break. The land around hadn't changed much since they started walking, fields of grass reaching out from one horizon to the next. A little more vegetation had started to appear, but nothing more than a few bushes and an occasional small tree, no bigger than a sapling, but enough to reassure Orson that they weren't just walking in circles. At first he had tried remembering some of the trees and bushes in case they needed to make a hasty retreat, but after an hour of walking one tree had blended into the next, one shrub indistinguishable from the previous one, and he stopped trying.

Soon after they had resumed their walk, Natalie stopped on the crest of a large hill without warning and Orson walked into her, nearly knocking her over. To the right of the path, the hill dropped dangerously steep towards a small grove of trees. Orson didn't like standing so close to the edge, but Natalie seemed nonplussed. "That's twice you've knocked into me today," she said.

"Why are you stopping?" he asked, wanting to be away from the hill despite the ache in his legs. Natalie set a wicked pace and he had to push himself to keep up with her. He hated admitting as much to Natalie; she already thought he was a wimp, and probably a whiner. He didn't need to add any more fuel to the fire. Still, his endurance had its limits and his had crumbled away about ten minutes ago, but he thought he could make it a little further, at least until they were on more level ground.

"I think it's gonna rain soon," she said. As if waiting for her words, a crack of thunder pounded in the sky above them. Orson looked up into the sky, which had become thick with dark clouds. Another crack of thunder echoed amongst the clouds and he shuddered.

"That can't be good."

"I think we should find somewhere to hide before the rain comes," Natalie said and Orson nodded.

"That sounds like a good idea, but where do we go? There's not much along this path. I doubt those little bushes will give us much protection."

"What about down there?" Natalie pointed down the hill to the right of the path.

The ground fell away a few paces ahead, rolling down the edge of a large hill that fell a good thirty feet before giving way to a large grove of trees. The hill looked pretty steep, and Orson moaned as he looked down it. He was afraid she was going to say that.

"You think that's smart?" he asked. "If it starts raining, that hill's gonna get pretty slippery. And it looks like a pretty long fall. I think we should keep walking."

"Not scared of heights, are you Orson?" Natalie asked smartly.

Orson was starting to get tired of Natalie's constant ribbing. It had been amusing for awhile, but he was tired from all the walking, let alone the butterflies that had been gnawing away at his insides since they had come into this strange world. That she was right didn't help his irritation, of course.

"Do you talk to your parents like that?" he asked testily.

"Of course. Doesn't everybody?"

Orson opened his mouth to respond when the first drop of rain splattered down on his nose. Another splashed on the lens of his glasses and he wiped them on the sleeve of his shirt.

"I think those trees are the best bet. I don't think we'll make it anywhere else in time, and I don't know about you, but I don't feel like spending the next few hours soaking wet." Natalie waved down at the hill. "Unless you're afraid, of course."

Orson growled and pushed past her. He was *not* afraid of a little hill, and would prove it to her. Large raindrops were hitting the ground every few feet around him now.

They had only managed to climb down a few feet when Orson's fears were realized and the skies opened up, pounding them with rain. The drops were heavy and soaking; with every step, the grass was becoming slicker and Orson could feel his control slipping. On one step, his foot skidded, and he barely caught his balance. Above him, Natalie was giggling mercilessly.

"How can you possibly think this is funny?" Orson growled up at her. "We might as well be trying to walk down a water sli...Oh cripes!"

Orson cried out as his foot slid completely out from underneath and he fell hard, somehow twisting around and landing on his stomach. He had barely hit the grass when he started skidding down the hill. Stretching out a desperate hand, he caught Natalie's ankle just as she started laughing at him and pulled her down with him. Together they tumbled end over end, bouncing and sliding along on the wet grass. Orson caught a quick view of the trees at the bottom, which were growing quickly larger and threatening.

There was no way they were going to miss the trees at the bottom, Orson thought despairingly. When they hit them, it was going to hurt. He screamed and closed his eyes, waiting for the pain to come.

⌐ TWELVE ⌐

Orson came to a rolling stop, his eyes closed so tightly he thought they must have sunken completely back into his head. There was no explosive pain, no sudden impact. The abrupt and rough stop he had expected at the bottom of the hill never came and as he lay motionless at the bottom of the hill, he gasped in a deep breath before opening his eyes. Barely an inch away from the end of his nose, the bark of a very large and mean looking spruce tree glared back at him.

He rolled over onto his back with a deep moan, letting the falling raindrops splatter on his face while he waited for his heart to slow down. A few feet away, he could hear Natalie struggling to catch her own breath.

"Natalie?" He sat up, ignoring his own aching body. Maybe she hadn't been as fortunate as him and had hit one of the trees. A knot of panic clenched at his belly; if she was badly hurt he didn't know what he would do. His fingers crept up to the scratch on his cheek. He had already learned that just because this was a dream didn't mean it couldn't hurt you in real life, and they were as far away from a hospital as humanly possible. Crawling on his hands and knees, he scuttled over to Natalie's quivering body, trying to steel himself for what he knew he would find. Maybe a broken leg, or a nasty and bleeding gash, or something even worse.

Natalie was curled in a ball, her feet pressed against the trunk of a tree. Orson didn't want to touch her, but had to see if she was okay. Reaching out a trembling hand, his fingers grazed her shoulder, and she rolled over onto her back. She was laughing so hard tears were streaming down her cheeks and she could barely hold a breath. "Can we do it again?" she gasped between sobbing gasps of laughter.

Orson growled as he fell back. "You're nuts, you know that? Absolutely nuts."

"And you scream well," she countered. "Are you alright?"

Orson nodded. He was sore and would have bruises on his body in places he didn't know existed but was otherwise fine; he suspected his pride had taken the biggest hit. His glasses were sitting lopsided on his nose, and he reached up to fix them.

"Great," he said, looking at the bent frame before trying to straighten it out. The glasses still sat a little crooked on his nose, but at least they wouldn't fall off.

"At least we won't have to look for water if we get thirsty," Natalie said, sitting up and resting her back against the tree. "We can just squeeze it out of my shirt."

"I guess we don't have to get out of the rain anymore," Orson said, and despite himself a smile broke out on his face. Natalie looked at him, her hair a tangled mess full of grass and dirt, and the two of them burst out laughing. By the time they were able to look at each other with a straight face again, Orson's sides felt like they were about to split.

"It's about time you had some fun," Natalie said, wiping a fresh tear from her cheek. "I was starting to think you were going to be grumpy the whole time."

"A near death experience shouldn't be funny," Orson protested, trying to make his face serious again, which only brought about another burst of giggles from both of them. The laughter soon turned into a loud grumble in Orson's stomach.

"Hungry?" Natalie said and Orson nodded, somewhat surprised. He'd been so worried about everything else that food hadn't crossed his mind even once. Now as they sat in the wet grass, his appetite had arrived with attitude. He quietly cursed himself for not thinking about that when they were back in his bedroom. Being in a dream, the idea that they might actually need to eat never even occurred to him.

"What are we going to do about food?" he asked, the laughter gone now. Whatever good humor he had found left just as quickly.

Natalie didn't answer. Her head was cocked slightly to one side and she was looking back into the trees. Whatever she was looking at, it seemed to have replaced any notions of appetite for her.

"Something's here," she said and Orson's heart jumped up into his throat almost immediately. "Did you hear that?"

"Hear what?" Orson squeaked just as a *snap* reached his ears. It sounded like a twig breaking. Eyes wide, he turned to look in the direction of the sound but couldn't see anything past the first few trees.

"It came from in there," she said, looking around one of the trees to see deeper into the grove. They waited for a few tense, quiet moments for any other sounds, but none came. Tired of playing the waiting game, Natalie quietly got to her feet and made to step around the nearest tree and into the grove.

"What are you doing?" Orson whispered, catching her wrist. "Don't even think about it!"

Natalie twisted away from Orson's grip and she pressed a finger to her lips, motioning for Orson to keep quiet. Her curiosity had gotten the better of her and she started walking around the tree, stepping carefully through the fallen leaves; the rain had soaked them enough to mask the sound of crunching leaves. Orson crawled to the edge of the tree and watched her.

She made it a few feet before turning back to Orson, curling her finger in a *come here* motion. He shook his head and she repeated the gesture with a stern frown. "I shouldn't have brought her to my dream," he grumbled to himself, walking gingerly towards her. "She's a magnet for trouble."

When he reached her, Natalie tried to direct him around one side of the tree. "Go that way," she whispered. "We'll circle around, maybe catch it off guard."

"No way," Orson protested. "If we're doing anything, we're doing it together. There's no way I'm walking into a trap alone."

"You're so paranoid, Orson," Natalie said, but didn't try to convince him any further. She instead pointed to what looked to be a large pine tree a few feet away from the one they were standing next to. "I think it's behind that tree."

"*Para*-what? I don't even know what that means!"

Raising a finger to her lips to shush him, Natalie cocked her head, listening for anything else that might give away whatever was there. Orson followed closely, gripping her sleeve as they stalked as quietly as possible into the grove of trees. They made it as far as the tree Natalie had pointed out when a low purring sound made them pause. Orson's stomach growled again, but it wasn't *his* food he was worried about.

"We're gonna end up as something's lunch, you know that, right?"

Natalie shushed him again with a heated look. Gathering in a deep breath, she lunged around the tree and ran straight towards the large pine, leaving Orson a step behind as he struggled to catch up.

"Natalie!" he called, chasing after her. "Don't...!"

He rounded the pine tree and nearly hit Natalie as she had come to a sudden stop. A strange sound was coming from her, and it took Orson a moment to realize she was giggling again. "It's so cute!" she exclaimed, and he peeked over her shoulder.

Standing on two ridiculously large feet easily five sizes too big for its tiny body, the strangest little creature Orson had ever seen stared at the two of them with beady black eyes that poked out from an impossible amount of red fur. Its fur was so thick Orson couldn't tell where its head stopped and its body began, if it even had a body.

"It's a dustmop with feet," he said. Natalie was already stepping closer to the thing with her hand outstretched. The red-furred creature was no taller than her knees.

Orson grabbed her arm. "Do you think that's a good idea?"

"C'mon, Orson," she said, pulling her arm free. "Look at it. Do you really think that little cutie could hurt us? It's like a big gerbil."

"Have you ever been bitten by a gerbil? It hurts."

The walking dustmop, as Orson had already named it, made a clucking sound and took a shuffling step closer to sniff at Natalie's offered hand. With a loud purring slurp, the thing licked her fingertips and she squealed in delight.

"See? It's friendly." She reached a little further, scratching its head and it leaned into her hand, purring like a little lawnmower. "Part gerbil, part cat."

"And part dustmop," Orson said again, shrugging when Natalie frowned at him.

"Be nice, Orson."

The thing looked up at Natalie, then Orson, before turning to look into the grove of trees. It made three barking sounds. A series of similar clucking sounds answered almost immediately.

Right before their eyes, the trees seemed to come alive with furry walking dustmops. A handful of the little creatures scurried out from behind trees and bushes, some with red fur like the first one, others orange and one a bright yellow. More dropped down from the leaves and branches of a few trees, and a couple seemed to come up right out of the ground. Orson tried counting but lost track after a dozen or so had appeared to join the first.

"There's so many of them!" Natalie exclaimed, but Orson wasn't half as excited to see them. He thought they could handle one of these things, but an entire pack? There must have been at least twenty.

"Natalie, I think we should go now. Maybe this wasn't such a good idea." The yellow one was looking directly at him and it made him nervous. There was something in the way it looked at him, something hungry.

"Relax, Orson. Look at these things. They're like little squirrels, or gophers. I bet they only eat berries and nuts, don't you, little guy? Haven't you ever fed squirrels in the park? They always come out in bunches when they think it's safe."

She stroked the first one again and it purred, looking up at her with adoring eyes. A small group of dustmops slowly formed a circle around her as she pet the first, each one hopping up and down, trying to catch her affection. All except the yellow one, which continued to stare at Orson.

"Something's wrong," he said.

"Something's always wrong with you, Orson. The mountains are dark, the hill is too steep, the little furry cuties are gonna eat us. Have some fun, already."

Orson took a step back instead and the yellow furball stepped with him. A tickle of goosebumps shot up his arms, a feeling he was starting to dislike immensely. He heard a shuffling sound behind him and risked a quick glance over his shoulder, only to find that more of the dustmops had come out of the trees to block his escape. The tickle of goosebumps became a full wave of butterflies in his stomach.

He was just about to yell at Natalie, insist that they get out of there *now*, that they could still make it as long as they moved immediately, when the strangest thing happened. The little dustmops began to sing.

The red one that they had first met opened its mouth first. Its voice was amazing and haunting, unlike any other singer Orson had ever heard before. One by one the others opened their mouths wide, their songs blending together into a wonderful melody, until every last dustmop had joined into the odd forest choir.

"Oh wow." Natalie clapped excitedly. "They're singing for us!"

Orson couldn't bring himself to share her excitement; there was something unnatural about the song of these things, almost as though they were simply a distraction, or... or...he growled. Why couldn't he think clearly? His thoughts felt muddled, like the song was keeping him from focusing. He looked down at the yellow dustmop. Its eyes watched him unblinkingly as it sang.

The song was so beautiful that Orson didn't notice when the warning bells in his head started to fade away. Natalie had closed her eyes dreamily and was swaying from side to side, lost in the hypnotizing tune.

"Natalie..." Orson started, but forgot what he was going to say. He could feel his own body starting to sway, growing amazingly light. He glanced down and for a moment was surprised that his feet were still on the ground rather than floating above it. His eyelids started drooping and he could think of nothing he wanted more than to listen to the song of these strange little animals. All of his worries were slipping away, carried off on a thick stream of music.

Something lingered at the edge of his consciousness, an annoying voice trying to pull him away from the music. He tried to ignore it—it was just getting in the way of that wonderful melody—but it was stubborn and refused to go easily. Nothing was as important as the music, so why was that stupid voice being so persistent? He vaguely recalled something about a girl, but what was her name? Why did remembering it seem so important?

S...

Sa...

Sar...

"Sarah!" he cried out, the name snapping in his mind like a stretched elastic band. As soon as he said the name, the music missed a beat and dropped out of tune; the clouds in his mind began dissipating inch by inch. Scratching and clawing at the mental block in his mind, he tried to push himself away from the strange trance that fought him note by note. Sarah. He was here to save his sister.

He forced his eyes open with great effort. Natalie was still surrounded by the singing dustmops but she was no longer standing. She was lying flat on her back in a pile of wet leaves, her face a calm mask, her eyes closed. Orson tried to move to her so he could pull her away from the singing dustmops. As hard as he tried, his legs wouldn't move. They seemed to have a mind of their own. He pushed harder, struggling to regain control over his own body, and was rewarded with a single step. The next step took a little less effort and the next even less.

The yellow dustmop saw that it was losing its grip on Orson and stared at him with furious eyes. It turned and yelled something at the other furballs that had gathered around Orson and they closed into a tighter circle around him. In unison they all began to sing again, this time swaying back and forth themselves, one big hypnotic wall of song and fur. The power of their song and dance took hold over Orson again and he felt himself slipping away for a second time.

He struggled valiantly but this time was unable to hold on. The wall in his mind started to tumble again, brick by mental brick. All thoughts of rescuing Natalie slipped away and he let them go without much of a fight. Sarah was next. In moments, Orson couldn't remember why he had been fighting this glorious song in the first place.

His eyes closed just in time for him to miss the shadow of the great form that stepped in front of him. Its roar was lost in the music.

⌊ THIRTEEN ⌋

Orson didn't realize the music had stopped until two big hands grabbed him by the shoulders and gave him a rough shake. The last resonating notes of the dustmops' song faded away and he was able to open his eyes, squinting into the suddenly painful dim light of day. A great shadow fell across him and he looked up into the golden eyes of a great wolf.

With a strangled cry, he fell backwards, landing in a pile of wet leaves. "Don't eat me!"

"Orson," Lupus said. "Relax, it's just me, Lupus. You're alright."

Orson scrambled backwards until he was at arm's length from the wolf while he tried to shake the last cobwebs from his head. Why was the wolf here? The last thing he remembered was walking into this grove of trees, spotting that red, furry little creature. Natalie had been with him and she had fallen to the ground.

"Where's Natalie?" he asked, trying to sound brave despite cowering against the tree. "You ate her, didn't you? Cough her up, right now!"

Lupus pointed off to the side. "If you mean the little she-human lying on the ground, she's fine. I really don't like the taste of human all that much. Leaves a very unpleasant aftertaste."

Orson cringed with wide eyes, wondering just how the wolf knew what a human tasted like until he saw Lupus was panting in short gasps and realized the wolf was laughing.

"That's not funny," he growled. He looked to his left and saw Natalie lying on the ground, curled up in a ball not ten feet away.

"Natalie," he called to her. "Wake up."

Natalie didn't respond, and Orson shuffled closer. Nudging her with his foot, he called out to her again, but she refused to move. He looked back at Lupus, eyeing the big wolf suspiciously.

"Is she...?"

Lupus panted again. "She's alive, Orson, but was knocked out by the Siren's song. She'll recover. She absorbed quite a bit of the song, though, and will likely be out for awhile."

"Sirens? Are you talking about those little walking dustmops?"

"Yes. They're called Sirens. Nasty little critters, if you ask me." Lupus's snout wrinkled in a wolfish scowl. "They use their song to trap their prey. It renders their food rather helpless."

"Their food?" Orson gulped.

"Of course. You didn't think they were just playing with you, did you?"

Orson swallowed again and started looking around, expecting to see more of the dustmops—the *Sirens*—come clambering out, hungry jaws snapping for them.

"Don't worry, they're gone. They're fierce around animals that seem like easy prey, but one roar and they scatter quickly. Little scavengers, that's all they are." He spat distastefully. "Most of the Siren's were around your friend, but there were enough of them to trap someone twice your size. You must have put up quite a struggle."

"I lost, didn't I?" Orson said. He hardly felt proud about falling into the trap of a knee-high hairball.

"You're still alive, aren't you?"

Orson didn't answer, instead gripping Natalie by the shoulders and trying to shake her awake, not wanting to think about how close he had come to being something's meal ticket. Natalie showed no signs of stirring.

"She'll be fine once we get her away from here. But we need to leave, and quickly. The Sirens are the least of our worries at the moment."

Orson looked back up at Lupus. The wolf was peering around the grove as though he expected something to come out at any moment. "What are you talking about?"

"That sky display when you arrived was spectacular, wasn't it?" Lupus asked.

It took a moment before Orson understood that Lupus must have been talking about the colours that had erupted above him and Natalie when they had first entered this weird land. "You saw that?"

"*Everybody* saw it. It's called the New Dawn, and doesn't happen often. But when it does, it's pretty hard to miss. It's only happened twelve times before today."

"Why only twelve times?"

"The coming of the New Dawn signifies something special in the Dreamlands, an arrival of sorts. Now, I must insist that we hurry, Orson. The New Dawn may have been glorious, but it also served as a beacon to your location and I am probably not the only one following it. I can think of at least one other who will not be far behind. I think you know of who I speak."

It took Orson a second, and when he did realize who Lupus meant it sent a shiver down his spine. "Sithyrus," he said, and Lupus nodded. "How would it be able to find me? That sky thing must have happened everywhere."

"The New Dawn would have been visible everywhere, but the center of it was right above you. Follow that and whoever may be looking would know where to start searching for you. Besides that, a New Dawn hasn't been seen in the Dreamlands in over one hundred years, so its coming has sparked a great deal of excitement throughout the land."

Orson shook his head. "This is more of that garbage you were trying to tell before, isn't it? It's all part of how I'm supposed to be some sort of hero."

"Yes. The time for explanations is later, though. For now, we have to leave, and quickly."

I can leave, Orson thought but didn't say it out loud. *I can leave this dream. I've done it before.*

Orson had met Lupus in his dreams three times and had managed to wake himself up every time. One more time shouldn't be that difficult. Just tell the wolf to go away, wake up, and be rid of all of this. Until the next dream. And the one after that. He had managed to escape each time, sure, but he had also ended up right back in the middle of one of these stupid dreams the very next time he fell asleep.

There was also Natalie to consider, and Sarah. If he left now, he would be abandoning both of them to whatever nightmares this place had in store. Natalie might wake up on her own, that was possible, but what if she didn't? And what about Sarah? If she was going to wake back up to the real world, wouldn't she have done so by now?

"What's going to happen to Natalie?" he finally asked. "Will she be all right?"

Lupus stepped closer, and Orson crowded protectively over Natalie's still body. "I can carry your companion until we are safe. And when she–Natalie–wakes up, she's going to want to be comfortable. Waking up from a Siren's song is not a very pleasant feeling. I imagine she'll have quite a headache."

"I feel fine," Orson said, though he was still feeling slightly muddled.

"You fought the spell and hadn't fallen fully under its effect when I arrived." Lupus placed a hand on Orson's shoulder and looked down with some concern at the boy. "Please, Orson, we must hurry. Sithyrus will be here soon, and it won't be coming alone this time. On a good day I may be able to handle the lizard, but a company of Nightmares would be a different story."

Orson was torn between the desire to wake himself up and the uncertainty of what would happen to Natalie. His sister was already missing because of him, and he didn't think he could handle the guilt of being responsible for another. For a moment Orson wondered if he would be able to bring Natalie with him if he did wake up, but quickly decided against trying. If he failed, the last thing he wanted was to leave her stranded and unconscious in the hands of an angry wolf.

"Alright," he said reluctantly. He didn't see any other choice at the moment. "Just be careful with her."

Lupus visibly relaxed. "Of course. She'll soon be in more comfortable surroundings."

Lupus stepped over them and Orson cringed, pressing down over Natalie for a moment before reluctantly stepping away. This was the closest he had been to the wolf since he had come out of the gym at Mardell in his dream. The wolf leaned down and gently picked Natalie up as easily as if she were a stuffed toy. When he had her cradled comfortably in one arm, he reached into a pouch that was latched around his waist and produced a small pearl.

"What's that?" Orson eyed the pearl suspiciously. Lupus held it down so he could see it better. The inside of the pearl was full of a swirling blue and white mist, and a strange light radiated brightly outward.

"It's a portice," Lupus said. "When it is burst, it creates a portal to another place to allow for quicker travel. You may want to cover your eyes."

Lupus looked deep into the portice and said in a firm voice: "Palace." With a quick flick, he hurled the pearl to the ground where it exploded brilliantly. Orson cried out and fell backwards, blinded for a moment by the burst of light.

"Ouch," Orson rubbed at his eyes until the spots disappeared from his vision. Lupus panted laughter.

"I told you to cover your eyes."

Once his vision cleared, Orson looked where Lupus had thrown the small pearl. The light had faded, but in its place stood a doorway twice the size of the one that had once been his bedroom mirror. Like the mirror, Orson could see his reflection in the shimmering doorway and saw that same strange blur. The reflection slowly faded and was replaced by what appeared to be an enormous room on the other side.

"This will take us directly to Aurora's palace," Lupus explained.

Orson looked at the doorway uneasily. He still wasn't sold on the idea of going anywhere with Lupus but had no choice now with Natalie snuggled in the big wolf's furry arms.

"I hope it's not like my mirror," Orson said with a restless sigh.

"Your mirror?" Lupus asked, cocking his head curiously.

"That's how we got here. Natalie was leaning on the mirror in my bedroom and she fell into it, or through it, or however it works. It was disgusting," he added distastefully. "Like stepping through a big bowl of cold pudding."

Lupus lifted his free hand, gesturing for Orson to go first. "I assure you, this one will be much more comfortable."

A thought occurred to Orson. "Won't they just follow us to the palace, using one of those portice things?" Orson asked.

"The palace is safe from their portices. They won't be able to follow us there, just as I wouldn't be able to follow them by portice if they were to find you. There are shields up, put in place hundreds of years ago, that prevent either side from penetrating the other's quarters through the use of a portice. The closest they would get is fifty miles from the palace. Besides, they would be foolish to try and invade the palace with only a small group. Strong as they have gotten, they would need a sizable force to conquer the Queen's palace. Now, if you would." He pointed again to the doorway.

"You first," Orson said, standing pat.

"If something happens, I would rather you were safely in the palace. With Sithyrus close behind, I would hope you feel the same."

Orson started to protest, but stopped. As unfair as it seemed, the wolf had a point. If Sithyrus did show up, he didn't want to be the only one on this side of the portal. Stepping up to the door, Orson pushed his hand through. Like his mirror, the image rippled around his hand. This time, however, there was no cold sensation or any feeling of thickness. His hand passed through easily and without much discomfort. He looked back at Lupus, who waved him on.

"Quickly, please. We really are in a bit of a rush."

Another idea hit Orson. It sounded absurd, but so did everything else in this strange land, so he decided to ask anyway. "Are you the Armed Sherpa?"

"Armed Sherpa?" Lupus's frown deepened. "Please, Orson, we don't have time for this."

Orson noticed something behind the wolf. A pocket of air had started shifting and a thin line appeared. It slowly began opening up, the mirror like surface growing. With a gulp, Orson thought he knew what was on the other side.

"Alright," he said. Pinching his nose, he stepped into the portice, Lupus close behind. For a moment he thought he heard a seething hiss before everything around him vanished.

⌞ FOURTEEN ⌟

Orson stopped dead in his tracks. His lungs didn't seem to want to draw a breath as he looked around his stunning new surroundings with unabashed awe. The realization that he had just been nearly eaten by a flock of walking puffballs slipped momentarily away from him as he gaped in astonishment at the incredible building he had just entered.

Through the guise of the portal, the trees of the Sirens' forest had transformed almost seamlessly into a marvel of architectural design; an enormous room bigger than any other Orson had seen in his short years, at least the size of a football field. The dynamic trees of the forest were now immense marble columns, stretching up to a vaulted ceiling at least fifty feet above his head. Heavy wooden rafters stretched from one side of the ceiling to the other, crisscrossing at great lengths to support the even heavier stone roof. Spaced at even intervals across the ceiling, giant gold braziers hung down like giant earrings, glimmering in the reflected light of the room.

The pockets of sky that had been visible between the branches of the trees were replaced by twenty-foot panels of stained glass windows, looming equally magnificent as the light from outside poured through in multi-colored streams. Below the windows, arranged in neatly pressed rows of intricately woven designs, glorious tapestries stared out into the room. Within each tapestry, a person—some of them male, others female—watched over the room like silent sentries. Looking at the tapestries was like looking through doorways into other worlds; the detail in the pictures was so lifelike, despite being woven from thread and needle.

In the center of the room, the grassy path through the forest had become a long red carpet, leading its way between the marble columns from one end of the room to the other. From where he was standing, Orson couldn't quite see where the carpet ended. Before he could step around to see, a shadow fell across him. Turning around, he looked up as Lupus joined him, still cradling Natalie in his furry arms.

"Where are we?" Orson asked the wolf.

"*The Palates dal Dremora*," Lupus answered. "The Palace of Dreams. This is the Great Hall. I take it you're impressed?"

Orson looked around, taking in as much of the hall with his eyes as he could. "It's...huge," was all he could breathlessly muster. "I've never seen anything like it."

Lupus smiled, his long pink tongue lolling out his mouth. "I would be surprised if you had. The Palace of Dreams has been around for nearly a thousand years. The architects who built it were masters in their craft, their secrets lost with them long ago. Many have tried in vain to duplicate the wonders of the Palace. None have come close."

Staring up at the stained glass windows high above them, Orson could believe it. In his own world, he had seen pictures of ancient churches and modern day buildings, and none of them carried the same effortless grace of this place.

Orson looked past Lupus at one of the tapestries hanging from the marble-tiled walls. It was a picture of a young man dressed in a black robe, holding a staff high above his head. The head of the staff was shining with a brilliance that seemed all too real within the thread-woven image. Beneath his feet, a horde of dark figures bowed low, staring up at the black-robed man in fear.

"Who is that?" Orson asked, finding himself drawn to the man. There was something wickedly fascinating about him; even in thread, the man radiated a power that Orson could feel through the tapestry.

"Oleandar," Lupus said fondly. "The first King of the Dreamlands. It was under his direction that the Palace of Dreams was constructed."

Orson looked up at the wolf in shock. "The first king? He looks like a teenager!"

"Sixteen, I believe, at the time he became king," Lupus confirmed. Orson shook his head in astonishment. A sixteen-year old king? That kind of responsibility and pressure was unfathomable.

"What are all those things at his feet?"

Lupus looked at the shadowy figures crowding Oleandar's feet and sniffed. "Nightmares. Before Oleandar arrived in the Dreamlands, the Nightmares had a strong hold over the Dremians that lived before us," Lupus explained. "Oleandar was not only the first king, but the first Dreamshaper as well, and led the Dremians out from under the dark shadow of the Nightmares. Under the reign of Nightmares like Sithyrus, the Dremians were little more than slaves. Oleandar led them out from that shadow, giving the Dremians a chance to live honestly and happily. It was a long, brutal war, but one that earned us the lives we enjoy now."

Nightmares. Orson peered at the painting and shivered. Even bowed at the feet of Oleandar they gave him the creeps. It was hard to imagine Sithyrus ever bowing down before anyone carrying a glowing stick, especially a sixteen-year-old kid.

Stepping back to get a better view of the tapestry in its entirety, Orson bumped into something. "Careful now," a raspy voice scolded him. Orson turned around to apologize but lost the words as he looked upon a creature with the head and fur of a skunk. The glowering little skunkman was about to say something else but froze solid when he looked up at Orson.

"Are you..." he stammered before turning to Lupus, "I mean, is that...is that *him*?" Lupus nodded and the skunk

99

took a step back. Grabbing one of Orson's hands, he shook it furiously. "So sorry, mate. I shouldn't be stepping behind people like that."

"That's okay," Orson said awkwardly as his arm was nearly shaken free of its socket. The skunkman walked away from them, apologizing and bowing with every step. "That was weird," Orson whispered to Lupus as he watched the skunk's retreat. "What was all that about?"

Lupus only smiled and shrugged. Orson turned back to the tapestry when a drop of water splashed down onto his head. Looking up, he gasped at the sight of two impossibly large grasshoppers clinging to the wall several dozens of feet above their heads. Each grasshopper held a bucket of water with one leg and a cloth with another as they busily wiped down the marble tiles. Another slosh of water escaped one of the buckets and splashed to the floor beside Orson's feet. One of the grasshopper's waved a spindly limb down at him, telling Orson to move back unless he wanted to get soaked.

"We're cleaning here!" the other grasshopper called out to Orson as though it was his fault that he was getting splashed. The grasshopper shook its head and went back to scrubbing.

Orson stepped out of range of falling water and looked back to the center of the Great Hall, watching as a pair of walrus-like creatures spoke closely to one another, staring in the direction of the boy and the wolf. When they realized they had caught Orson's attention, the walrus-things quickly hurried on their way.

Here and there in the hall, other strange creatures moved in scattered clumps. Some carried piles of cloths and blankets, others held bundles of important looking parchment. One lady—at least Orson assumed it was a lady, though she was covered head-to-foot in coarse grey fur—was holding a basket of strange looking fruits. She offered one to Lupus, a crescent-shaped, red-tipped fruit that looked to Orson like a miniature banana—but froze when she noticed the wolf's companion. Babbling something Orson couldn't comprehend, she quickly left the two of them alone, casting wide-eyed looks at them as she hurried on her way.

"What are they?" Orson whispered up to Lupus; his voice carried in the cavernous room if he talked too loudly.

"Dremians," the wolf answered, not at all concerned with keeping his voice low. "The people of the Dreamlands. In better days, the Grand Hall would be full of them, bustling about, trying to gain an audience with the Queen. These days, however, most are too afraid to be outside of their houses for too long, and I can't blame them. The Palace is safe, but the nearest town is a few miles to the south and nobody wants to be caught out on the open ground by the Nightmares. Ambushes are incredibly rare, but they *have* happened, even this close to the Palace."

"Why don't they just use those portals, like the one we used?"

"Townsfolk are no longer permitted to carry portices with them," Lupus explained. "The last thing we need is a Nightmare getting its dirty hands on one and sneaking inside the Palace. From the outside, the Palace of Dreams is nearly impenetrable, but if one of them ever got inside it would cause a great deal of trouble."

"That makes sense," Orson said. "Have any Nightmares ever gotten inside?"

"Once," Lupus answered. "It took a month to clean the hallways of its stink."

That was something Orson could understand. He had experience firsthand the foul odor of Sithyrus. Of course, he had a feeling that the wolf wasn't only talking about the smell. Another trio of Dremians passed, and this group didn't even try to hide their stares. Frowning, Orson stared back until they were out of sight.

"Why do they all keep looking at me like that?"

Lupus shrugged. "Probably for the same reason that you stared at me when you first saw me. It's not everyday a human walks these halls."

"Some of them don't seem very happy to see me,"

Orson remarked, thinking of the basket-carrying creature.

"Unfortunately, the presence of a human in the Great Hall is usually surrounded by suspicious circumstances. Most humans aren't able to enter the Dreamlands this deeply. You are as strange to them as they must be to you."

Orson had a feeling Lupus wasn't being completely open with him. The skunkman's words echoed quietly in his head for a moment. *Is that him?* The skunkman hadn't appeared hesitant to see a human in the Palace; he had seemed downright awestruck. Before he could ask, Lupus nudged him into motion.

Walking along the walls of the Great Hall, Orson counted eleven tapestries in all, each one much more extravagant than the next and certainly more interesting than anything he had seen in the museums he had visited with his mother. Like Oleandar's tapestry, each picture depicted a prominent figure in the center, surrounded by shadowy forms. The one furthest from where they had entered the palace showed a man dressed in shining armour and wielding a sword high above his head. Dark shapes stood around the man, encircling him but seeming more terrified than terrifying. The next tapestry showed a man slightly hidden behind a large tree, holding a glowing orb of light in one hand and pushing it into the darkness of the trees.

One by one, Lupus identified the figures in the pictures. There was Alexander, fighting through impossible odds with only his sword. David, stalking through an icy forest that Lupus called the Frozen Woods. There was a picture of a man standing on the ramparts of a large castle. Another showed a tiny, lean man in a ripped shirt using an axe to cut down a large, ominous looking tree.

Lupus walked him through each wall hanging, patiently explaining who the people in them were each time they stopped. When they finally reached the last one, Lupus smiled down at the boy. "I know you're full of questions, but we've got an important matter to attend to still. There is someone who would like to meet you, and I think we've kept her waiting long enough."

"Who's this?" Orson asked, studying the last tapestry. A young man stared out from the fabric, wearing little more than a pair of shorts, his body covered in dozens of scars as he held a shield high above his head. His mouth was open as though he were screaming at something. The man's face was shadowed too darkly to see what he really looked like, but as Orson stared into the tapestry he felt a weird sense that he had seen this man before. There was something about the way he stood. Orson shook his head; he had seen countless numbers of action hero movies. This man probably looked like someone from a movie he had once seen.

"Ah, that would be Derek," Lupus answered and Orson thought the wolf sounded almost sad as he looked at the picture. "He was the next-to-last Dreamshaper. During a battle with the Nightmares two generations ago, he was lost to us, but not before he managed to drive the Nightmares back from an assault on the Palace."

"Lost? Where did he go?"

Lupus shrugged. "Nobody knows. Derek went out in search of the Nightmares, intending to put a stop to their attack on the Palace. A few days after his departure, the Nightmares retreated back to the Haunted Mountain, but Derek never returned. The Dremians spent months searching for him, but found no signs. Most believe he died during a great battle that ultimately forced the Nightmares into retreat."

Orson stared at the tapestry a moment longer. He still couldn't shake the feeling that there was something he wasn't seeing quite right in the picture, but before he could look any closer Lupus hurried him away.

"We really should go and see her, Orson. She's been waiting quite awhile now."

"See who?" Orson asked as they moved back towards the center of the Great Hall.

"Queen Aurora," Lupus answered and Orson paused.

"The Queen?" he said, barely mouthing the words. "The Queen of all...*this*...wants to meet me?"

"She's quite eager, actually. And you should never keep a Queen waiting. It's simply not polite. Besides, my arms are starting to get tired from carrying your friend. She's heavier than she seems."

Orson couldn't suppress a sharp laugh, despite the dark situation that had left Natalie unconscious. "I'll make sure I tell her that when she wakes up."

Orson followed Lupus as he stepped onto the red carpet and walked down the Great Hall between the immense columns. Finally able to see down to the far end of the carpet, Orson saw it led to a large stone platform at the far end of the Great Hall. A large chair rested atop the platform. Someone was sitting in the chair, watching them approach down the carpet. Orson didn't need to be a rocket scientist to figure out who the person in the chair must be.

As they reached the foot of the platform, Orson looked up at the girl in the chair and barely suppressed a gasp. Beautiful wasn't a strong enough word for the girl—and she couldn't be *more* than a girl, Orson realized. Wearing a simple white gown that shimmered in the light of the Hall, she was the most spectacular girl Orson had ever seen. An ocean of golden hair flowed freely over her shoulders, decorated by a small silver tiara encrusted with tiny purple gems. Bright blue eyes that glimmered magically looked down at them and Orson felt his cheeks start to blush under her gaze.

"Orson Bailey, welcome to the Dreamlands," she said when they were standing before the platform. "I am Aurora, Queen of the Dreamlands."

"Buh..." was all Orson managed to squeeze out. The Queen giggled lightly before looking up at Lupus. Standing on the red carpet, the wolf still stood at eye level to the Queen in her chair up on the platform.

"Who is the girl?" she asked the wolf.

"A friend of the Orson's," Lupus said and held Natalie

up higher so the Queen could get a closer look. "She is under the Siren's spell. Orson managed to break it momentarily, but the girl wasn't so lucky."

When Aurora looked at Orson this time, her eyes were open wide in amazement. "You escaped the Siren's song?" she asked him.

"I don't know if I would say escaped," Orson said in a voice barely above a whisper. "Lupus showed up just in time."

Orson felt ridiculously small under the Queen's intense gaze. How could this girl be a Queen? She couldn't be more than thirteen years old, yet she radiated with power and confidence that belied her young appearance, much the same as Oleandar had from his place in the tapestry. He had never seen a Queen before; girl or not, she was still incredibly intimidating.

"Can you help Natalie?" he squeaked.

Aurora looked at Natalie again and smiled. "Lupus, will you please take the girl where she will be comfortable? I wish to speak with Orson alone for a few minutes."

Lupus gave the Queen a slight bow and turned away, leaving Orson alone with the Queen of the Dreamlands. As Lupus disappeared around one of the columns, Orson turned back to Aurora and swallowed hard.

"Your friend will be fine. You'll see her very soon, and I'm sure she will be happy to see you as well."

Orson nodded, his voice failing him once again.

"You have no idea how happy I am to see you here, Orson. We have been searching long and hard for you, and I worried that the Nightmares would reach you first. Unfortunately, your sister was not so lucky as you seem to have been."

The mention of Sarah snapped Orson back to reality. "Are you going to save her?" he asked.

Aurora smiled sympathetically. "We are going to try, but we need your help. Without the Dreamshaper, we don't stand a chance against the Nightmares.

"Orson, you are the only chance your sister has."

⌞ FIFTEEN ⌟

"Nope," Orson shook his head from side to side. "No way. That's impossible."

Aurora sat patiently as Orson balked at her words. "The signs all point to you," she said when he had settled slightly. "The arrival of the New Dawn confirmed it, as I'm sure Lupus explained. The New Dawn coincides directly with the arrival of the next Dreamshaper into the Dreamlands. The Eye of the Dawn opens up directly above the head of the Dreamshaper. Kind of like your own fireworks welcoming party."

"This has to be a mistake," Orson shook his head. "I'm just a kid. There's no way that I'm this Dream-thinger. I've never even stood up to the bullies in my school. I'm kinda the school dork. Even my baby sister is cooler than me."

"The Red Dawn doesn't make mistakes," Aurora said simply, as though that should be enough to convince him. Clearly, it wasn't.

"What about the other Dreamshapers? Why can't they help?"

"The Dreamlands have been without a *true* Dreamshaper for several years now. Now, the signs have finally come again to show us the next Dreamshaper, and just in the nick of time. The Nightmares..."

"The signs are lying," Orson interrupted in protest. "The skies and whatever else is telling you this is wrong. I'm a ten-year-old kid, a *small* ten-year-old kid. Do you really think I'm gonna be able to fight a bunch of bogeymen and dinosaurs? Even in a dream I'm smart enough to know how crazy *that* idea is."

Aurora smiled sadly. Her blue eyes shone brightly, but the dark bags beneath them loomed just as prominent. It was easy to see she hadn't slept much lately; the stress of whatever was happening in this strange world was clearly weighing down on her. When she spoke again, her voice was tired and strained.

"I had hoped to avoid the conversation turning this way, Orson, but I need you to understand. Time is short and as much as I would like to make this easier on you, I can't. I understand how shocking this is to you..."

"I doubt that," Orson interrupted but Aurora ignored the comment, fixing him instead with a tired but penetrating gaze. Orson clamped his mouth shut. Tired or not, this was a Queen, and probably wouldn't tolerate much more rudeness, not from a simple boy.

"I know more than you may believe at the moment," she told him and, despite his protests, Orson knew she wasn't lying. She was the Queen here, so she must know quite a lot about what was happening—but that didn't mean she was right about all of it. "What I tell you now is not a trick, but the honest truth. A hard truth that I wish I did not have to see, but one you would do well to think about. Without your help, without the *Dreamshaper's* help, you may never see your sister again."

"That's not fair," Orson said meekly.

"It's not a matter of being fair. Without the Dreamshaper, we're simply not strong enough to stand against the Nightmares. Your sister is no doubt a captive deep in the Haunted Mountain, the home of the Nightmares, and without a Dreamshaper we have little chance of rescuing her. And it gets worse."

"Of course it does," Orson grumbled, feeling deflated. What good was a Queen if she couldn't use her power to save a little girl? That feeling of awe over being in the presence of a Queen was quickly fading. Orson supposed that this was what happened when you let a girl only a few years older than him run a kingdom. Shouldn't they have a King or something? In the movies, it was always a King that ruled the kingdom. The Queen was just there to keep him out of trouble.

Aurora rose from her chair and stepped off the platform. Guiding Orson down the red carpet, she continued talking as they walked. "The Nightmares have grown strong over the past few years. We have fought to keep them back, but our strength is fading and will not hold much longer. Soon they will attack the Palace. If we are not ready, if *you* are not ready, the Palace of Dreams will fall."

"Why is this place so important?" Orson asked.

She was close enough now that Orson could have reached out to touch her if he so chose. He caught a whiff of scent that made him think of his mother's lilac tree, a pleasant aroma. "The *Palates dal Demora* has always represented the power of the Dreamlands, and more specifically the power of the Dreamshaper. As disorganized as they have been, the Nightmares have always been intimidated by that power. But now they have a new leader, someone who has organized the Nightmares, and someone that has made them understand that without a true Dreamshaper the Palace of Dreams is much weaker."

"So just find this leader and deal with him," Orson suggested, as though it were that simple. "Get rid of him and the Nightmares will leave you alone, won't they?"

"If only it were that easy," Aurora chuckled dryly. "We've never actually seen him, only heard about him through our spies in the Haunted Mountain. From the information we've gathered, we don't even know if he actually *lives* in the Haunted Mountain with the other Nightmares. Whoever he is, he covers his tracks quite well. And that's just the start of the problem."

"It gets worse?" Orson moaned. This was all starting

to sound like the plot for a really bad movie.

"The Nightmares are constructing a new device, a Machine. Once it is completed, stopping the Nightmares will be nearly impossible."

"A machine? What kind of machine?" Images of tanks and planes paraded through Orson's head, spaceships and weird alien crafts that he had seen in those same bad movies; strange computers with thousands of flashing buttons and twisting dials.

"Yes, a terrible Machine that will allow them to enter the waking world. Your world."

Orson froze. This really *was* the plot for a horribly bad movie. He almost reached across to pinch his own arm, thinking he must be dreaming, but stopped. Of *course* he was dreaming. He wouldn't be in this predicament if he wasn't dreaming.

The thought of Sithyrus walking around freely in his world was mind numbing. He could almost hear the click-click of the lizard's claws on the floor of Mardell as it stalked his classmates, munching on them one-by-one. He could smell the rotten stench of the lizard's breath, breathing down his neck as it stalked him in his own house.

Queen Aurora put a gentle hand on Orson's shoulder and looked deeply into his eyes. "We haven't had a Dreamshaper in nearly fifty years. Twelve have come before you, each one leading the Dremians against the Nightmares in order to maintain the balance of good and evil. You, Orson Bailey, have been chosen as the thirteenth. You are the one to lead us through this next battle. Without you, the Dreamlands will fall back under the shadow of darkness, and it will take your world with it."

Her words hit him like hammer. Here he was, a scrawny little boy who couldn't even face the bullies in his classroom, who had barely escaped the Nightmare Sithyrus not once but twice, and he was being asked to help save two worlds. He had already proven he wasn't up to the task against a single Nightmare. What was he supposed to do against an army of them?

The nagging voice was screaming in his head, telling him to get out now, before it was too late. Find Natalie and run. Leave Sarah here; she was just a baby, it's not like she would really know what was happening. All he would have to do is stay awake for the rest of his life. It would take a lot of coffee, but he could do it.

Looking into Aurora's brilliant but tired blue eyes and sighed. His mom had let him try a sip of her coffee once. He couldn't stand the taste of the stuff.

"How do we save Sarah?"

⌐ SIXTEEN ⌐

Sitting on the edge of a chair in one of the palaces many spare rooms, Orson shifted nervously as he watched Natalie rub her eyes and groan miserably from the couch. She had only woken up a few minutes ago but was clearly feeling the effects of the Siren song, just as Lupus had said she would. Still, as sorry as he felt for her, Orson was nervous for an entirely different reason. Her headache would fade, but his was just beginning.

He was still having trouble believing he had just come face-to-face with an actual *Queen*—not just face-to-face, but had had a conversation with her. He doubted anyone else in his family could say they had met royalty, even if technically it was in a dream. And so what if she looked like she was only a few years older than him? It was still an experience he would never forget.

Watching his friend rubbing the pain from her eyes, Orson felt awash with conflicting emotions. On one hand, he had just met the most important person in the Dreamlands. On the other, she had just told him that *he* was now the most important person in the Dreamlands, and that his baby sister's fate rested in his clumsy, ten-year-old hands. Hands that couldn't even catch a dodgeball in gym class.

"What happened?" Natalie asked, the first time she had spoken in the past few minutes. She rubbed her temples gingerly, trying to soothe away her headache.

Orson gave her a quick update of what had happened

since the Siren attack. He skipped over the unimportant things, skirting around parts he didn't understand—which were many—focusing instead on what the Queen had told him about the Nightmares and the inherent threat to the Dreamlands and apparently their own world. Natalie listened quietly with her head in her hands.

"At least we finally know *something*," she said after he finished, running a hand through her tangled hair. "Do you really think you're this Dream-thingamajig they've been waiting for?"

Orson shrugged. "I dunno. Not really, but what choice do I have? If they can help me save Sarah, I have to at least try. At least until we get my sister back."

Natalie nodded, wincing with the movement and burying her face in her hands. "Tell me more about this Queen," she mumbled between her fingers. "What's she like?"

"Different. I can't explain it, but even though part of me wants to keep away from her I just can't. She seemed really tired, but there was something more about her. You'd have to meet her first, I suppose, but there's something in her eyes...or maybe it was her voice..."

Natalie peeked out between her fingers. "Is she pretty?"

"Beautiful," Orson said, quicker than he had intended. He felt his cheeks blush immediately. "I mean, I guess. Nothing special, though. No different than any other girl."

"Beautiful, huh?" she said and Orson could hear the smile in her words. He shook his head and frowned.

"Oh, get off it. I didn't mean it like that. I mean, she's nice and all...but...well, she's a Queen, and I'm...I'm just a boy. Besides, I don't even like girls. They're just...just..."

"Just what?" Natalie pressed, looking over her fingertips.

"Icky. Girls are icky."

Natalie dropped her hands from her face and frowned at him. "We're icky?" she asked sharply.

"That's not what I meant," Orson tried to recover.

"Then what did you mean? Please, I'd love to know."

Orson shook his head with a light growl. "I didn't mean...I mean...How are you feeling now? How's your headache?"

Sticking her tongue between her teeth, Natalie made a croaking sound. "It feels like someone's been pounding on my head with a hammer. Why didn't this happen to you?"

Orson shrugged. "Lupus said it was because I didn't get knocked out as quickly as you. He told me it was because I'm supposed to be the Dreamshifter."

"Dreamshaper," a dry, raspy voice corrected from the doorway. They both jumped at the voice, Orson landing clumsily on the edge of the chair and tumbling to the floor.

Pulling himself to his feet, Orson stared at the empty doorway. Without warning, a head appeared at the top of the door frame, followed by an upside-down face. It was hard to make out any real facial definitions from the creature's midnight skin besides a pair of curved, pointed mandibles that clicked together in rapid succession. With a graceful twist of its decidedly ungraceful body, the creature dropped to the floor, landing with almost no sound on four long, spindly legs. Four equally spindly arms gripped the inside of the doorway as the thing stepped—*slid*—into the room.

Beneath the light of the room, the children had a better view of the spider-like beast. Two eyes stared back at them like dead lamps, completely black save for a deep red glowing center that moved from Natalie to Orson and back again. The creature's skin was dotted sporadically with small tufts of carefully groomed hair. On either side of a set of strangely humanoid black lips, its cruel looking mandibles clicked together again.

"Nightmare!" Orson cried out, grabbing the chair he had spilled out of and throwing it at the spider-thing. The chair was heavier than he expected and would have fallen well short of the creature, had the spider not shot two thin streams of webbing from two of its hands and ensnared the chair, yanking it from midair to its other two hands. Setting the chair down gently beside the door, the spider looked disdainfully back at the two children.

"Please try not to—*click click click*—wreck the furniture," it said in its dry voice, the mandibles clicking in disapproval. "It's not cheap."

"Orson, what is it?" Natalie asked, grabbing a pillow from the bed and holding it in her hands like a baseball bat.

"I think it's a Nightmare," he said, his heart thumping in his chest. "I don't know how it got in the Palace, but..."

"I am most certainly *not* a—*click click*—Nightmare," the spider said irritably. "I am an Arachnan. My name is Ariadas, First Servant to Queen Aurora. I have been assigned to make sure you and your—*click click click*—female companion are well-nourished this morning."

Orson stared at the spider. This thing was a Dremian? Thinking back to the two grasshoppers that had nearly spilled their soapy water on his head in the Great Hall, he realized that not all Dremians were likely to be cute and fluffy, but a spider? He had always thought of spiders as sinister little bugs. If anything deserved to be a Nightmare, it was a spider.

"Aria...da..." Natalie tried to sound out its name.

"Ariadas, Miss Natalie—*click click*—," the spider servant said, sounding annoyed at having to repeat itself. The way its mandibles clicked every time it spoke was very unnerving. "I assure you, Master Bailey, I won't—*click click click*—tangle you in my webs, so you don't need to stare so unabashedly."

Orson flushed at having been caught staring. "You're a servant?"

"For over fifty years, now, Master Bailey. You seem surprised."

"No, it's just...well, I hate spiders."

"I can't imagine why," Ariadas said. "Now, are you—*click*—ready to eat, Master Bailey, or shall I come back at a—

click click click click—more convenient time?"

"Please don't call me *Master*," Orson said. "I'm not a master of anything. But I am hungry." His stomach agreed loudly, grumbling hungrily at the thought of food. Until the spider had mentioned it, he had forgotten that he hadn't eaten anything in several hours now.

"Naturally," Ariadas said, as though it had already known the answer. Dremian or not, Orson was finding it quite easy to dislike the Arachnan. For a servant, he was clearly full of himself; the constant *clicking* when it talked wasn't helping either. "I have taken the liberty of—*click click*—arranging a meal for you. If you'll kindly follow me I will take you to the dining hall."

Without another word, Ariadas turned on its four legs and disappeared into the hallway. Following the servant through the twists and turns of the Palace, he led the children to a large dining room. Huge rectangular tables formed a long line along the outskirts of the room, surrounding the smaller, circular tables in the middle. At the far end, an enormous oval table on a huge platform was buried beneath a gloriously elaborate tablecloth of blue and gold lace. Orson imagined that particular table was reserved for the Queen herself.

One of the tables in the middle of the room was stacked with an assortment of silver and gold covered trays. Ariadas went to each of the trays and removed the cover, revealing plate after plate of delicious looking food to the palace's two newest guests.

"I trust you will find—*click*—everything to your liking," the servant said after he had opened the final platter. A delicious array of aromas sifted into Orson's nostrils and his stomach responded with a hungry growl that was immediately echoed by Natalie.

On one tray a pile of small and strange fruits glistened at them, freshly washed and still dripping: Orson reached out and plucked a purple heart-shaped berry from a tiny branch that reminded him of a grape stem and popped it into his mouth. The purple heart burst delightfully with juice as he bit into it.

"Tastes like kiwi," he tried to speak around the fruit; it came out more like *tashtes lk kwi*. Natalie giggled before picking up a fist sized ball of red. She bit into it and moaned in pleasure as a trail of juice dribbled down her chin.

"What is this?" she said before taking another large bite.

"That is the pocopo fruit, from the Red Trees of the—*click click*—Euclypt Forest to the west," Ariadas informed her as he poured them both a glass of what looked like lemonade. "They grow only one week of the year and are considered something of a delicacy in the Dreamlands. Naturally, we keep a healthy stock of them in the Palace stores."

"Naturally," Orson imitated over another purple heart.

"Pocopo," Natalie spat through a mouthful of fruitflesh. A tiny piece of chewed pocopo spattered on Ariadas's hand and the servant flicked it away in distaste. "It tastes a little like a peach, but better."

The two of them went through each tray, barely listening as Ariadas explained each of the strange foods while they shoveled bite after bite into their mouths. One tray held a steaming pile of multicolored breads, some covered in dark seeds, some in a white powder that tasted like coconut, and some filled with a tender cream that spurted out over Orson's fingers as he took an oversized chomp. Another tray held slices of meat that loosely resembled smoked ham but had been cured in a sauce that tasted of peanuts. Natalie helped herself to a large chunk of the meat, which Ariadas identified as "*click click*—mirboar."

After fifteen minutes of devouring everything but the trays, Natalie belched and Orson plopped his plate on the table. "I think I'm officially stuffed," she said, the words coming out in gasps as she tried to breathe around the food that was piled up all the way from her stomach to her throat.

"Mmhmm," Orson agreed, too full to speak as he rested his hands gingerly over his swollen stomach. He doubted he would need to eat again for days, possibly weeks.

Lupus came into the dining room just as Ariadas started tidying up the dishes. The big wolf greeted the Arachnan before walking over to the two children. "Have you had enough to eat?"

Natalie let out another low belch.

"Well spoken," the wolf said with amused approval. "How is your head?"

"Better," Natalie said, surprised that she had completely forgotten about her headache while they were eating. Lupus looked down at the core of a pocopo fruit on the table before her and nodded knowingly.

"The pocopo usually helps with headaches," he said. "Well, if you are finished with your meal, I would like to show you something."

Rising from their chairs, a feat that was remarkably hard due to their grotesquely full stomachs, they followed Lupus from the dining hall and through the Palace. Orson thought it would take him a few years to learn all the passages; he silently hoped he wouldn't be around long enough to test that theory. Rounding a corner and entering through a set of doors that brought them back into the Great Hall, Orson watched Natalie's eyes open in astonishment as she saw the splendor of the Hall for the first time.

They walked past the Queen's platform at the front of the Great Hall and Orson glanced at Aurora's chair. His stomach dropped when he thought about the conversation they had shared only a few hours ago. "That's a pretty fancy seat," Natalie said as they passed by.

"The Queen's." Orson nodded. Despite the knot in his stomach over what Aurora had told him, he couldn't help but feel a little disappointed that she wasn't sitting there at the moment. That feeling would likely pass quickly the next time he saw her; she would probably want to start talking to him about that Dreamshaper nonsense again.

Despite his doubts about the whole thing, Orson did have to admit there was a part of him that was a little excited about all of this. It made him nervous and frightened, but a part of him liked being told he was important. It was a nice change from always being the weak link. Even when he did disappoint them, as he was sure he eventually would, at least he would have had an adventure of sorts.

Lupus led them through a door that opened into a lavish, outdoor garden. The garden was as long as a soccer field and brimming with botanic life: a chain of rainbow flower beds grew along a grey stone wall, disappearing into a tiny grove of sapling trees that Orson didn't recognize. A perfectly squared, finely pruned hedge dotted the other side. Each branch of the hedge carried a bundle of tiny orange berries that looked dangerously inviting, like the poisoned berries his mother always told him not to eat.

They followed a path through the center of the garden. A tiny stream rustled underneath a small stone bridge, the water sharp and clear as it gurgled past in tiny sweeping waves. On the other side of the bridge, a polished marble gazebo stood brightly in the afternoon sunlight. The back end of the gazebo was sheltered under the branches of long thin trees that made Orson pause. Golden leaves glimmered reflectively, fanning out from the branches of the strange trees.

"This place is wonderful," Natalie breathed as the three of them took seats inside the gazebo.

"What are these trees?" Orson asked, picking a few golden leaves off the branches of the trees hanging above his seat.

"Delilah trees," Lupus explained. "A rare and glorious tree. It was once found in great numbers throughout the Dreamlands, but since the taint of the Nightmares the Delilah has become badly endangered. Some of the Dreamland creatures believe it can still be found in a few small groves to the extreme north, along the Hills of Borell, but I have yet to see any proof of that."

"What makes them so special?" Natalie asked.

"When crushed and mixed with the juice of most

fruits, the leaves of the Delilah create a powerful healing potion. There have even been rumors of Delilah leaf potions strong enough to pull creatures back from the brink of death. I haven't seen it myself, but it is certainly within the realm of possibility. Because of this, the Nightmares have been harvesting and destroying any trees they come across. Most of the Delilah groves are to the East of the Dreamlands, near the Haunted Mountain, which gives the Nightmares easy access to them. Thankfully the Delilahs here are still young, barely even two hundred years old. They will come in handy for the upcoming battles."

Orson nearly choked. "Two hundred? You call that young?"

"The Delilah can live up to three thousand years. Another reason why they are so valuable and important to maintain here in the Palace."

"Those shiny little leaves can do all that?" Natalie asked, staring at the leaves in Orson's hands. "We don't have anything like that in our world."

"What happens if you eat the leaves without any juice?" Orson asked.

Lupus hesitated. "I'm not sure," he finally answered. "I've never seen them used in such a manner. I suppose they could either be more potent, or perhaps have no effect whatsoever. Without being mixed, they may even be poisonous."

"Poisonous?" Orson started to let the leaves slide from his hands.

Lupus laughed. "Touching them with your hands won't hurt you," he read the worry on Orson's face. As the first leaf tipped off Orson's fingertips, he closed his hand instead, abruptly shoving them into his pocket where they nestled against the picture he had drawn of Sithyrus and the note he had written with the strange message from his dream: *Armed Sherpa*. The meaning of the message was still unclear; Orson wondered if they had a library in the Palace where he might be able to research it.

They sat in silence for a few moments, enjoying the sounds of the bubbling stream and rustling trees. In the quiet, Orson's mind wandered back to Sarah, trapped in whatever pit the Nightmares had placed her in, a baby alone in the clutches of monsters. Sighing deeply, he looked up at the wolf.

"Can you really help me save my sister?" he asked. "Can you help us rescue Sarah?"

Lupus rested a heavy hand on Orson's shoulder. "We will do our best, Orson. I wish I could promise you more than that, but take heart in knowing that with you at our side, the chances of saving your sister are greatly increased. Once you learn to harness your powers as the Dreamshaper, anything is possible."

Orson sighed under the weight of Lupus's false bravado. That was the problem; he didn't think he had any power to harness. He just couldn't shake the feeling that the wolf was wrong; that Aurora was wrong. They were following a false hope that he couldn't even begin to understand. Sitting quietly in the gazebo, the three of them stared out into the garden of the Palace of Dreams, wondering what lay ahead.

⌐ SEVENTEEN ⌐

The day had taken a gloomy turn as they left the garden. The sun still shone brightly overhead, but clouds of doubt had settled inside Orson. Queen Aurora was waiting to talk to him again, unleashing a fluttering of butterfly wings in the pit of his stomach. He wasn't sure what made him more nervous, knowing they would have to talk more about all of this Dreamshaper business or having to look into her enchanting blue eyes and seeing the disappointment when she found out he wasn't who she thought he was. Just looking into those eyes again, those beautiful blue eyes, was enough to make him dizzy.

Natalie nudged him in the ribs. "You okay, Orson? You look like you're ready to throw up everything you ate."

"I'm fine," he said quietly.

"Nervous about seeing your lovely Queen again? The most beautiful girl in the kingdom, the enchanted ruler of boys' hearts and..."

"Go stuff yourself," Orson answered, his face burning.

Natalie patted her stomach fondly. "Been there, done that."

Orson growled and looked away. Beside him, Natalie chuckled and gave him a light-hearted punch on the shoulder. Why did she have to be *so* annoying, he wondered; if all girls were like that, he was never getting married. Girls just made everything complicated.

Lupus led them back through the palace's winding

hallways, stopping after several minutes in front of a simple wooden door. It hardly looked like a door for a Queen's room, yet Lupus turned to them both with a smile on his snout. "Here we are," he said, gesturing to the door.

"I believe her Majesty is expecting you, sir Orson," Natalie said in a rather sad attempt at an English accent, embellishing her words with a mock curtsy. "'Twould be best to not keep her waiting."

Orson glared at her as she giggled. Lupus looked at the two of them, not understanding the hidden teasing. "Actually, she would like to speak with both of you."

"Me?" Natalie's amused smile dipped. "Meet a Queen? Oh, I don't know about that."

Orson, surprised by the sudden crack in Natalie's composure, sneered at her. "What's the matter, Natalie. Afraid to meet someone more important than you?"

Natalie punched him hard in the shoulder. "Shut up, Orson. I'm not afraid of your new girlfriend."

Orson rubbed his arm. "She's not my girlfriend," he said. "And you are so afraid." She gave him another punch.

"You two are very strange creatures," Lupus said before opening the door.

The room beyond the doorway was very plain, a far cry from the splendor of the Grand Hall, and reminded Orson of the gymnasium at Mardell as they stepped inside. Its cold white brick walls and tiny slits of windows high above that let in only the barest hint of outside light brought back uncomfortable memories of dodgeball with Big Jimmy Scrags and his cronies.

Aurora was standing on the edge of a square rug in the center of the room, her hands clasped behind her back and red hair pulled into a tight bun on top of her head. An array of objects was lined up on the rug: mostly small yellow cubes and a couple of pieces of fruit. The fruit looked ripe and inviting, but Orson had a feeling that they weren't there for eating.

"Welcome," Queen Aurora greeted them. She looked

at Natalie and smiled. "You must be Natalie."

Natalie didn't return the smile. "Yup, I am," she said rather informally. "Aren't you a little young to be a Queen?"

Orson looked over at Natalie. "Natalie, don't be rude. She *is* a Queen," he whispered harshly.

"That's quite all right, Orson," Aurora waved him off. She turned to Natalie. "Appearances can be deceiving, as I'm sure you learned from the Sirens."

Natalie sneered. "Nasty little things," she shook a fist. "They better hope I don't see them again."

"They were just following their nature," Aurora answered patiently. Natalie scowled lightly at the Queen. Orson felt her body tense up beside him. Natalie had always seemed so cool; he didn't understand why she was suddenly acting so out of sorts. He could almost feel the hidden tension in the room the moment she met the Queen. Orson made a mental note to ask her about it later, when they were alone.

"I'm sure they could find a better nature than eating people," Natalie growled, crossing her arms over her chest.

"So what are we doing here?" Orson switched the direction of the conversation. If Aurora had noticed Natalie's hostility—she would have to be blind to *not* feel it—the Queen was doing a wonderful job hiding it.

"Unfortunately, Orson," she said, waving for them to join her at the rug, "time is short and we need to make the best of it if we're going to stop the Nightmares and save your sister. Are you prepared to start training?"

Orson's jaw dropped. "Right now? Shouldn't we talk first, make sure I'm really this Dreamshaper? It seems a little quick to start training, whatever that means."

"It's the *lack* of time that has me concerned, Orson," Aurora countered. "I would love nothing more than to take our time with all of this, but your late arrival has put us in a slight bind, I'm afraid. We need to get started as soon as possible if we are to have any chance to succeed.

"As I already told you," Aurora continued, "the New

Dawn announces the arrival of the new Dreamshaper, and it has spoken about you. There is no doubt about whether or not you *are* the one who is destined to lead us against the Nightmares. The only question is whether or not we have the time to prepare you for the upcoming struggle."

"I can already tell you the answer to that one," Orson muttered.

"Before we can really start with anything big, you first must learn to gather the power of the Dreamshaper within you. We'll start with a few small tasks, which is why I have assembled these objects on the carpet."

Orson looked down at the cubes and fruit. "What am I supposed to do with these?"

"I want you to move them," Aurora answered. Orson thought it must be a trick. Reaching out, he started to pick up one of the cubes with his hands.

"Not with your hands, Orson," Aurora stopped him. "With your mind."

Orson snatched his hand away. "With my mind? I can't move things with my mind."

"You can," Aurora said matter-of-factly. "You just have to clear your head and focus on one of the shapes before you."

Clear my head? Orson thought sharply. His sister was missing, lost in the world of dreams, and he was stuck here in a strange land surrounded by weird spiders and wolves and little singing furballs. She expected him to clear his head? He had no idea how to even *start* to do that. With a deep sigh he tried pushing at the scattered thoughts weaving around his brain. It was hopeless; with everything going on around him, it was an impossible task.

"I can't do it. I can't clear my head."

"Be patient," Aurora said calmly. "I don't expect you to get it on your first try. It takes practice and patience."

"Shouldn't he have a wand or something?" Natalie said, clearly lacking the aforementioned patience. "You know, a magic stick to wave around while he says *abracadabra* or something like that, like in those *Harry Potter* books?"

"Harry who?" Aurora shook her head questioningly. "In any case, some of the past Dreamshapers have used wands, but it's more out of aesthetics than necessity. An instrument may help you focus a little easier, but it doesn't affect the power of your ability. The power of the Dreamshaper comes purely from within."

Orson's second effort produced little more than the first, except for a discomfort in his chest. He realized he was holding his breath and let it out with a whoosh.

"Don't push so hard, Orson," Aurora said. "Breath. Just let the thoughts go. The more you force it, the harder it will be. Let go of your doubts; as long as you hold onto them, clearing your mind will be out of the question."

Orson felt an unexpected rage start to fill him up. Couldn't she see that he couldn't do it? He couldn't even throw a baseball, much less move a little yellow cube with nothing more than his mind. Wasn't that proof enough that he wasn't this Dreamshaper?

"I can't do it," he said. "I can't move it."

"Try again," Aurora answered calmly. "Focus all of your energy on the cube. Don't ask it to move, *tell* it to move. You're in control, not the cube."

"I can't!" Orson protested. "I don't have any power, can't you see that?"

"But you do, Orson. You've already used it several times, in fact."

"That's impossible," he argued.

Aurora smiled. "Is it? Think about when you first met Sithyrus. How did you escape?"

"I woke myself up," Orson said.

"Think harder. What happened *before* you woke yourself up?"

Orson thought about his first encounter with the giant lizard. Something else *had* happened, just after Sithyrus had broken into his room and attacked him in his bed. Orson had yelled at the lizard to stop, and Sithyrus had suddenly been frozen in mid-air, long enough for Orson get away.

"I froze it," he said. "I yelled for it to stop, and it froze right in the air."

"See?" Aurora smiled again. "You have used it. And more than once, in fact. You used your power each time you sent Lupus away. You've also used it to call Natalie into your dreams, haven't you? What did you do differently before that you're not doing now?"

Orson thought back over the times he had encountered both Lupus and Sithyrus in his dreams. Natalie had been there the second time Lupus had found them; the first time he had shared a dream with her. He certainly hadn't been thinking with a clear mind then: anything but. He had been afraid—*terrified*—and had known only that he needed to get away. All he had known at the time was that he needed to escape or he was dead. In a sense, his fear had made him more determined. He hadn't made it a choice for Lupus or Sithyrus to go away; he hadn't given Natalie a choice as to whether she should come to him in his dream. He had made it happen through sheer determination.

Looking at the Queen for a moment, he dropped his eyes down to the cubes. Ignoring Aurora's advice to clear his mind, he instead let his frustrations build, let the anger over being unable to move the items fill him.

"Move," he told one of the objects, one of the fruits this time. "I want you to move."

The fruit didn't respond. Rather than let his frustration over not being listened to get the better of him, he instead let it fill him even more. Glaring at the fruit, he focused all of his anger at it. Nothing else mattered but getting the fruit to do what it was told.

"Move," he repeated, stronger now. The fruit didn't move, but it did start to tremble, as though it were alive and suddenly afraid. He should have been shocked to see the fruit shivering, but instead it only made him angrier. He hadn't told the fruit to shake, he told it to move.

"Move!" he commanded, nearly shouting now. "I want you to move!"

Orson whipped his hand off to the side. The fruit leaped into the air and followed the movement of his hand, hurling itself against the far wall of the room where it exploded with a violent, juicy impact.

Beside him, Natalie let out an astonished gasp that broke Orson from his trance. Her mouth hung open as she looked at him with wide eyes then back at the wall. Orson followed her gaze, looking at the juice stained wall in shocked astonishment.

"I did it," he breathed. "I made it move."

Aurora was smiling.

⌐ EIGHTEEN ⌐

"That was cool," Natalie said as she sat down in the desk across from Orson, who was sprawled out in his own chair. Dark bags pulled at his eyes as he restlessly rolled a pencil on his desk. "I mean really cool. I didn't actually expect you to be able to do it. No offense."

"Don't worry." Orson rubbed his eyes tiredly. "I didn't expect to be able to do it either. I don't even know *what* I did."

Orson was physically exhausted. He felt tired and sore, though he wasn't sure why he would feel sore, unless he tossed and turned something awful during last night's dream. In any case, he wished he could share Natalie's excitement over what he accomplished in the session with Aurora, but all he really wanted to do was go back to sleep. After discovering he actually *did* have power in the Dreamlands, it was disappointing to be stuck here in the waking world where he was plain ol' Orson Bailey.

"So, what else do you think you can do?" Natalie asked, absently chewing on the end of a pencil.

"I have no idea," Orson sighed. Hopefully smashing fruits against walls wasn't the extent of his newfound talent. That would just be cruel—Orson Bailey, Scourge of the Citrus Fruit.

"Do you think you could fly?" Natalie asked. "I've always wanted to fly. Now *that* would be something else. Just imagine, being able to float up in the air, free as a bird.

You should try it next time, see if you can fly."

Orson smiled ruefully. "I think I'll take it a few steps at a time, Nat. The last thing I need is to go jumping off a cliff only to discover that the only power I have is painting the rocks below a nice shade of red."

Natalie sighed and bit her lip in disappointment. "Fine. But if you can fly, you'd better take me up with you. If you don't, I'll give you the worst pink belly you've ever had; good enough to make Big Fat Jimmy Scrags jealous."

To emphasize her point, Natalie mimed giving an imaginary person lying across her desk a pink belly; her hands flipping up and down sharply as she made a wet slapping sound with her lips. Orson couldn't suppress a chuckle at the image.

"I can barely lift Sarah from her crib. What makes you think I'd be able to carry you?"

"You'll find a way," she said, then raised an eyebrow at him. "You'd better. Just remember. Pink belly."

The image of Natalie giving someone a pink belly—her hands slapping the kid's stomach so hard and quick that it turned a bright shade of pink—with Jimmy Scrags looking over her shoulder, nodding in approval, set them both off in a fit of giggles. Mr. Pratt, standing at the front of the classroom, turned and directed a dark scowl at them both.

"Something you'd like to share?" he asked them. They immediately pinched their lips tightly closed.

"No, Mr. Pratt," Natalie answered for them. Orson couldn't speak for himself; he was shaking with the effort of swallowing his laughter.

"What's so funny, freaks?" Jimmy Scrags demanded, scowling at them from his seat near the window.

"Your face," Orson said without thinking, still picturing Jimmy's face watching Natalie's pink belly with approval. The moment the words crossed his lips his face went ashen as he realized that he may have just signed his own death warrant. The rest of the class sucked in a deep, collective breath. Even Natalie had stopped laughing; she was looking at him with that same look of amazement after he'd smashed the fruit.

Orson looked at Jimmy. The bully's face had become a shade of red nearly equal to Mr. Pratt's, minus the scary vein at his temple. There was murder in Jimmy's eyes. "I'm so dead," Orson said.

Just when it seemed the classroom would implode from the sudden tension, someone let out a choked laugh and Orson looked back to see Mike Spencer cupping a hand over his mouth. Jimmy was out of his desk in an instant.

"You think that's funny, Mikey?" Jimmy demanded, puffing himself up like some sort of mutated blowfish. Mike tried to shake his head, but a single tear trickled out his eye as he struggled to hold his laughter back. The look on his face as he struggled to control himself brought another chorus of small chuckles from a few other students. He finally couldn't hold it in any longer and let out a loud guffaw. Within moments the laughter had caught hold of everybody and the class was consumed by an ambitious case of the giggles.

"That's enough," Mr. Pratt scolded at the front of the room. Jimmy started walking towards Mike's desk, his hands scrunched up into two meaty fists.

"Let's see how funny you think it is without teeth!"

"Oh sit down, you dummy," Natalie said, her own cheeks flushed from laughing so hard. "It was just a joke."

Jimmy turned to her. She was closer then Mike; he snatched her ponytail in a deathgrip and yanked down hard, pulling her head back wickedly. Natalie cried out and Orson was on his feet in a flash, pushing Jimmy as hard as he could. Big J stumbled back a few steps, his ample posterior nearly knocking over the desk behind him.

"Don't touch her!" Orson said. He didn't even realize he had picked up the pencil from his desk and was holding it between himself and the bully. When he saw what he was holding, both he and Jimmy stared down at it, stunned. At the front of the room, Mr. Pratt's face had turned an uglier, darker shade of red and the vein was throbbing madly at his temple.

"Sit...down...now," he seethed.

"You shouldn't have done that, Strings," Jimmy hissed, batting the pencil away from Orson with a ham-sized hand. "Now you're *really* gonna get it." Jimmy pulled a fist back, fully intent on introducing Orson's face to the back of his head. Everything was moving in slow motion to Orson as he waited for the hammer to come crashing down.

"JIMMY SCRAGS AND ORSON BAILEY, SIT... DOWN...NOW!"

The entire classroom jerked to a halt as Mr. Pratt's bellow pounded through the room. Even Jimmy jumped back quickly, sliding back into his desk with his fist still clenched at his side. The bully's eyes bore into Orson and he dragged a thumb across his throat. Orson understood the threat clearly. Mr. Pratt had only delayed the inevitable.

Orson swallowed hard, wondering if his powers would allow him to teleport himself into the Dreamlands while he was awake. He had the feeling that Jimmy would help put him to sleep soon enough anyway.

Mr. Pratt glowered over the class, daring anyone else to utter so much as another peep. Nobody did; they had all turned back to their notes like nothing had happened. Orson looked down at his own blank page then up at the clock on the wall. Notes were the least of his worries at the moment. Recess was only a few minutes away. After what had just happened, they might as well rename recess to *hunting season*.

Somehow, though, he managed to avoid Jimmy at recess, finding a quiet little corner in the library to hide out until the bell rang. Ironically, he noticed it was the same end of the library Jimmy had been cornered by Sithyrus.

At one point he saw Jimmy walk past the library window and ducked under a table. When Madame Blanchette glared at him from the librarian's desk he faked as if tying his shoe. When he straightened up, Jimmy was gone. Back in the class, Jimmy didn't even look at him, which made Orson even more nervous. He and Natalie shared a few glances; at one point Orson looked back to where Mike Spencer sat, but the other boy was suddenly absent from class.

At lunch, Orson sat close to the teacher's table in the cafeteria—even Jimmy wasn't stupid enough to try something around the teachers. The bully sat at the next table, talking just loud enough for Orson to hear him say Mike Spencer's name, followed by a cruel chortle as one of Jimmy's friends—Frank Ciccone, a greasy haired boy with thick, bushy eyebrows—clapped the head bully on the back. On the other side of Jimmy, Barton Spinkerton, a tall, gangly boy with freckles all the way down his neck, looked at Orson and grinned cruelly. Frank and Barton had been running the playground with Jimmy for the better part of two years now; his wicked but not-so-smart cronies. When the three of them looked at you, walking away wasn't an option. You ran for your life.

When the bell to start the lunch recess rang, Jimmy strode past Orson and bumped him hard enough to nearly knock him from his chair. The bully didn't even look back as he left the cafeteria. Orson watched him leave, a knot establishing itself tightly in his stomach. Jimmy could be waiting for him anywhere: at his locker, on the playground. Right outside the lunchroom door. Orson tried to use the cafeteria as a sanctuary for lunch recess, feigning an upset stomach, but Mr. Pratt was still angry with him and kicked him outside.

The hallway was clear and there was no sign of Jimmy when he got to his locker. Orson wasn't naive enough to think Big J was satisfied with a simple shoulder bump in the lunchroom. There was an ambush waiting for him somewhere. It was just a matter of when the trap would be sprung.

As it turned out, he didn't have to wait long. Stepping outside, Orson had just enough time to marvel at how quiet the fifth-grade exit was before a huge fist buried itself in his stomach. The breath left his lungs with a whoosh and he doubled up, clutching his stomach as a large shadow loomed over him.

"Still feel like making jokes, Strings?" Big J pushed Orson off the steps to the dusty ground.

Orson sprawled in the dirt, winded and trying to climb to his knees. Jimmy jumped off the steps and kicked him hard in the ribs. Orson cried out, rolling over on to his back. Standing above him, Jimmy pushed a heavy foot down on his chest, pinning him to the ground.

"You shoulda just left it alone," Jimmy said with a mean smile. "Now I gotta hurt you, just like I hurt Mikey. I never seen you at recess, but I seen him. He never shoulda laughed. Nobody laughs at Big J. I helped remind him of that, and now I gotta remind you."

Orson tried to say something but could do little more than gasp for breath with Jimmy's anvil foot squashing his chest. He was done for; he should have known Jimmy would be waiting for him. Now he was going to pay for opening his big mouth.

Orson closed his eyes and waited for the next blow, the one that would finish him off. Jimmy made a heavy *hunf* sound and Orson knew he was about to get his face kicked in. Instead, though, the pressure on his chest lifted. Opening his eyes, Orson saw Jimmy stumbling away, holding a hand to his head. Beneath his meaty fingers, Orson could see a tiny trickle of blood.

"Leave him alone, Jimmy," Mike Spencer said from a few steps away. He was holding a club-sized stick in one hand. He was also sporting a nasty looking black eye, no doubt the result of a run-in with Jimmy at recess. It was pretty clear why Mike hadn't been in class since recess; he had probably spent the last few periods with the school nurse and an ice bag.

Beside Mike, Natalie bent down to pick up a stick of her own. Jimmy looked at the two of them furiously. The bully's entire body was shaking with rage. He stepped over Orson and towards the two fools who had dared to interrupt his business.

"Didn't get enough at recess, Mikey? You must be a sucker for pain. And you brought String's little girlfriend with you, too. How sweet." He stepped closer to the pair, but stopped when Mike cocked his club like a baseball bat, ready to swing if the bully took another step closer.

"Your pals aren't here to back you up this time, Jimmy," Mike warned. "I told Mrs. Blondin about the black eye you gave me and she pulled Frank and Barty into the office. She'll be looking for you next, if there's anything left of you. Let's see how you like being outnumbered for a change." He wiggled the end of the bat. "C'mon, I dare you to take another step."

Natalie was waving frantically at Orson. "Would you get over here already?" she said, holding her stick awkwardly above her head. Orson scampered over slowly, his stomach and ribs aching from the pounding he had taken. Jimmy could do little more than watch as his target escaped. Eying Mike's stick, the bully didn't seem in any hurry to get another whack. Mike and Jimmy were both on the same baseball team, and Jimmy knew how good Mike was with a baseball bat.

"I'm gonna get you for this, you just wait and see," Jimmy snarled before jumping backwards with a startled cry to avoid being hit by a wild swing from Natalie.

"Just get going, trashmouth!" Natalie told him. Jimmy unceremoniously turned and ran. He didn't stop until he reached the corner of the school and disappeared.

With Jimmy gone, Orson was finally able to catch a breath and get to his feet. Mike and Natalie kept a tight grip on their branches in case Jimmy changed his mind and circled back. Mike's black eye looked horrible; the skin around his eye was puffed out and throbbed terribly.

"Are you okay?" Orson asked him.

"I'll be fine," Mike answered, finally dropping his stick

to the ground when it was clear Jimmy wouldn't be back. "Frank and Bart caught me from behind at recess, that's all. Jimmy sent them after me again at lunch, but I managed to give them the slip. They're probably still looking for me in the playground."

"But Mrs. Blondin," Orson inquired.

"I'm no tattle-tale. I never told her what happened, but I knew the dumb oaf would fall for it. Me and Natalie knew he'd be looking for you next. Sorry we didn't get here before he started in on you."

"That's all right," Orson said, trying to sound like it was no big deal; like his ribs didn't feel like he'd just been hit by a bowling ball. If Mike was tough enough to take a black eye and keep going, he could take a punch to the stomach. "He just surprised me is all."

"I'd watch your back for a few days," Mike said. "Jimmy'll be looking for blood. We're gonna have to find some quiet spots where they won't be able to find us."

Orson and Natalie nodded in agreement. Jimmy wasn't going to just let this go, especially now that Natalie and Mike were involved. Still, despite the knowledge that they had pushed themselves to the top of Jimmy's must-kill list, Orson couldn't help feeling a twinge of excitement. Who would've thought it? Last week, nobody in their right mind would have helped him with so much as a math problem. Now here he was, standing side by side with not one but *two* classmates, and they had just chased the biggest bully in Mardell from pounding him into the dirt. He was finding unexpected allies all over the place these days.

The bell rang and the three of them started back towards the school. Along the way, Natalie leaned over and whispered into Orson's ear. "You sure you're okay, Orson?" she asked.

Orson looked at her and smiled brightly. He wasn't okay; his ribs were throbbing, his stomach bruised, and there was a hole in the knee of his new jeans that would make his mother furious. Yet for the first time since he started at

Mardell he felt something other than fear and loneliness. He felt *good*. He had stood up to Jimmy Scrags and lived, and had made a new friend in the process. If a few scrapes and bruises were the cost, then they were well worth the reward.

"Yeah, I'll be alright," he said, trying to sound as brave as Mikey had been about his black eye. Natalie looked at him strangely and laughed. Beside them, Mike looked around, checking every few steps to make sure the coast was clear.

"At least until the end of the day."

⌐ NINETEEN ⌐

The next few days were nothing short of exotic, a nice change from the normal glum existence Orson had become accustomed to. During the evenings, he spent the greater part of each night in the Palace of Dreams with Aurora, trying to figure out his new abilities, hoping that making pulpy fruit juice wasn't the total extent of his new skills.

One night, he had returned with Natalie to find Aurora waiting for him in the same room with a new set of objects in front of her, heavier objects that she wanted him to move just as he had moved the fruit. He was disappointed to find that none of them were fruits; exploding fruit was much more exciting than lifting and dropping cubes, but the spider-servant Ariadas had complained about the sticky mess on the wall. Harnessing his power came easier than last time, and Orson was quickly lifting and dropping the objects, perhaps not naturally, but with much more confidence. After an hour of lifting and setting them back down, he started moving them shakily around the room, once nearly crowning Natalie with a twenty-pound stone. That had earned him a sharp comment with by an even sharper punch to the shoulder.

The next evening, Aurora brought some transparent orbs that reminded Orson of a larger version of the portice that Lupus had used to get them into the Palace. Unlike the portice, however, these orbs had no blue and white mists in their centers, but rather were filled with a strange looking liquid that could well have been Coca-Cola. Aurora instructed him to try and concentrate a thin stream of energy into the globes rather than forcing everything into it.

Using only a small amount of energy should have been easier, Orson suspected, and was surprised to find it quite difficult. In moving the objects, he had taught himself to channel his anger into a command, using the force of his emotions to manipulate the cubes and stones. When he tried using the same tactic on the first globe, the angry energy was too much for the fragile glass and it exploded, showering the three of them with brown liquid. Standing at the far side of the room, Lupus had laughed at the site of the three of them dripping on the carpet until the Queen had quieted him with an annoyed glance. The liquid in the globe was nearly impossible to get out of clothing, and the Queen had made the mistake of wearing one of her favorite cloaks that day. Natalie, seeing the Queen's frustration with having her cloak ruined, had spent the remainder of the session with a secretive smile that only Orson noticed.

The next attempt worked a little better. Orson managed to confine his energy slightly, and the new globe only cracked, the liquid draining out onto the carpet but not exploding everywhere. Seeing the improvement lightened his spirits, and by the third attempt Orson finally managed to control the energy enough to not break the orb. Instead of exploding, the liquid within began to glow, a dim light at first, barely as bright as a candle flame. Excited, Orson fed more power into it, trying to make it brighter. With a hissing crack, the orb broke open, spilling the liquid onto his shoes and effectively ending the lesson.

The next couple of nights with Aurora were much the same: lifting and moving; lighting candles and lanterns (and once accidentally lighting the tip of Lupus's tail on fire; the wolf hadn't found this funny in the least); forcing a quill to write across a piece of parchment with his mind rather than by hand. During a break in which he and Natalie had been given a few hours rest in the Palace garden, Natalie had begged Orson to use his power to lift her into the air. A reminder of pink bellies to come had finally convinced him to try, and after a few strained minutes he managed to levitate her two feet off the ground. She giggled frantically as he held her suspended above the ground, moving her forward and backward as though she was flying.

When the Queen came out to talk to them—looking particularly stunning in a satin blue gown and sparkling tiara —Orson lost his concentration and let Natalie fall, her face landing splat in a puddle of mud along the bank of the small stream beside the gazebo. Aurora smiled, but Natalie had not found the incident the least bit amusing. She made a point of reminding Orson of that fact for the next few days.

In the waking world, the daunting knowledge that Jimmy Scrags and his bunch of hoodlums were hunting them forced Orson, Natalie and Mike to spend the majority of their school breaks huddled up behind the hill at the edge of the playground or in the library. Still, for Orson it was just nice to finally have some friends, even if it meant—as it likely would—that he would be on the receiving end of another beating should Jimmy catch up with them.

At one point, Natalie suggested telling Mike about the Dreamlands, but Orson didn't think it was a good idea. He had just gained Mike's confidence and didn't see the point in risking that by telling the other boy about something that sounded like it came from a Saturday morning cartoon. Though he didn't say as much to Natalie—whose company he still enjoyed immensely—it was nice having another boy to talk to.

One afternoon, Orson introduced Mike to Sergeant Sharpe, bringing a stack of his best comics for Mike to see. With great reverence, he showed Mike the very first issue of the comic series, which had cost Orson three week's allowance to buy.

"Look at the size of his knife," Orson said as the two of them read through a battle between the Sarge and a particularly nasty enemy.

"So much blood," Mike responded excitedly. Beside them, Natalie rolled her eyes.

"Those comics are disgusting," she commented. "Don't you have any Archie comics?"

"Who'd wanna read stupid Archie comics when you have the Sarge?" Orson said, frowning at her. Mike nodded his agreement. Natalie groaned and lay back on the hill, muttering something about "stupid boys" and needing more girlfriends.

The only thing that dampened Orson's spirits was his time at home between the end of school and bedtime. His house had become quiet and lonely since Sarah had been taken to the hospital. Suppers were usually nothing more than made-for-TV dinners or canned pasta meals. Afterwards, Mrs. Bailey would sit on the couch by the phone, half-heartedly watching television while waiting for any news from the hospital. The sight of his mother hurting so badly troubled Orson deeply, but he didn't know what to do for her. Feeling helpless, he escaped after his suppers to his bedroom under the pretense of needing to finish some homework.

Orson knew that Sarah's condition wasn't going to change, not until he saved her from the Nightmares. The sight of his mother walking around the house in such a state of constant worry drove him to work hard on developing his abilities in the Dreamlands. The sooner he rescued Sarah, the sooner his family would become whole again.

After another night of doing the same things with Aurora, lifting the same objects, lighting the same globes and candles, Orson expressed his concern over the slow progress they were making. The simple tasks the Queen forced him to repeat night after night were becoming easy, almost effortless, and he was eager to move on to something more difficult. At first, Aurora didn't like the idea of rushing into any harder lessons, but she was forced to admit that Orson was right. Time was running out.

"We'll pick up the pace tomorrow," she promised.

"Get some rest tonight. You'll need all the energy you can muster for your next lesson."

Orson woke two hours before his alarm was set to ring. Lying in bed, his mind whirled excitedly as he tried to think of what the next step would be. Whatever it was, it was sure to bring him closer to rescuing Sarah. Thinking of how nice it would be to have his family back, to seeing his mother smile again, he drifted lightly back to sleep.

⌐ TWENTY ⌐

As always, Aurora was already waiting for him when he entered what he now called the training room. He had decided to let Natalie rest rather than calling her into the Dreamlands this time; if the next step in his training was going to be as difficult as the Queen had made it sound, he didn't want any distractions. Not only that, the growing tension between the two girls made him more than a little uncomfortable. Natalie would probably box his ears in school tomorrow when she realized she'd been left behind, but he wanted some time alone with Aurora without having to worry about Natalie's snide comments.

Natalie's odd behavior had not gone unnoticed by the Queen, either. When Orson sat down across the carpet from her, Aurora looked questioningly at the empty spot that his friend normally occupied.

"Natalie decided not to join us?" she asked.

Orson shrugged. "I thought it might be better if I came alone this time. Less distractions."

Aurora nodded knowingly, before adding: "I get the impression that she isn't very fond of me. Have I done something to upset her?"

Orson shrugged. "Natalie's a little strange that way. Even I don't understand her half the time. Maybe she's jealous that you're training me to be the next Dreamshaper and not her."

Aurora smiled lightly. "Perhaps there's more to it

than that," she said quizzically, but didn't elaborate any further. "It's too bad. If I still lived in your world, I think Natalie and I could have been great friends."

"If you lived in my world you'd probably get a kick in the guts by Jimmy just for talking to me...waitaminute, what did you just say?"

"That Natalie and I could have been friends?"

Orson shook his head. "No, the part about if you still lived in my world. You lived in the waking world?"

Aurora smiled. "I *am* human, Orson, in case you hadn't noticed. It's been awhile since I've been home, but that doesn't make me any less human, I would hope."

Looking at the Queen, Orson couldn't believe he hadn't thought of it before. It was such an obvious coincidence, he couldn't believe he hadn't noticed it.

"But how...I don't understand..."

"Think back, Orson. Do you remember the images of past Dreamshapers that line the walls of the Great Hall?" She waited for Orson to nod before continuing. "What did you notice about all of them?"

"Well, they all looked pretty impressive." Orson struggled to recall the pictures in his head. "And older than me."

Aurora shook her head. "Think deeper. There is one similarity they all share, something that stands out amongst all the Dreamshapers. Something you see every time you look in a mirror."

Orson tried to gather the images from the tapestries in his mind. There was Alexander, wielding his sword as he cut through the Nightmares. David, leading the Dremians through some forest to surround the enemy. His thoughts drifted back to the earliest Dreamshaper, Oleandar, standing tall above the Nightmares, his muscles huge as he held his staff aloft. The sheer look of determination on his face, the beads of sweat glistening on his brow. Derek, with all his scars and shadowy face.

He pictured them all standing alongside each other,

fighting over the course of the Dreamlands' history, and the answer became suddenly apparent.

"Human," he whispered, then more loudly: "They were all human."

Aurora smiled brightly. "Every single Dreamshaper has been human. One painting for all of them, made in honor of their legacies after they finished their time in the Dreamlands."

Something Lupus had told him suddenly snapped back into his thoughts. "Lupus said there were twelve Dreamshapers so far, that I was supposed to be unlucky number thirteen. But I only counted eleven pictures in the Great Hall. What happened to the twelfth one? Doesn't he get a picture?"

"In due time," Aurora answered. "A Dreamshaper's legacy is only added to the Great Hall once the next one has arrived to take their place. It has been a tradition since Oleandar's time."

Orson stared at the Queen, feeling the teeth of some hidden knowledge biting at him. There was something more to this, something she wasn't telling him. Was this another one of her tests? He hated tests. He failed a good deal of them in school every year. Mulling it over, he tried to connect the pieces.

"If the Dreamshapers only get their pictures hung when the next one shows up, than that must mean there's still another Dreamshaper around somewhere," he said, thinking aloud.

"There *was* another," Aurora corrected him. "The moment you arrived in the Dreamlands, the other lost that title, along with much of her abilities. The Red Dawn isn't just a beacon displaying the arrival of the new Dreamshaper, but also a symbol of the transition from one to the next."

Orson felt a twinge of disappointment. For a brief moment, he had thought that he wasn't alone in all of this, that there was another Dreamshaper, someone who could help him. Like it or not, he seemed destined to be alone one way or another.

So what had happened to this other Dreamshaper then? Maybe he—no, the Queen had said *her*, not he—could still give him advice on what he needed to do. If only he could find her...

The realization hit him like one of Jimmy's club-sized fists, right between the eyes. He remembered something else Lupus had told him. The Palace of Dreams had been built by Oleandar, which would have made him the first King of the Dreamlands. Orson suspected that there had been several more kings since Oleandar's time: eleven, to be exact. Only the last king wasn't a king at all. The last one was actually a Queen, just like the last Dreamshaper was a girl, a *human* girl.

One Dreamshaper, one human, one Queen.

"You," he whispered, as though saying it any louder would make it less possible. "You're a Dreamshaper."

"I *was* a Dreamshaper," Aurora countered with a smile. "I'm afraid the title no longer applies now that you're here. Now I am simply the Queen of the Dreamlands."

Simply a Queen didn't sound as disappointing as her mild tone of voice suggested. One just didn't claim to be *simply* royalty any more than the leader of Canada claimed to be *simply* the Prime Minister, or the President of the United States was *simply* the President. Still, from his time here he had gathered that the Dreamshaper was the most important person in the Dreamlands at any given time, possibly even more important than being royalty.

"Does that mean," he swallowed hard, "that I'm the next King?"

Aurora laughed, a silvery, pleasant laugh. "Not yet, it doesn't. You don't have to worry about that duty right now. Being a Dreamshaper doesn't necessarily mean you have to rule over the Dreamlands. In fact, only five of us *have* taken the title of king or queen. That isn't something you need worry about, at least not until our current problems have been dealt with."

Orson let out a sigh of relief. Being the next Dreamshaper was enough. He wasn't sure he even had that in him, let alone taking over as ruler of the world of Dreams. Besides, it was very possible—likely, even—that he would be the last Dreamshaper, if the Nightmares had their say in matters.

"But how could you be the last Dreamshaper?" Orson asked as he looked at her across the carpet. "You can't be much older than me. Lupus said that the last New Dawn was over a hundred years ago."

"One hundred and thirteen, actually," Aurora answered.

"One hundred and..." he started, his voice breaking up before he could finish his sentence. "You mean to tell me that you're over a century old? That's impossible. *Nobody* lives that long, not even my grandpa, and *he* was about as old as they get before he died last year."

"I came here first on my thirteenth birthday," Aurora explained. "I stumbled into the Dreamlands much the same as you, unexpectedly falling through a portal. In my case, the portal happened to be a swimming pool in my great grandfather's backyard. I can still remember the pool even now. I was terrified of it. It was U-shaped with cracked and worn tiles that were covered in mold The water was murky and disgusting and smelled of rotting leaves. My grandfather had never bothered to care for his pool properly."

"And you still swam in it?" Orson stuck out his tongue in disgust. "Gross."

"Swam is hardly the word," Aurora said. "I remember stepping outside to get some fresh air, walking along the edge of the pool. I remember the smell more than anything else; the disgusting stench of decaying leaves and stale water that had turned the pool into a swamp. The edge was wet, and I slipped into the water."

Aurora shivered at the memory. "Everyone was inside, so nobody heard me screaming in the water. I hadn't learned to swim, and the water was too thick and dirty for me to reach the edge. I probably would have drowned had my father not come outside looking for me.

"That was a week before my thirteenth birthday. For the next few days, my dreams were haunted by my grandfather's pool right up until my birthday, though I never saw it in the waking world again. The night I turned thirteen, I once again dreamed I was standing at the edge of the pool. I would stand there, staring into it and trying to see the bottom, but the water was endless, or so it seemed from where I was standing. It was like staring into a void, one that terrified me at the same time it lured me closer."

"You fell in again?" Orson asked and Aurora shook her head.

"No, I jumped."

This revelation took Orson aback. "You jumped? But I thought you were scared! What on Earth would make you jump?"

"Something not *on* Earth. As I stood on the edge of the pool, a Nightmare found me, much as Sithyrus found you. The water was my only escape. I've often wondered why I believed the water would save me; after all, it was only a pool. If nothing else, it should have been little more than a trap. But I was only a girl and didn't know any better, so I jumped."

Orson's mind raced as he listened to her story. "What happened?"

"The pool turned out to be a portal into the Dreamlands, like your mirror. When I arrived, I found myself in a small village, a few miles north of the Palace of Dreams. Like you, the New Dawn erupted above me and I became the Dreamshaper."

Orson's head was burning with questions and he didn't know where to start. "What happened to your powers now? Did they disappear when I showed up? Are you human again?"

Aurora frowned lightheartedly. "I've always been human, just a little more as well. And no, my powers aren't gone, at least not completely. As a Dreamshaper, you never lose everything. But they are no longer strong enough to deal with the new threat of the Nightmares. My role has changed now. Now my responsibility is to train you and make sure you are prepared for the struggles ahead."

"What else happened to you? Why was there a Nightmare chasing you? What did you have to do in the Dreamlands? Who trained you?"

"Stories for another time," Aurora shook her head. "We've wasted enough time as it is, but I needed you to know where I came from. To know that I've been through much the same as you, that I understand how hard this must be for you. Hopefully it will help you find the confidence to lead us against the Nightmares. Like you told me before, the time for silly tricks is over. It's time we move on to more challenging things. Are you ready?"

Orson looked at the Queen—the previous Dreamshaper—and thought his mind might explode with a thousand unanswered questions. She was right, though; knowing that he was being trained by a Dreamshaper *did* give him more confidence, though whether that could be translated into anything more was yet to be decided.

Letting out a heavy sigh, Orson looked at the Queen and nodded. "Let's get started."

⌞ TWENTY ONE ⌟

Orson wiped droplets of cool sweat from his forehead. A small trickle ran under his glasses, stinging his eyes. Rubbing his fingers under his glasses, he glanced at Aurora; she was watching closely, adding to the pressure he already felt.

"Concentrate, Orson," she told him. "This isn't going to be like moving cubes or fruit, or lighting globes. You need to find the source of power within you, to learn to channel it: to slip into it. Anger won't work this time. It's not enough to force your will on it; you have to become one with it. Let it be a part of you. Try to clear your mind."

Clear his mind? Orson was ready to give up, but forced himself to give it the "old college try," as his father used to say. As hard as he pressed, he just couldn't seem to quiet the roving thoughts that kept disturbing his attempt.

Frowning, Orson thought he would try a different approach. Closing his eyes tightly, he picked one thing in his thoughts and tried to focus all of his attention on that. If he could keep his mind limited to one single thought rather than a thousand different ones, maybe he could bring himself closer to accomplishing the task at hand.

Aurora refused to tell him exactly what that task was; at least, not yet. First, she wanted him to find a way to grab his power, to contain it and let it become part of him, if only for a moment. She told him that in order to accomplish anything more difficult than what he had done thus far he would need to gain a firmer control on his ability.

Trying to find the right thought, Orson finally settled on the only one that made sense. There was one thing he had always turned to in times of need, when he needed to find some strength to get through a difficult situation. The Sarge. Squeezing his eyes even tighter, Orson turned all of his thoughts to Sergeant Sharpe. He thought of his favorite cover, where the Sarge was standing on top of a building, calmly appraising the situation as a dozen enemies aimed up at him from the ground below. The Sarge looked confident and in control, just what Orson needed now. He needed a boost of confidence against the enemies in his head.

Even with his mind focused on Sergeant Sharpe, Orson could feel the shovels of distraction digging away. He pushed harder, trying to force them away, refusing to let them gain the upper hand. His anger and frustration started to slowly fade: an ebbing tide leaving a smooth calm beach in its wake.

It was in that quiet where he heard the Queen's voice.

Orson, you've done it! She was talking in his mind, Orson realized, not out loud. This should surprise him, he knew, yet somehow it seemed natural. *Open yourself up to your gift. Let it come into you, but be careful. You aren't fully ready and to allow too much power at once can be dangerous.*

All at once Orson was aware that there *was* power there, and not a small amount but a huge pool, hiding within his mind, trying to find a way inside. Orson felt a twitch of apprehension. What if it meant to hurt him? What if this wasn't power at all, but some sort of sinister spell, like the song of the Sirens?

There was only one way to find out.

Biting his lip—unaware he was doing so—Orson forced himself to relax. He let the power come to him, start to wash over him. He could feel it seeping into every pore, joining with him, connecting to his life force. The wave of power felt so good, so refreshing.

Too much! Aurora called out to him. *You have to control yourself, Orson! You're not ready for it all yet.*

Orson listened to Aurora and closed himself off. It felt wrong, holding out all that energy when it was dying to get inside of him. He reminded himself that Aurora was his teacher for a reason; she had been a Dreamshaper before. She was familiar with the feelings coursing through him at that moment. Sighing, he pulled himself back, refusing to let any more inside.

"Open your eyes." Aurora was no longer in his head. Orson opened his eyes and gasped. Everything around him was radiating energy; the room was filled with a heavenly glow that made even the darkest corner seem light.

"How do you feel?" she asked him.

"I feel...good," he answered and was surprised at the cool, monotonous tone of his own voice. "Like my entire body is filled with electricity."

"Good. Now get rid of your glasses."

Orson reached up to pull his glasses off, wondering what this was supposed to teach him. His fingertips grazed the frame of his familiar round-framed spectacles when Aurora caught him by his wrists and brought his hands down. "Not with your hands, Orson," she said. "Use your mind."

Frowning, Orson started lifting the glasses from his nose, the same way he had lifted the fruit and cubes. Aurora stopped him again.

"I didn't say *lift* your glasses. I said get rid of them."

"But I need them to see," Orson protested lightly.

Aurora shook her head. "Only if you think you do. As the Dreamshaper, you have the power to fix that, if you want. You can make it so you don't need your glasses."

"That's impossible. I'm pretty much blind without them. The last time I tried moving without them I walked into a lamppost."

Aurora smiled but remained persistent. "Impossible is such a strong and misleading word. Using a mirror as a doorway should be impossible, yet you've done it. In dreams, impossible is just another word. Whether you believe it or not is entirely up to you."

Believe the impossible? Was everything a riddle in this place? Orson sighed. How was he supposed to believe that he could decide whether or not he wanted to wear glasses? His eye doctor had already decided that for him.

Still, the thought of getting rid of the glasses he was so irritatingly dependent on was a pleasant thought. What did he have to lose by trying? Closing his eyes, he let a trickle of energy flow through him, directing it up towards his face, forming an invisible bubble over his eyes. As the bubble closed, he felt a not unpleasant tickle over the surface of his eyes. The frames of his glasses grew momentarily warm before they vanished altogether, disappearing completely from his face.

Orson opened his eyes and gasped.

For the first time in his life, Orson looked out through perfect eyes. The glasses that had once hung slightly twisted from the end of his nose were gone, evaporated into thin air.

"My glasses," he whispered, staring at Aurora. "They're gone." He ran his hands over his bare face in disbelief. "Are they gone forever?"

Aurora sat back down on the floor across from him. "Only for as long as you want them to be gone, and only in the Dreamlands, I'm afraid. You will still need them in the waking world."

Orson felt a little disappointment that he would only be free from his glasses in the Dreamlands, but the disappointment was nothing compared to the exhilaration of actually making them disappear in the first place. "Will they still be gone when I come back next time?"

Aurora shook her head sadly. "Your magic only works while you're in the Dreamlands. Once you return to the waking world, your ability disappears until you come back to the Dreamlands. But it's a small task to eliminate them when you first re-enter our world."

Orson nodded. He was sure it would be an annoyance when he woke up, but for now the idea that the spell wouldn't last hardly seemed important. Everything around him seemed new, fresh. Losing his glasses felt like a new awakening. He felt strong, confident. For the first time since he had been unwillingly dragged into all of this, he felt as though he may be able to handle it.

He was starting to believe.

⌐ TWENTY TWO ⌐

"One-hundred years old," Natalie breathed in disbelief. A candy rolled out of her mouth, landing in her juice-filled thermos. She didn't bother fishing it out. "You're kidding me."

Orson and Natalie sat together at recess on the crest of what had become *their hill*. Natalie had brought a small beach towel to school and they had set out a small snack buffet: half a bag of nickel candies, a ham sandwich, some orange juice and a chocolate-chip granola bar that they broke between them. The wind was starting to cool off; the leaves on the trees behind the hill had started to change, a sign that autumn was just around the corner.

"One-hundred and twenty-six, actually," Orson corrected her over a mouthful of sandwich. "She was thirteen when she got into the Dreamlands, a hundred and thirteen years ago."

"Wow." Natalie shook her head. "So I guess a date is out of the question for you. Unless you like dating someone's great-great-great grandmother."

"Don't be gross," Orson sneered. He slipped his house key from around his neck and laid it in the grass beside him.

"I guess that explains the wrinkles," Natalie said under her breath, just loud enough for Orson to hear.

Orson frowned. "She doesn't have wrinkles. What is it with you and her, anyway? Why does she bother you so much?"

Natalie scowled at him. "She doesn't bother me," she said. Orson gave her a doubtful look.

"It's pretty obvious that you don't like Aurora, Natalie. She may not hear all your stupid little comments, but I do. What's she ever done to you?"

Natalie bit into her half of the ham sandwich before answering. "I told you, she doesn't bother me."

"*Something* about her bugs you. I don't see why. She's been really nice to me."

"Of course she has. You're the *Dreamshaper*." Natalie bit angrily into her sandwich, ripping off a huge mouthful and chewing it loudly.

"What's that supposed to mean?" he asked her, peeling the wrapper back off the granola bar. He broke off a piece and took a bite.

"You're the Dreamshaper," Natalie growled. "You figure it out."

"I don't understand you sometimes," he said. A piece of granola flew out between of his mouth and landed wetly on Natalie's lap. She stopped halfway through a handful of candies and stared down at the pulpy remains of the granola bar plastered to her pants, complete with a soggy chocolate chip.

"That's disgusting," she cried, glaring at Orson. With a grimace, she flicked the granola from her pants. The wet piece shot straight up into the air, hitting Orson on the cheek. Orson peeled it off and popped it into his mouth.

"What?" he said when Natalie flashed him a look of total disgust. "I'm not wasting a perfectly good piece of chocolate."

"Boys." Natalie rolled her eyes.

The bell rang and they gathered up their small picnic, Orson shoving the last half dozen candies into his pocket for later. He was wearing the same pants as yesterday but had taken the Sithyrus picture and note out and buried them under the clothes in the top drawer of his dresser.

As they approached the door, Orson reached up to

finger the house key that was normally attached to a string around his neck. It was gone. Digging through his pockets, he sifted through the skittles, candy wrappers and notes but came up empty. The key was missing.

"What's wrong?" Natalie asked, pausing at the top of the steps leading into the school.

"I think I left something at the hill. I have to grab it."

"Do you want some help?"

Orson shook his head, already turning away. "No, it's cool. I'll just be a minute. Let Mr. Pratt know I'll be right there."

Natalie shrugged and went inside.

Racing up the hill, Orson started searching through the grass where they had spread out their light picnic. The key should be easy to spot; a bright orange string had a tendency to stand out no matter where it was. That was the main reason he hated wearing it around his neck—nothing said geek like a bright orange string around your neck.

There was no sign of the key. Orson wondered if he was looking in the wrong spot, but a few scattered candies marked where they had been sitting only moments before. He had placed the key in the grass beside the blanket; it should have been easy to find. Scratching his head, he didn't notice the shadow fall across him until it was too late.

"Looking for something, Strings?" a voice said. Orson turned on his knees and looked up into the sneering faces of Jimmy, Barton and Frank. Jimmy was holding Orson's orange string in one meaty fist. The bully swung the key around like a sling.

"Give me back my key, Jimmy," Orson said, not actually expecting them to give it back.

"Gimme my key back," Barton said in a mock whining voice. "Aw, the baby wants his key, Jimmy. Mebbe you should give it to him."

"Better give it to him quick," Frank added, "before his mommy gets mad at him for losing it."

The smile grew on Jimmy's face. "Oh, I'm gonna give

it to him, all right. I'm gonna give it to him good."

Orson knew what was coming. Kneeling in the grass as he was, he wouldn't have enough time to jump to his feet *and* start running before they were on him. He could have tried rolling away, using the slope of the hill to gain some momentum, but Jimmy and his thugs were already standing in his way, anticipating he might try something like that.

It was hopeless. He was in deep trouble.

Orson opened his mouth to say something, to call out in the hopes that someone would hear him. A couple of kids were still running to get inside the school before they were late. Before he could make a sound, Jimmy kicked him hard in the stomach, knocking the breath from his lungs with a whoosh. Orson toppled backwards, clutching his stomach and gasping for air. Lurking above him like an overstuffed troll, Jimmy twirled the key around hard, letting go and launching it deep into the trees behind the hill. Orson could do little more than watch it disappear in the thick bushes.

"Not so tough without your friends, are you, Strings?" Jimmy laughed. "But don't worry. We'll get the other two soon enough."

Orson rolled up into a ball in the grass. This was going to hurt.

Dreamshaper

When Orson walked into the classroom—fifteen minutes late —all eyes turned to him. Someone in the back of the class gasped when they saw the blood dripping from Orson's nose and lip. His glasses sat lopsided on his face and parts of his clothing were torn from rummaging through the bushes looking for his key. One arm rested gingerly over his bruised stomach. The orange-stringed key was back around his neck. Jimmy was already back in the classroom, sitting at his desk as though nothing had happened. When Orson looked at him, he smiled innocently and shrugged.

When Natalie looked over at Orson, her face went pale. "Oh, Orson," she whispered as he sat down heavily in his desk. "I'm sorry, I never should have left..."

Orson waved her off. Looking over his shoulder, he saw Mike's face, his eye still slightly puffed, glaring at Jimmy's back. Mike knew what had happened; his eye was still feeling the effects of an earlier meeting with the bullies. They had been so careful to not get caught alone since Mike's black eye and Orson's close encounter. All it took was one careless minute for the bullies to catch one of them off-guard.

"What happened to you?" Mr. Pratt asked, coming to Orson's desk to examine him more closely.

Jimmy eyes never left Orson; the smirk on his lips grew. The bully had to expect that Orson would tell what happened. If he told Mr. Pratt that Jimmy and his band of merry makers had given him the bloody nose and lip, Jimmy would be sent down to speak with the principle. Mrs. Blondin may even suspend them a few days.

But in the end, Orson knew that was exactly what Jimmy wanted. If Orson told, it would be an admission in front of everyone that he couldn't handle Jimmy, that the bully had gotten the better of him and his friends. That once again, Jimmy had beaten his enemies into submission.

"Well?" Mr. Pratt said. Orson shook his head. He kept his eyes fixed on Jimmy. The corners of Jimmy's mouth dipped down as the smile fell away. Rather than looking at him with the normal amount of fear that the bully expected, Orson's brow furrowed angrily and he shook his head.

"Nothing," Orson said. "I had an accident in the playground at lunch."

"That's some accident," Mr. Pratt said. Orson shrugged.

"I lost my key in the woods and slipped when I was trying to find it. Hit my nose on a root."

Mr. Pratt watched Orson carefully for a moment,

clearly not believing the story. It was plain for everyone to see that Orson hadn't gotten the bleeding nose from a trip in the woods; someone had given it to him. When it was apparent that Orson wasn't going to change his story, Mr. Pratt sighed.

"Go clean yourself up. Stop in to see the nurse. You should have that nose looked at."

Orson nodded and got up from his desk. His face hurt and his stomach ached; he tried his best to keep from showing his discomfort. He didn't want Jimmy to see how hurt he really was. Before leaving the class, he leaned over to Natalie, who was watching him sadly.

"One of these days," he whispered harshly to Natalie, "Jimmy Scrags is gonna get his."

⌐ TWENTY THREE ⌐

Orson sat up in bed with the feeling that someone was watching him. Something shuffled faintly in the shadowy corner of his room, so quiet it might have just been the sounds of the house breathing. Orson's father had taught him when he was younger—when he was just a toddler—about how houses sometimes breathed. Orson had been terribly frightened of the sounds in the dark when you were lying in bed, the creaking in the walls and floor. His father told him that the sounds were really just the house breathing at night, watching over the family as they all slept. Back then Orson had accepted his father's words as true, forgetting about the monsters in the shadows.

Now he knew better. Now he had seen the monsters in the shadows.

Reaching for his reading lamp, Orson clicked it on, feeling foolish as he looked over to see if something was hiding in the corner of his room. For a moment he thought he saw something move beside his bedroom mirror—there was a momentary blur in the air itself, almost like a giant bubble of air shifting before settling into place and becoming invisible once again. Orson frowned, reaching for his glasses. Sliding them into place over his ears, he looked back into the corner, but it was empty.

Orson climbed out of bed and stretched his arms. He knew he was dreaming—he had started to recognize the feeling of being in a dream. There was always something in

161

the air, some hidden thickness, not uncomfortable but not normal, either. Touching his face lightly, he was surprised to find it swollen and sore even in the dream; apparently Jimmy Scrags's fists were far reaching.

Closing his eyes, Orson concentrated on his power, letting a small trickle of energy flow into himself. He directed the light flow of energy into his lip, wondering if he could use the power on his swollen lip the same way he had on his glasses. Under his finger, he felt the bump slowly shrink. It didn't disappear completely, but it stopped hurting. Opening his eyes, he walked over to the mirror in the corner and looked at his reflection. The mirror was a portal into the Dreamlands, making his reflection blurry, but it was clear enough to let him see that his lip was nearly healed, at least in his dream. When he woke up, it would still be swollen and bruised.

Even with his glasses on and the lamp glowing, Orson couldn't shake the feeling that he was being watched. He looked over beside the mirror where he had seen the air shifting and bit his lip. The corner was still empty, but for some strange reason still raised the small hairs on his arms. He started reaching out into the empty air, sure his fingers would find something waiting in the corner, invisible to his naked eye, but stopped. He was just being paranoid— spending so much time in the Dreamlands had played with his mind. He had much more important things to do than chase imaginary monsters hiding in plain view.

Staring into the mirror, he prepared to use it to get back to the Palace. He hated going through the mirror; he would never get used to the feeling of stepping into the jelly-like portal. As exciting as it was to discover his newfound magical abilities, if there was one thing Orson wouldn't miss when this was all over, it was having to step through these portals to get into the Dreamlands. There had to be a better way to travel.

For now, he resigned himself to using the portal. Sighing lightly, he stared into the mirror, remembering what

Aurora had taught him about using it. Concentrating on where he needed to go, he looked straight into the mirror and said: "The Palace of Dreams."

The mirror rippled lightly. For a moment Orson considered calling Natalie to come with him. That feeling of being watched wouldn't go away, and he was starting to feel more than a little unnerved. Maybe the beating Jimmy had given him had scrambled his brains a little and had put him on edge. Telling himself he was being silly, he decided to leave Natalie out of his dreams tonight.

Natalie would probably only distract him from his lesson, anyway. He was glad she was there to help him, but for some reason she had developed a dislike for the Queen of the Dreamlands, and he wasn't in the mood to deal with it tonight, not after everything that had happened in school.

Orson didn't know why Natalie hated Aurora; the Queen had certainly done nothing to earn the irritating comments Natalie made. It must be a girl thing, he thought. Girls were always acting so weird. Sarah would probably be the same when she got a little older.

"I wonder where Sarah is right now," he said when the thought of his sister struck him. Wherever she was, he hoped she was okay. The irony of such a thought wasn't lost on him. A few short weeks ago he would have done anything to get away from his baby sister. Now that she was gone, all he could do was worry he may never see her again.

Orson swallowed the thought and dipped his hand into the mirror. The cold immediately traveled up into his arm. It was better to get this over with quickly. Sucking in a deep breath, he stepped into the mirror.

Just before his head slipped into the portal, he thought he heard a whispering sound behind him. Something tugged on the collar of his shirt, trying to pull him back into the room. Yanking himself away, Orson opened his mouth to cry out and felt the cold seep down his throat and into his lungs, choking him. The fingers tugging on his shirt slipped away and he tumbled through the mirror.

The ground vanished beneath his feet as he fell through the portal. The moment he emerged on the other side, he knew something was wrong. Rather than stepping into the Great Hall, he found himself flailing into complete darkness.

As he hit the ground hard, sputtering and gasping over the choking cold he had swallowed in the portal, Orson knew he wasn't in the Palace of Dreams. He was somewhere different, a place enshrouded in darkness that stank of moldy danger.

Something had gone terribly wrong.

⌐ TWENTY FOUR ⌐

The darkness was suffocating.

Frozen on his hands and knees, Orson was too alarmed to move. The ground beneath him was mercilessly hard—his hands were raw from the rough landing and his knees throbbed painfully. The cold in his throat was finally fading and he was able to take in a few gasping breaths. In the darkness, his breathing echoed eerily, matched only by the thumping of his pulse in his ears. The room was humid; even though he couldn't see anything, Orson could smell the dank odor of mold on rock. The air tasted heavy and old, like the air deep in the back of a cave. It tasted like air that hadn't been changed in a very long time.

Even worse, Orson's glasses had fallen off as he hit the ground hard. The sound of breaking glass had been unmistakable, even in the daunting darkness. Grazing the ground tenderly with his fingers—the last thing he needed was to cut his finger on broken glass—he found his frames and confirmed what he thought. One lens was broken in half and the other had completely fallen out of the frames. Even if there was light, he'd be blind.

"Great," he said, not liking the sound of his voice in the dark.

Orson got to his feet. This was all wrong. The portal was supposed to take him to the Palace of Dreams. Why had it brought him here—and where *was* here? Orson reached behind to adjust the collar of his shirt, which had been pulled snuggly against his throat. Something *had* been in his room, hiding in plain light, which should be impossible. It had tried to grab him as he entered the mirror: had it pushed him here?

Even worse, had it followed him here?

As if waiting for him to think just that, something moved in the darkness behind him. Orson turned blindly around. If the thing from his room had followed him, it wouldn't need to hide here in the dark. He hoped that whatever was following him was as blind in here as he was, but doubted he would be so lucky. His attacker could probably see him quite well in the dark; why else would it have chosen a place like this?

Bending down, Orson felt carefully along the floor for a stick or makeshift weapon. There were no sticks, but he did find a handful of rocks. Shoving a couple in his pocket, he kept one in each hand, ready to throw. With a stick he could swing wildly with some chance of hitting anything close. It would be optimistic to think he would be able to hit anything in this darkness with a rock, but it was better than nothing. If nothing else, he might be able to hold the rock and use it to bash anything that got too close.

Feeling all too helpless, Orson wished he had some light. An idea struck him.

Remembering the globes he had trained with, Orson closed his eyes and tried to send out a little wave of energy, searching for some source of light. He felt the power seep into him—it was getting easier finding his power, but using it was a different story. Another shuffling sound behind him broke his concentration.

Alone or not, if Orson didn't find a way out of here, he was in big trouble, and to find a way out he was going to need some light. Closing his eyes, he tried to focus around the sound in the darkness and sent out another wave of energy. This time he was able to hold on long enough for a dozen light orbs scattered around the floor to catch and glow, dimly illuminating the room. His eyes blurred without his glasses,

Orson looked around.

The room was empty.

Confused, Orson wasn't about to waste the opportunity. Using his ability to fix his eyes, he gave his vision a moment to clear up before looking around.

Surrounded by heavy rock walls that were awash in creepy shadows from the light of the globes, Orson figured he was a cave of sorts. The walls were damp and covered in thin patches of dark mold, the source of the smell in the air. There was only one way out of the cave, a narrow passage to the right. With nowhere else to go, Orson made his way to the opening.

The passage lengthened into a tunnel carved into the thick red rock. Light globes hung from the walls every half dozen feet, attached to large wooden support beams nearly as thick as Orson's waist. Touching the beam closest to him, Orson thought the tunnel looked like an old mineshaft. Under his hand, the beam groaned miserably and a large piece of rotten wood flaked away.

Orson backed away quickly. If these rotten beams were all that was keeping the rocky ceiling from crashing down, it wasn't very encouraging. He looked up nervously, envisioning the ruined supports giving way and burying him under a ton of rubble. It didn't take long for Orson to decide that this probably wasn't the safest place to be.

The mineshaft twisted and turned several times, almost like a twisted relative to the corridors in the Palace of Dreams. Luckily there was only one path to follow, a far cry from the branching halls of the Palace. Every so often the sensation of being watched would return, but whenever he turned to look the tunnel behind him was empty. Orson wondered if this was what it was like to be a deer during hunting season. Constantly checking over his shoulder, he certainly felt like he was being stalked.

The air in the mineshaft was horribly dry and polluted from years of dust and mildew. It only took a few minutes before Orson's head was starting to spin from drawing in shallow, searing breaths. Every breath he took threatened to choke him; he could feel the beginning traces of panic building but forced himself to march on. There had to be a way out of here.

Turning around the next corner, Orson froze. The wall ahead was completely sealed. The tunnel had led him to a dead end.

Had he missed a turn somewhere? Coughing up a lungful of dust, he growled, frustrated and concerned. He retraced his steps in his head and was sure that he hadn't missed anything. There hadn't been any doors or turns other than the way he had come, not unless they were ridiculously well hidden. There didn't seem any other choice but going back, but doing so would only lead him back to where he had started, and possibly right into the arms of whatever was hunting him.

"If anything's hunting me," he tried to reassure himself. There had been no other signs that anyone else was down here with him, but if there was one thing he had learned in the Dreamlands thus far, it was that not everything was always as it appeared.

He pressed his hands up against the dead end, desperately hoping for a secret door. In the movies, these kinds of places always had a secret door that the hero didn't find until the last possible moment. There was no door, but his fingers did slip inside a small hole in the wall, oddly smooth compared to the rough wall around it. A second hole was cut into the wall a few inches higher and to the left, and another an equal distance above that.

It was a ladder of sorts, carved into the wall of the tunnel. Following the ladder with his eyes, he could have cried when he saw a trapdoor directly above his head. With tremendous relief, he began to climb, his foot just able to squeeze in the holes as he pulled himself upward.

Straining his shoulder against the trapdoor, Orson winced as it creaked open, the noise sounding incredibly loud in the otherwise quiet tunnel. Thankfully it wasn't hinged, so instead of having to let it drop with an alerting bang he was able to slide it sideways enough to let him peek his head through.

The air above the trapdoor wasn't fresh, but it was a great deal better than the air below. Orson took a few deep breaths, feeling the choking sensation filter out of his lungs. It would have been a relief had each breath not sounded as loud as the creaking door in his ears.

As Orson pulled himself out of the underground tunnel, he noticed the new hallway was lit by the same globes as beneath, but was missing the wooden supports. The red walls—though still carved into the rock itself—were smoothly polished but barren of any other decoration. There was something disturbingly familiar about this place, something he couldn't quite put his finger on it.

At least until he saw the small metal door glimmering faintly in the wall ahead.

Seeing the little door—like the door of a hotel laundry chute—brought back a wave of dread that stood the hair on the back of Orson's neck on end. This was where he had come when he first escaped Sithyrus, before this Dreamshaper nonsense had started. He could almost hear the roar of the lizard chasing him down the hallway, nearly catching hold of his pajama shirt before he dropped down that same chute in the wall ahead. He knew what he would find at the bottom if he climbed through now: a pile of disgusting sludge. He had no interest in seeing if he was right.

The feeling of being watched suddenly came back strong. Orson thought he could smell something, an oily scent that faded quickly. He whipped around, expecting to see Sithyrus right behind him, ready to pounce. The hallway was still empty. Orson ran a shaking hand through his red hair—he had never felt this scared before, not even in the moments leading up to a dodgeball game against Jimmy Scrags.

"Hello?" he called out softly, not liking the way that

even a whisper seemed incredibly loud in here.

Movement sounded from around the corner at the far end of the hall. "Ay, 'oo's there?" a gruff voice called out. "'Oo's there, I sez?" the voice called again, followed by heavy footsteps. "Oy! You better answer, 'cuz I knows yer there!"

Orson wanted to bang his head against the wall; he couldn't believe he'd been stupid enough to call out in here. Not wanting to see what was coming around the corner—more importantly, not wanting whatever was coming to see *him*—Orson dropped back down the trapdoor in the floor, pulling it closed behind him, careful to do so quietly. It shut not a moment too soon; moments after it clicked lightly shut, he heard the sound of heavy footsteps come pounding down the hallway above.

Not wanting to risk a fall and alert whatever was chasing him that he was down below, he squeezed himself tightly against the rock wall, clinging onto the holes tenaciously.

"Wha's go'n on 'ere?" the voice was right above him now. The stale air of the mineshaft had already started filling his lungs again, and Orson was forced to take controlled, shallow breaths to keep from coughing.

"'Ey, you idjit, what're you goin' on about?" another voice joined the first. There were two of them now. The other one must have heard the commotion and come to investigate.

"Thought I hears somethin,'" the first voice said, "Sounded like talking. Thought I should checks it out, make sure ever'thing's tip-top."

The second voice snorted, even closer to the trapdoor. "Are you some kinda stupid? What, something here, in the Mountain?" A heavy foot thudded hollowly on the trapdoor. It creaked and curved dangerously inward. For one desperate moment Orson was certain it would come crashing down on his head with the full weight of whatever was standing above him. Thankfully it held, but not without spilling a shower of dust down onto him. "Who'd be dumb enough to come sneaking 'round in 'ere?"

"I ain't no stupid," the first one answered hotly. "I hears talking, I knows I did, like someone was whisperin'."

The foot on top of the door shifted, sprinkling Orson with a new trickle of dust, which immediately floated its way up his nose. Crinkling his face, he shook his head from side to side, using everything he had to keep from sneezing. Even through the dust and stale air, he could smell a foul odor that reminded him of his gym socks after a month.

"You prob'ly just heard a rat," the second voice snarled. "You really think someone could have gotten in here? That someone, other than you, per'aps, would be that stupid?" There was another groan as the thing on top of the door smacked the first one.

"Well that's nice," the first one growled. "Suppose it could been a rat, pretty noisy little feller, though. Musta been a big one. How d'you explain the talking, if yer so smart?"

"Get yer head screwed on straight," the second one said, shifting again and giving Orson another mouthful of dust. He was choking on a sneeze now. He wasn't going to be able to hold it much longer. "A talkin' rat. Sith'rus would have yer head if he heard you being so stupid."

"Maybe I'm just a little worked up," the first voice said after a moment. "That human babe won't stop cryin' and it's startin' ter drive me crazy! How can some little thing make so much noise? And let's not talk about the stink! You ever seen a mess like that? Right in its clothes, too."

Crying and stinky. They had to be talking about his sister. Craning his ear up, he tried to listen closer.

"She'll be done soon enough," the second voice answered. "Sith'rus sez the Machine's almost ready and then we can get rid of the little pink beastie."

"Wha' about the Dreamshaper?" the first asked and Orson tilted his head a little more, so that his ear was nearly touching the wood; the stink from the feet above nearly brought tears to his eyes.

"Wha' about the Dreamshaper," the second one mocked. "Well, when the Machine's goin' we ain't gonna need to worry about him, now are we? Sith'rus will just find him in his own world and take care of 'im there. Is your brain even plugged in just yet?"

The first one growled low but Orson was no longer paying attention. The Machine was almost working. Were they talking about the Machine Aurora had told him about, the one that would let the Nightmares out of the Dreamlands and into the waking world? If they were close to finishing it, then the things above him were right: they wouldn't need Sarah anymore. Orson seriously doubted that meant they would just take her safely back home.

The door shuddered again. "I told you, I ain't no idjit!" the first voice roared. Its foot came down heavy and a cloud of dust exploded around Orson's head. He couldn't hold back the sneeze any longer. It erupted from his nose and nearly knocked him from the stone ladder. The movement above him stopped.

The trapdoor was ripped open, exposing Orson to the monsters above. He cried out as they stared down at him, gawking as much in disbelief at the intruder perched below as he was at them.

One of the Nightmare's looked like little more than a large dog with black, pointed ears pinned tightly back against its head. The other one was much more frightening. A large mass of oozing goo dripped down its face, plunking off the tip of its nose and just missing Orson as it splattered into the tunnel below.

"I told you I 'ears something," the dog-thing growled. "It don't look like no rat to me, now do it?"

The second one made an odd clucking noise. "Sure it do," it said. "Looks like a big ol' pink rat to me. Only question is, wha's a big pink rat do'n 'ere in the Mountain?"

"Guess we should ask it," the other one said cruelly.

In desperation, Orson let go, hoping to fall back into the tunnel below. The creatures above were quicker. Just as he started to topple from the wall, they both reached down and grabbed him, yanking him from the hole.

"Looks jes' like that baby," the dog snarled, holding Orson at arms' length like he was diseased. "But older."

"Whatcha doin' here, ratty?" the second one asked, leaning in close.

"I..." Orson stammered, trying to think of something. He tried to gather up his power to use against them, but he was too terrified to focus. He was at the mercy of these monsters. "I wasn't doing anything, I promise!"

"'ey, you suppose he's, you know, *him*?" the dog asked, his beady eyes widening.

"If he is, we're gonna be heroes," the second one said. "We'd better not let anyone sees 'im until we get 'im back to Sith'rus."

The dog's eyes lit up considerably. "You think he's dan'grous?"

"Naw," the oozing Nightmare answered. "Looks pretty useless to me..."

The Nightmare didn't get a chance to finish its sentence. As Orson looked on in horror, a dark shape seemed to materialize from the wall itself. In one smooth motion, the thing had grabbed both Nightmares by their necks. In the same motion, it cracked their two heads together with a sickening sound. As they fell apart, Orson tumbled out of their hands to the floor.

Standing over him, the black thing was even more terrifying than the Sithyrus. Looking into it was like looking into death itself. Orson couldn't make out its features, only a dark mask that seemed to absorb all the light around it, drawing it into darkness as though it were a hungry shadow feeding on the light.

"Stay back," Orson managed weakly. The thing didn't respond. In one quick movement it had him by the shirt, lifting him clear off the ground. With its other hand, it held up a small orb that Orson recognized immediately as a portice.

Smashing the portice to the ground, the dark shape opened up a gateway and tossed Orson through.

⌐ TWENTY FIVE ⌐

Orson stared up at the terrifying monster—if anything deserved to be called *monster* it was this thing—unable to take his eyes off of it. Its skin was a deep blue, so dark it was nearly black. Orson had thought it had a plate of spiked armour covering its back; looking closer, Orson had been shocked to discover that the spikes weren't armour, but were actually *part* of the creature, sticking right out of its skin.

The dark beast watched Orson intently through a mask that must have come straight out of one of the science fiction movies his mother was always forbidding him to watch. The eye slits glowed bright green and a bundle of dreadlocks hung from the back of its head. As Orson watched, the shadow creature opened and closed its hands with a creaking sound like old leather.

Dream demon: that's what Aurora had called it. Orson could see why. The word *demon* sounded just about right for this nightmarish thing. It certainly didn't look like anything that had come from up above the clouds.

"Does it have a name?" Orson asked Queen Aurora.

"*His* name is Mange," she answered. The demon didn't react to his name being spoken.

"Mange," Orson repeated. "He looks like he should be one of *them*." It was hard for Orson to picture the demon as anything but a Nightmare. He certainly fit the bill of evil creatures—Mange looked as though he was created from the same mold that produced Sithyrus. "What was he doing

175

there, anyway?"

Aurora pulled on a long braid as she looked across the table at him. "Guarding you, of course."

"Guarding me? From what?"

Aurora frowned. "From yourself, it seems," she said slyly. Orson didn't need to ask what she was talking about.

"I thought Lupus was supposed to be watching out for me."

"There are many people watching out for you, Orson," Aurora assured him. "Some of them more directly than others, like Lupus. Mange, however, has certain abilities that enable him to protect you in a much more efficient manner."

"Abilities?"

Aurora gestured to the dream demon. Orson turned around to look at the black-skinned beast—at least, he thought he was turning to look at him. The demon had vanished. All he could see was the wall on which Mange had been leaning a moment ago.

"Where did he go?" Orson said, surprised. He whipped his head this way and that, searching for Mange, but the demon was nowhere to be seen. When he looked back at the Queen, Aurora simply smiled and nodded for him to look again. Frowning, Orson turned back around.

Mange was standing in the same place as before.

"What...?" Orson stammered, jumping at the sudden reappearance of the dream demon. "That's impossible. Do it again," he demanded. As he watched, Mange disappeared and reappeared in a matter of seconds.

"You can turn invisible?" Orson asked him. Mange only shrugged and shook his head.

"Dream demons don't speak," Aurora informed him. "At least, not in any language we can hear or understand."

Standing up, the Queen walked around and patted Mange on the arm, a gesture that seemed awkward for such an imposing creature. "Mange doesn't exactly turn invisible. It's more of a camouflage, like a chameleon. A dream demon's skin, while heavily armoured, works like a sponge. Instead of absorbing water, however, it absorbs the colour of the surrounding environment, giving the impression of turning invisible. As you found out back in the Haunted Mountain, it's a skill that comes in handy."

It had been a strange blend of relief and fear; Orson watched the demon step through the portice and had thought it was a Nightmare invading the Palace. When Aurora had showed up, completely unconcerned about this sudden Nightmare in her midst, Orson had nearly fallen over, until the Queen had told him that Mange was on their side.

"Are there more dream demons?" he asked Aurora, keeping his eyes fixed on Mange in case the demon was going to disappear again.

Aurora shook her head sadly. "If there are, they haven't been seen in years. As far as we know, Mange is the last of the dream demons."

"What happened to them all?"

"The same as everything else." Aurora tugged on her braid. "When the Nightmares began spreading their evil, even the demons weren't immune to it. When they refused to join the Nightmares' cause, they were overwhelmed in their own homes. Mange managed to escape, but we haven't heard from any others."

Orson thought back to the ease in which Mange had dealt with the two Nightmares that had caught him. If that was how dangerous one dream demon was, he could only imagine the force that would have been necessary to stop an entire race of them. If the Nightmares could erase an entire race from the Dreamlands, what hope did Orson have of stopping them? Especially with the Machine near completion...

Orson froze. He had almost forgotten about what he had overheard in the Haunted Mountain.

"The Machine is almost ready," he burst out. Aurora paused, her hand gripping her braid tightly.

"What?" she asked carefully. "What are you talking about, Orson? That's impossible. The Machine should be weeks away from completion."

"Before those things caught me, I heard them talking about Sarah. They said they wouldn't need her much longer because the Machine was almost done."

The Queen's face went pale. "Did they say how long?"

Orson shook his head. "No, but from the way they were talking, I don't think it's a few weeks."

"That's just not possible," Aurora said again. "They can't have gathered everything they need, not yet. You must have misheard them."

"I know what I heard," Orson insisted.

"Maybe, but you didn't hear them say when. You could be wrong."

Orson shook his head. Why wasn't she listening to him? "But what if I'm right?"

"It's just not possible," Aurora repeated. "This is too soon. We're nowhere near ready to deal with this yet. It shouldn't be possible that the Machine is that close, but you're right. I can't ignore the risk that what you're saying is true."

"What are we going to do?" Orson asked. Behind him, Mange shifted, his skin creaking softly as he flexed. The dream demon looked ready to go battle the Nightmares right now—Orson didn't think he would pass at the chance if it showed itself.

"I don't know." Aurora shook her head. "I just don't know. But for all of our sakes, Orson, I hope you're wrong."

⌐ TWENTY SIX ⌐

Natalie joined Orson on their hill at recess. Orson, twisting his fingers nervously, told Natalie about his recent trip to the Dreamlands. Natalie listened quietly, frowning at Orson the entire time. She sat a little farther apart from Orson than normal; he had a feeling that she was upset with him for some reason. If she was, she didn't say anything, at least not right away.

"A meeting?" Natalie asked after he finished. "After what you told her, the most she plans on doing is setting up a meeting?"

Orson sniffed. The cut on his lip was back now that he was in the waking world again. It still lightly stung as he brushed it with his finger. "Aurora said she needs to talk to a committee, or something like that, before she makes a decision. Something about politics. I didn't really understand what she was talking about."

"My dad always says politics make life harder than it should be," Natalie replied, shaking her head. "So what are you gonna do?"

"Well, Aurora thinks the Machine won't be done for a few weeks," Orson shrugged. "She said they can't be that close to completing it yet. She said we can't do anything until she's had her meeting."

"*She* said this, *she* said that," Natalie mocked. "She's got you wrapped around her finger, doesn't she? You're the one who heard the Nightmares, Orson. Do you think the

179

Machine's gonna be done in a few weeks?"

Orson stared at his hands for a long moment, wishing he were anywhere else just then. Things had been going so well up until the moment he wandered unwillingly into the Haunted Mountain. As the Dreamshaper, he had finally started getting an identity—he had become *somebody*, even if it was only in his dreams. The idea that he, Orson Bailey— *Strings*—had magic made him feel important for a change. That feeling was tainted now by the memory of what else that magic had brought. Because of him, Sarah had been kidnapped. Even if he hadn't known about the magic, he still felt it was his fault she was in trouble.

"Well?" Natalie asked again. "What do you think? Do we have that much time?"

Orson looked at his friend. Finally, he shook his head. "I guess not."

"I didn't think so." Natalie took a long sip from a water bottle she had brought outside for recess. "So, what are we gonna do?"

"We? I don't think..."

Orson was abruptly cut off by an all too familiar voice at the bottom of the hill. Jimmy Scrags had found them on the hill, and as usual, the bully wasn't alone. Frank and Barton were standing on either side of the bigger boy, sneering up at Orson and Natalie.

"Look what we found, boys," Jimmy leered at them from the bottom of the hill, bending down to pick up a fist-sized rock. Barton and Frank already had one in each hand. "Looks like we found us a couple lovebirds kissing on the hill."

"And without little Mikey Spencer to protect them," Barton added cruelly.

"Yeah, without Mike," Frank echoed. "What d'ya figure we should do, Big J?"

"Big J?" Natalie called down before Jimmy could answer. "They must call you that for your fat stomach, because it sure can't mean the size of your brain."

"Natalie," Orson warned, but Natalie was on a roll.

"Takes a pretty tough guy to beat up on someone when you outnumber them, doesn't it, Jimmy?" she asked mockingly.

Jimmy snarled up at her. "Way I remember it, you three dorks ganged up on me last time. I'm just returning the favor." Jimmy had clearly forgotten about his attack on both Mike and Orson, or had chosen to push the memory aside.

Orson started to tug at Natalie's arm, wanting to get away before it was too late. He wanted to make Jimmy Scrags pay for the things he'd done, but now wasn't the time, not with only the two of them against all three bullies. Natalie, however, had other ideas.

"Aw, what's-a-matter, Jimmy?" she shot back at him. "Still bug you that you got beat up by a girl?"

"You ain't no girl, Natalie," Jimmy retorted, seething now. Orson thought he could actually see steam coming from the bully's ears. "You're more boy than your new boyfriend!"

"Well, c'mon then, you fat lump," she stung back and Orson groaned again. A little diplomacy probably wouldn't have made any difference, but Natalie's hot-headedness was going to bring them a world of hurt. "If you're so good with a rock, let's see what you've got. I bet my grandma's got a better arm than you sad soggy softies!"

Jimmy cocked his arm and let loose with a bullet. His rock hurtled dangerously towards Natalie and Orson thought she was done for. She dodged the missile easily, however, jumping nimbly to one side and laughing as the rock flew harmlessly past. She looked down and stuck her tongue out at Jimmy, who roared in return. The three goons started up the hill towards them, Jimmy's face a shade of red that would have made Mr. Pratt proud.

"Maybe I said too much?" Natalie said and Orson groaned again. Grabbing her elbow, the two of them ran for their lives.

They ran until they were winded, rocks flying past their shoulders and ears every now and then. One rock hit Orson in the shoulder and he cried out, more in shock than pain. Thankfully, Jimmy wasn't much of a runner, and they quickly put some distance between themselves and the gang of thugs.

Racing around the corner of the school, they paused for a moment, leaning against the wall to catch their breath. They had managed to lose Jimmy in the playground, but it was a short way around the school, and someone would have noticed them running. Jimmy was no doubt shaking down some unfortunate soul right at that very moment to find out what direction they had gone.

"That was way too close," Orson said and Natalie chuckled.

"Just be happy they can't sing, like those Sirens in the dream," she said with a chuckle. "If those three donkeys started braying, it probably would've knocked us out cold."

Orson didn't feel much like laughing at the moment. He was a little more concerned with living for another day than cracking jokes. "We've gotta put a stop to him, Natalie," he said. "Before he really hurts one of us."

"You could always bring him into your dreams, like you do with me, and deal with him there."

Orson shook his head. "I've got enough to worry about when I'm there. The last thing I need is Jimmy running around the Dreamlands. He'd probably end up joining the Nightmares."

Natalie nodded. "Probably. Hey, do you think he had anything to do with your sister?"

The question caught Orson off-guard. "Why would Jimmy have had anything to do with Sarah?"

Natalie shrugged. "Well, you said Sithyrus was talking to him in your dream once. What if he talked about Sarah? Maybe he put the idea in Sithyrus's head."

Orson was stunned. He hadn't even considered that possibility. He certainly wouldn't have put it past the bully to do something so cold-hearted—or cowardly, considering how Jimmy was behaving when Sithyrus had trapped him in the library. The thought infuriated him, but he pushed it aside for the moment. Whether or not Jimmy had anything to do with Sarah's kidnapping was a matter for another time. He had much deeper problems to deal with.

"Maybe," he said. "But right now I have more important things to worry about, like how long it's going to take Aurora to have her meeting."

Natalie rolled her eyes. "How can you just sit around waiting for the Queen's stupid little meeting? What if your sister doesn't have that much time left?"

Orson looked at her. "What can we do? Aurora won't be happy until she's had the meeting, so there's nothing we *can* do. Why do you hate her so much, anyway?"

"I don't hate her," Natalie said indignantly.

"You're lying, but one of these days you're gonna have to tell me what's going on. It's probably just some sort of crazy girl thing—you girls are *all* crazy, as far as I'm concerned."

Natalie bopped him lightly on the shoulder. "Watch it, or Jimmy Scrags won't be the only one you need to worry about."

"I'm just saying," he answered.

Natalie's brow furrowed. "What is it about her that you like so much? All she's done since you started this Dreamshaper stuff is try to tell you what to do. She may be a Queen, Orson, but she's not *our* Queen. You let her boss you around like you're her little slave or something."

Orson couldn't believe what he was hearing. Is this what she was mad about? "She doesn't *boss* me, Natalie. She's trying to help me. She knows what's going on in the Dreamlands. We wouldn't have a chance of saving Sarah without her."

"Are you sure?" Natalie said, looking Orson straight in the eyes.

Orson paused as he looked into Natalie's face. "What

183

do you mean? Of course I'm sure."

"Think about it, Orson. You've just been in the home of the Nightmares, and you got out just fine.

"With a little help from Mange," he corrected her.

"Even still, what if we went back in, together? Maybe we can get her out."

"Maybe we can get ourselves killed," he countered. "Besides, I don't even know how I got there in the first place. Even if I could get us back, what if something was waiting for us? I don't know what happened to those two Nightmares Mange knocked out, but if they're still alive, they probably told Sithyrus I was there. The Nightmares will be watching for me now."

"What if Sithyrus decides that they don't need Sarah anymore? What if the Machine is almost ready? You were the one down there, Orson, not Aurora. You heard what those things said. Now you have to decide what to do next. Do you want to sit around waiting for your Queen's meeting, or do you want to save your sister before it's too late?"

Orson shook his head. "I can't take on an entire army of Nightmares alone."

"Who said you have to fight them? Maybe we can sneak in and grab her. And you won't be alone. I already missed out on your last trip. Do you really think I'm missing the next one?"

"I don't know," Orson said, a lump building in his throat. "I just don't know."

⌞ TWENTY SEVEN ⌟

Orson stared into the muddled surface of the mirror. His glasses were gone, but his eyes worked just fine, thanks to his gift. His image wavered back at him, twisted like a Pablo Picasso painting, amplifying the worried grimace on his face as he wondered if it was too late to change his mind.

"This isn't a good idea," he said. Natalie, standing beside him, patted him on the shoulder.

"Well, we're here now, aren't we? No sense backing out."

"What if the Nightmares are waiting on the other side?" He looked over at Natalie; she was standing with her arms crossed across her chest, looking cool and calm in the face of impending danger. "How can you be so calm about this?"

"Calm?" Natalie sniffed. "I'm absolutely terrified right now. So, how do we get it to take us back to...what did you call that place again?"

"The Haunted Mountain," Orson said with a shiver. Even the name seemed somehow darker at that moment— *The Haunted Mountain*. Why couldn't it be called something else? Something with a nicer tone to it: The Rocky Mountain, or even the Fuzzy Pink Bunny Mountain. Anything would be better than the word *haunted*.

In any case, Orson had no idea how he had gotten there the first time. He had thought at first that something had pushed him in, but that something had turned out to be the dream demon, Mange. As one of Aurora's best soldiers, Orson doubted that the demon would have pushed him through. Mange was probably trying to *stop* him from going through.

He thought back to what Aurora had told him about using portices. When you were using one, you needed to concentrate on where you wanted to go. Maybe he had simply lost his concentration.

Orson froze. He knew what had happened. "My thoughts slipped," he said. Natalie stared at him in confusion.

"What?"

"My thoughts slipped," Orson repeated. "Last time I was here, I was planning on going to the Palace of Dreams. Aurora told me when I wanted to use the portal, I just had to tell it where I wanted to go. That's how Lupus brought us to the Palace after the Sirens' attack, and that's how I've been getting back there for training."

"I'm still not following," Natalie said.

"When I was going to go back to the Palace last time, I told the mirror to take me there. But just before I stepped through the mirror, I got distracted. I started thinking about Sarah and where she might be. It was my last thought before I tried to use the mirror. What if that's what brought me to the Haunted Mountain? What if the portal read my thoughts?"

Natalie shrugged. "There's only one way to find out."

Orson nodded. If they were going to do this, they had to go now. The nerves had quieted down for a moment, but they would be back. "Alright, let's do this." Stepping up to the mirror, he looked into the glass again and swallowed loudly enough for Natalie to hear and chuckle lightly. Closing his eyes for a moment, he thought about the mineshaft, about the darkness waiting for them. "Take us to Sarah. Take us to the place you brought me before."

He opened his eyes. The two of them looked into the mirror, searching for any sign that it had worked. Orson knew they wouldn't be able to see anything; the mirror looked the same as it always did: blurry but otherwise normal.

"Did it work?" Natalie asked.

"Only one way to find out. If it did, the cave on the other side should be completely dark. Just stay close until I can turn on the lights."

Natalie reached out and took Orson's hand. Her fingers felt warm and not altogether unpleasant. "This way we won't get separated," she said, and for the first time Orson could see just how frightened she really was. She looked right at him for a long moment. "You look different without your glasses," she said, touching his cheek lightly. "I like it. You should think about getting contacts in our world."

"We have to make it back to our world first." He squeezed her hand reassuringly and prepared to take the first step when another thought occurred to him. Motioning for Natalie to be quiet, he waited, listening to nothing. Feeling nothing. No hidden eyes, no invisible presence: No Mange. He couldn't feel the dream demon hiding in the room, which didn't necessarily mean he *wasn't* there, but it was a bit reassuring. If Mange knew what he was doing, the demon would likely try to stop them, or race back to tell the Queen. Reaching out with his free hand, he waved it through the empty air beside the mirror. There was nothing there.

"What are you doing?" Natalie asked, eyeing him curiously.

Orson drew his hand back. "Just making sure," he said. "That's where Mange was hiding last time."

Turning his thoughts back to Sarah, he looked back into the mirror. He had to focus and think of nothing but the Haunted Mountain, so he didn't make another mistake. The last thing he wanted was for the two of them to suddenly show up in Mange's bedroom. He doubted the dream demon would be very appreciative if that happened.

"Sarah," he said again. "Take us to Sarah."

Orson pulled Natalie through the mirror, letting the silver liquid swallow them. Hopefully it would be the last time.

When they passed through to the other side, Orson was ready for the drop this time and landed on his feet, stumbling only when Natalie slipped to her knees. Her hand nearly slipped free but she squeezed tighter, not wanting to let go in the sudden enveloping darkness.

"This is definitely the place," he whispered, his voice harsh and loud in the still darkness. Within moments he was already feeling the choking air polluting his lungs.

"The air tastes terrible," Natalie coughed in the darkness. "Lights?"

As he had done before, Orson sent out a stream of energy, searching for the light orbs that had been on the floor before, hoping that they hadn't been moved. They were still there; within a few moments the cave was dimly light by a dozen faintly glowing orbs. On the floor at his feet, a pair of broken glasses gleamed in dull reflection of the orbs.

"It may have been better in the dark," Natalie said, scanning the cave with her eyes. "This place is creepy."

"Imagine being here alone," Orson said. Natalie's hand slipped away from his and he felt an unexpected pang of disappointment over the lost contact.

"Is that the way?" she asked, pointing to the opening several paces ahead. Orson nodded.

"Yes. Just don't touch the wooden beams. They might break if you breathe on them." Leading the way, he guided Natalie out of the cave and into the sunken, rotting mineshafts.

"How long does this go on for?" Natalie asked after they had been walking for a few minutes.

"Not much longer," Orson said. "There will be a dead-end soon...There, straight ahead." The wall with the ladder appeared around the next corner. "There's a ladder we have to climb and a trapdoor at the top."

"Good," Natalie coughed. "I don't know how much

more of this I could take. My throat is burning."

Orson ran his fingers over the wall, sure that the holes would be gone. Surely the Nightmares would have filled them in after his last narrow escape, if they had survived the thrashing Mange had given them. There was no sign that the Nightmares had been down in the tunnels, though, and his fingers found the first hole. He let out a sigh of relief. Gesturing to Natalie to wait quietly at the bottom, he climbed carefully up until his head was nearly touching the trapdoor. Reaching up, he pushed lightly and the door opened a crack. Two for two.

Pressing his ear to the door, Orson listened for any sounds. When he heard nothing, he carefully slid the door aside and peeked out. His heart pounded heavily in his chest. The hall above the door was empty. There were no Nightmares in sight.

Natalie coughed. The sound echoed blazingly loud up to Orson's ears. He winced, remembering his sneeze that had caught the attention of the Nightmares before. He looked down at her and she shrugged apologetically. Ducking down in the hole, he waited for a few moments in case something had heard her. When he was satisfied her cough had gone unnoticed, he pulled himself up through to the hallway above. Helping Natalie up, they took a moment to let the slightly fresher air soothe their aching lungs and throats.

"Not much of an improvement, is it?" Natalie said, studying the hallway. She pointed to a small metal door in the wall. "What's that?"

"Some sort of chute," Orson answered, not bothering to tell her about the mess that was undoubtedly still at the bottom.

Natalie nodded. "Which way now?"

Orson bit his lip as he tried to decide. Now came the hard part, finding out where the Nightmares were holding his baby sister. The small metal door in the wall to their right gleamed softly in the dull light of the hall. Orson shrugged, then pointed down in the direction of the metal door. It seemed as good a place to start as any.

"That way."

Natalie nodded. "Lead on, Dreamshaper."

"Don't call me that."

They walked slowly and carefully, trying to make as little noise as possible. At each corner they paused, taking a small peek around the edge to look for any signs of danger. After several twists and turns, Orson paused, biting his lip as he leaned in to whisper to Natalie.

"I wonder if we took a wrong turn."

"Is there a *right* turn in this place?"

"Good point," Orson conceded, and they continued walking.

They rounded a corner and the corridor in front of them widened, opening up into an enormous, circular room. Stopping just inside the entrance, Natalie gave Orson a light pat on the back.

"Finally, something different," she said, stepping past him into the chamber.

Orson sniffed. "Different doesn't always mean good."

Glowing orbs shone from the walls of the room, but the cavern was big enough that the light from the orbs didn't completely fill it. The floor in the center was untouched, a dark puddle just waiting for someone to come and get their feet wet in its murky depths. Orson felt a cool chill tingle down his arms as he looked into the enormous shadow. Something about the shadow made him very nervous.

"Something's wrong," he whispered, pulling at Natalie's hand.

"There's a lot wrong with this place," Natalie said. "All the more reason to find Sarah and get out of here as quick as we can."

Orson nodded, but there was something else. Something he was missing. This room, more than the hallways or the tunnels below, made him very nervous.

Natalie stepped forward, her foot dropping into the

edge of the shadowy puddle in the middle of the room. When her foot was about to press down, Orson felt something overflow inside of him, spilling over his nerves. His mind was assaulted with visions of darkness, with the sounds of hissing and crying. He cried out, trying to call her back from the shadow on the floor.

"Don't put your foot down!"

It was too late. The ball of Natalie's foot hit the floor. The shadow crunched under her foot like it was made of porcelain. A line of white cracks spread out from her footstep like a spider's web, streaking and zigzagging across the shadow. One by one, the orbs flickered out, submerging the room into choking blackness.

"Orson?" Natalie found his hand again and squeezed tightly. "What happened?"

"I think we just stepped into a trap." The hairs on the back of his neck were standing on end, tickled by the foreboding feeling biting into his nerves.

"What do we do now?" Natalie asked.

Get out of there as fast as possible was Orson's first thought, but how could you escape when you couldn't see where you were going?

Something brushed up against his leg. He jerked sharply, but it was impossible to see anything in the shroud of black. More stuttering steps ran past and Natalie gasped.

"Something just touched me," she said, her voice quivering.

There was more movement ahead of them, then behind. Orson thought he heard a small rock clattering along the floor somewhere to his left.

"They're surrounding us," he suddenly realized. Natalie gripped his fingers painfully tight.

"What are we going to do?"

"I don't know," Orson said. His heart felt like it was working overtime. "I just wish I could see..."

The orbs flared back into life. Natalie screamed.

⌐ TWENTY EIGHT ⌐

"What are they?" Natalie cried out, pressing against Orson's shoulder.

"I don't know," Orson said helplessly. Herding the two of them into the middle of the room, a crowd of small but dangerous brutes surrounded them, staring hungrily. They were no taller than Orson's waist, but his encounter with the Sirens had cleared him of the misconception that size mattered.

The sharpened teeth protruding from their over-sized lower lips were another clear sign of just how deadly these things were. The beasts looked like deeply mutated cats. They were almost completely bald, save for patchy clumps of dirty brown quills that poked out in odd angles and quivered as they breathed. The quills looked startlingly similar to a porcupine's. Beneath the quills, the grey skin of the monsters was drawn back tightly over a disgustingly skeletal frame. Nearly white eyes bulged from their heads, all focused on the two intruders.

One of them hissed angrily. The others echoed the sound as they started to close in.

"What are we going to do?" Natalie asked, pressing back against Orson.

"I don't know," Orson repeated, trying desperately to think of something. "There's so many! We can't beat all of these things with just two of us. We need to even up the odds. Wait, that's it!"

"Whatever you're thinking, you'd better do it quick. I don't think they're gonna wait for an appetizer." Natalie kicked out a foot at one that had stepped almost within range. It jumped back, but only for a second.

Swallowing hard, Orson closed his eyes and tried to force back the fear, focusing on what he needed to do. He would only have one try at this. If it didn't work, they were done for. Listening to the gurgled purrs of the terrible monsters, he wondered if they were done for anyway.

"Lupus, we need you!" he cried out. One of the creatures reached out and clawed at his pants. He kicked it away.

Natalie was whimpering beside him. "Orson!" she cried out, but Orson ignored her and refused to open his eyes.

"Lupus!" he called again. He had been able to bring Natalie into his dreams. He prayed that the same would work for the big wolf; if anyone could help them fight off these horrid things it was Lupus. They should never have come here without him to begin with.

Something growled to his right and Natalie screamed again.

"*LUPUS, WE NEED YOU RIGHT NOW!*" Orson opened his eyes.

The things were at their feet now; their twisted mouths open wide as they started to bite at their legs.

Something roared violently. Every head—human *and* cat—turned to see a huge shape charge directly at the circle of creatures. Lupus's eyes were wild as he threw himself into the crowd of monsters, flinging them every which way as he forced his way to the trapped children.

"Orson," the wolf boomed when he finally reached the two of them. "Are you all right?" One of the brutes lunged for Lupus's leg and the wolf kicked out sharply. The crack of breaking teeth made Orson cringe as the brute was sent flying back into its crowd of brethren. "You shouldn't be here!"

"You're telling me," Orson answered, missing with a kick of his own. "What are these things?"

"Shadowcats," Lupus answered with obvious distaste. "Nightmare pets. Nasty things. What in the world are you doing here?"

"We came to save Sarah," Natalie answered, striking out at a shadowcat with more success than Orson. Her hand thumped it soundly on the head and it let out a hiss as it backed away. She gasped as a quill from between the cat's ears pricked her finger. The area around the prick immediately swelled into an ugly red bump.

They may have been caught off guard by the sudden appearance of the wolf, but the shadowcats were recovering quickly. Most of them had fixed their white glares on Lupus, judging him to be the biggest threat, for good reason. Each time the wolf lashed out, a handful of shadowcats were sent flying back in a flurry of teeth and quills.

Lupus stopped long enough to turn a surprised look on Orson. "Save Sarah? I thought Aurora told you to wait until after the meeting."

"I know, but Aurora didn't hear what those Nightmares were saying! I couldn't just sit back if Sarah was in danger. She might not have time for meetings."

"You should have talked with her, Orson..."

"Um, guys?" Natalie interrupted, kicking another shadowcat away. "There's more important things to worry about right now, in case you forgot."

The shadowcat swarm seemed to have doubled in size; there had to be at least thirty of them now. Sweating with the effort, the three of them struggled to keep the horde at bay, but Orson knew it was only going to be a matter of time. There were simply too many of them and the three trapped intruders were quickly tiring.

"Why won't they stay down?" Orson screamed as he punched another back to the ground. It hit the floor hard but didn't scurry back like the others. Landing beside Orson's foot, it opened up its mouth and bit down on his shin. Orson screamed as he felt the teeth rip through his pants and bury deep in his leg.

Natalie brought the heel of her foot down hard on the thing's head. With an angry yowl it let go of Orson's leg, but the damage had been done. Blood dribbled out of the bite marks in Orson's leg, staining his pants crimson around the wounds. Before it could scamper away, Orson grabbed it and hurled it back into its companions, scattering five of them like bowling pins.

The shadowcats regrouped again and started circling around them. Panting for breath, Lupus stared them down.

"There's too many," the wolf said. "We'll never get past them this way."

"What do we do?" Orson asked. His leg throbbed as the blood trickled lightly from his wound.

"There's got to be a way to distract them," Natalie suggested. "Long enough so we can get away."

The shadowcats were closing in. Lupus took stock of them with his eyes. The fur on the big wolf's neck quivered as he growled, trying to think of a plan.

"There might be one chance," he said, his voice strangely quiet.

Natalie and Orson both asked the same question. "What?"

"When I tell you to run, you go as fast as you can, and as far as you can, do you understand me?"

Orson looked up at the wolf. There was a look of cold determination in Lupus's golden eyes. "What are you gonna do?"

"Just get ready," Lupus answered, his voice low and dangerous. "As soon as I put you down, you run for your lives, got it?"

"Put us down," Orson started. "But if you pick us up..."

Before Orson could finish, Lupus had grabbed both him and Natalie in his great, furry arms. With a terrible roar, the wolf lunged straight through the crowd of

195

shadowcats, stepping on some, kicking some out of his way. Fighting his way towards the opposite entrance of the room, Lupus didn't stop until he was clear through the shadowcats. After he had forced his way past the last few, he tossed Orson and Natalie into the next hallway and turned to face the oncoming horde of shadowcats.

"Lupus," Orson began.

"RUN!" Lupus yelled back over his shoulder. "NOW!"

With his big frame nearly filling the entire entrance to the room, Lupus readied himself for the advancing monsters. Orson was frozen in place, stunned into disbelief.

"Orson, you heard him, get moving!" Natalie urged, but Orson remained still.

"We can't just leave him here alone with those things. He won't have a chance! They'll eat him alive!"

"They'll eat all of us alive if you don't get going," Lupus growled. He stomped down directly on top of a shadowcat. "You're the Dreamshaper, Orson, you need to get out of here. Get your sister if you can, but get out...of... here!" His last words were strained with the effort of holding back several shadowcats at once. "If you die here, then we are all lost, and all of this has been for nothing."

"But Lupus..."

"*GO!*"

Grabbing him by the elbow, Natalie jerked Orson into motion. Together they raced down the hall, the sounds of the battle fading behind them. Rounding the next corner, Orson heard Lupus give out one last roar.

They ran around several more corners, not stopping until they were sure they weren't being followed. Taking a moment to catch his breath, Orson looked down the hallway, hoping that the big wolf would appear at any moment. He knew better. Lupus wasn't coming. There was no way the wolf could have survived against all of those monsters. A tear welled up in his eye, leaving a dirty wet streak down his cheek.

"He should have come with us," he said quietly.

"He couldn't." Natalie put a hand on his shoulder. "He did what he had to do to save us."

Shrugging her hand away, Orson glared at her. "He shouldn't have *had* to save us. We never should have come here in the first place. Now, because of us, Lupus might be dead. How are we going to explain that to Aurora? Because of us, her best soldier is gone."

"If we don't get moving, those things are going to come and find us. Lupus didn't sacrifice himself just so we would get caught anyway. We need to move."

Orson didn't say anything, but followed Natalie down the hall. The adrenaline from the fight had evaporated and his leg hurt fiercely from the shadowcat bite. He walked with a noticeable limp—every so often moaning in discomfort—but they couldn't stop, not until they were well away from the shadowcats—and Lupus.

"Are you okay, Orson?" Natalie asked when she was finally satisfied that they were safe for a few moments. "That bite looks pretty bad."

"I'm fine," Orson said.

"We should wrap it to stop the bleeding."

Orson grunted. His face was a stony mask. Bending down, Natalie grabbed the tattered remains of the pant leg around Orson's wound and tore a long strip, using it as a bandage around the bite. Orson winced a little when she tightened it, but otherwise said nothing.

"I shouldn't have let you to convince me to come here," he said after a moment of awkward silence.

"Orson, I..."

"I knew you didn't like Aurora. Was this all a plan of yours?"

"What are you talking about?" Natalie asked.

"You know exactly what I'm talking about. You've had a problem with Aurora since the moment you met her. That's why you were so desperate for us to come here alone, isn't it? So that you could finally show her up and prove that we didn't need her help."

Natalie didn't know what to say. Orson's words stung because she knew they were true, at least to some degree. Sighing, she finished tightening the bandage on his leg and leaned back against the wall. "I don't have a problem with Aurora."

Orson's face darkened. "How can you say that..."

"Just listen, Orson," she interrupted. "Look, ever since this all started happening, it's been you and me. We shared that first dream together, in Mardell, when this whole adventure started. Since then, it was you and me, working together. We started exploring the Dreamlands together."

"What does that have to do with anything?" Orson asked, not sure what she was getting at. "What does that have to do with the Queen?"

Natalie tugged on a strand of hair. "It has *everything* to do with the Queen. When you learned about being the Dreamshaper, I was there to help you, to share all of this with you. Then Aurora showed up, and suddenly I wasn't important anymore. You didn't need me."

Orson shook his head. "That's not true. You're here with me now."

"It *is* true. As soon as we got to the Palace and Aurora got her claws on you, you didn't need my help anymore. *She* started training you. *She* was the one you talked to about what was happening. *She* was the one you went to for help with Sarah. *She* was a Dreamshaper and knows everything about this world. What possible reason could you need me, a normal girl from the waking world? Just look at what happened the other day, the first time you came to this mountain. You didn't even bother telling me you were coming here. I had to find out *after* you were almost caught."

Natalie was on the verge of tears. Orson listened to her, suddenly feeling a little ashamed. He had no idea she felt this way. It certainly wasn't what he intended.

"Even in the waking world—in *our* world—you didn't need me anymore. Now you have Mike Spencer to help you fight Jimmy and his cronies. To talk about silly boy stuff, like those stupid comics of yours."

"Natalie," he said when she finally stopped. "You're being stupid." Natalie's eyes sharpened as she opened her mouth to respond, but he gestured for her to keep quiet. "Of course I need you. I wouldn't be here if it weren't for you. You're a bigger part of this—*all* of this—than Aurora or Mike. I wouldn't have even made it into the Dreamlands if you hadn't fallen through the mirror. Why do you think I hang out with you in the waking world *and* the Dreamlands? I trust you more than anyone else."

Natalie smiled up at him. "Really?"

Orson nodded. "Really."

Natalie straightened up. "Well then, let's get a move on. We're not gonna find Sarah just sitting around here being all mushy."

Orson smiled. Natalie was right; Lupus had sacrificed himself so they could get away, but he wasn't going anywhere without Sarah. He had come here to save her, and that's what they were going to do.

Together.

⌊ TWENTY NINE ⌋

"We need a map," Natalie muttered as they walked down what felt like the hundredth corridor in the Haunted Mountain. They had taken so many twists and turns that Orson had no idea how to even get back to the trapdoor. For all he knew, the next corner may even bring them all the way back.

"Or a tour guide," he said. "One that wouldn't try to eat us."

They walked to the edge of the next corner and stepped around. On the other side, they both froze. A Nightmare was staked out not ten feet from them, holding a thick length of rope tied to a collar around the neck of a shadowcat. The Nightmare was covered in slick, greasy fur, so thick it was nearly impossible to decide if it was facing them or the other direction, especially in the dim light of the hall. The thing didn't react at all to their sudden appearance, so it must have been looking the other way. The shadowcat scratched irritably behind its ear.

Clapping a hand over his mouth, Orson hustled Natalie back around the corner before they were spotted.

"What do we do now?" Natalie asked in a hushed whisper.

Orson bit his lip, trying to think of something, anything. He supposed they could go back the way they'd come; of course, retracing their steps in this place would be as likely as finding a needle in a haystack. Add to that the risk of stumbling back into the pack of shadowcats they had encountered earlier put a serious damper on the idea of retreating. That didn't leave them many other options.

Their options decreased even more when they suddenly heard a growling hiss. The shadowcat.

"'Ey, what's that, you stupid thing?" a gruff voice answered the hiss. "Somethin' down there? A'right then, lead the way, dummy."

The sound of scratching claws on the ground grated in their ears as Natalie and Orson listened to the shadowcat pulling the Nightmare towards them. The Nightmare would see them before they could make it around the corner at the other end of the hall they were at. They could try to run, but the shadowcat would catch them easily.

Without even thinking about what he was doing, Orson grabbed Natalie and pressed her against the wall. In desperation he closed his eyes and called his magic and spread it out, using it like a blanket to cover the two of them as they huddled tightly against the wall. Natalie gasped as she felt his power cover her. Orson opened his eyes.

Natalie was gone. He could feel her there with him, standing right beside him against the wall, but couldn't see her. Surprised, he looked down at himself. He couldn't even see his feet.

He had turned them invisible.

Orson swallowed the alarm over what he had just somehow done, not wanting to lose his focus and bring them back into view. A moment later, the patch-quilled head of the shadowcat peeked around the corner, its tongue lolling from its mouth and white eyes bulging as it struggled to pull its master.

"Calm down, would ya?" the Nightmare growled. The shadowcat tugged harder, pulling until they were right beside the invisible children, inches away from where they were pressed against the wall. The Nightmare's greasy fur was rank with a foul, choking odor that threatened to make Orson cough. He swallowed the cough, holding his breath tightly. The guard was so close that he was sure it would brush up against them and find them hiding there in plain sight.

Miraculously, the Nightmare continued past them. When it was several steps away, Orson urged Natalie to move, slowly and quietly towards the near corner. A few more steps and they would be safely around the corner.

Down towards the other end of the hall, the shadowcat stopped. It lifted its prickled head and sniffed at the air. With a vicious hiss, it turned and looked back down the hall, white eyes glaring in the direction of the invisible children.

"'Ave you lost your marbles?" the Nightmare aimed a kick at the shadowcat. "There ain't nuthin' down there."

The Nightmare's kick missed, throwing it off balance. Feeling the sudden shift in weight, the shadowcat took the opportunity to lunge forward, yanking the rope out of the Nightmare's hand. The greasy-furred guard fell forward and lost his grip on the rope. Free from restraint, the shadowcat launched itself down the hallway.

"'Ey, get back 'ere!" the Nightmare cursed from the floor.

Orson watched as the shadowcat plunged down the hall, moving right towards them. Grabbing Natalie's elbow, he yanked her forward. "It knows we're here," he cried. "Run!"

Losing focus on his magic, they were suddenly visible as they started to run. He heard the Nightmare yell in confusion over the sudden appearance of two children. Pulling Natalie's elbow, he yanked her around the corner and down the next hallway in a full sprint, the shadowcat in quick pursuit.

As they raced down the hall, Orson saw a heavy wooden square in the floor up ahead of them. It was the trapdoor. In the wall a few feet further, the small metal door gleamed in the dim lighting of the orbs. In their wanderings, they had managed to circle completely back to where they had started. Orson felt a momentary pang of frustration; if they were back at the start, it meant they were nowhere near finding Sarah. He pushed that thought aside—they had more pressing matters to deal with at the moment.

The shadowcat was right behind them. Orson's bitten leg throbbed mercilessly as they ran. Eying both doors, he knew they would only have time to open one of them before the shadowcat caught up with them. He knew where the trapdoor would take them—back into the tunnels below—but didn't think he would have time to close the door before the cat leaped down after them. Even if he did manage to get it closed, they would be trapped down there. He might be able to wake them up before they were caught, but then this entire journey—including Lupus's sacrifice—would have been for nothing.

"The chute," Orson said, pointing to the small metal door in the wall. Natalie nodded. They could hear the shadowcat hissing and panting only a few feet behind them.

Orson turned to look just as the shadowcat launched itself into the air, flying right for them, all claws, teeth and quills. Without thinking, he shoved Natalie back and grabbed the handle of the metal door. Swinging it open with as much strength as he could muster, he slammed the door into the shadowcat with shuddering force at the last possible instant. The metal quivered as the beast hit it hard, sending a numbing shudder down his arm. The shadowcat dropped to the floor and mewled softly, stunned from the impact.

"Get in!" Orson yelled to Natalie. The cat was already starting to climb slowly to its feet. Natalie didn't hesitate; she clambered through the door and dropped down the chute. When she disappeared, Orson climbed in after her, feet first so he could close the door behind him. As the door clicked shut, he heard the claws of the shadowcat scratching at the metal. He could hear it howl in frustration as he slid down to the room below.

Orson landed right on top of Natalie, knocking her facedown into the disgusting sludge on the floor, the same stuff that had cushioned his fall during his first visit. It smelled even fouler than his first experience with it.

"This stuff is really nasty," he said with a grimace. Natalie wriggled helplessly beneath him, unable to answer as he had her pinned down into the muck. He scrambled off and helped her out of the sludge. Her face had turned a pale green under the mess of slop.

"Are you okay?" he asked her.

"No," she breathed heavily. "I'm gonna ..." Her face became a mask of distress. "I'm gonna be sick." She turned away and threw up right on the pile of slop. Orson wrinkled his nose and turned away. When she looked back at him, her eyes were watery but fierce.

"If you ever say a word about this to anybody—just *one word*—even to your Queen..." she punched a fist into the palm of her other hand. Orson understood the implied threat implicitly.

"You secret's safe with me," Orson said, solemnly holding up his right hand.

The room was exactly as Orson remembered it. Besides the chute in the roof, there was no way out except for a single wooden door, the same one Sithyrus had broken through when he had first met the nasty lizard. The door had since been repaired, but there were still sharp wooden slivers scattered near the foot of the doorway, leftover pieces from the original door.

Orson swallowed. Being in this place again twisted his stomach into an uncomfortable knot.

"What do we do now?" Natalie asked, the colour slowly returning to her face.

"I guess we go through there," Orson gestured at the door. "Last time I came here, it was locked, but that didn't stop Sithyrus from nearly getting me."

Natalie approached the door. Taking hold of the handle, she twisted her wrist and it turned fully. "It's open. What's on the other side?"

"No idea," Orson admitted. "I didn't get to look last

time. I was a little busy trying not to get eaten."

Natalie, her hand still on the handle, pulled it open a crack. As it opened slightly, her nose wrinkled up in disgust. "We must be in the garbage rooms," she said sourly, looking at the gross pile of sludge she had just climbed out of. "First that stuff, and whatever's past this door doesn't smell much better. It smells like someone dumped a bunch of rotten meat in the next room. I don't think I want to go in there."

Orson smirked. Of course they would have fallen into the Haunted Mountain's garbage disposal. They'd had lousy luck so far, why would it change now? What was next, a room full of...

Orson paused. Natalie's words rang in his head. *Smells like someone dumped some rotten meat.* That was a smell he knew all too well.

Sithyrus.

"Natalie, get away from there!" he cried, but it was too late. She had already opened the door wider. As she turned to look back at Orson, something long and sinewy snared her around the waist. With a cry, Natalie was yanked into the room and out of sight. The smell of rotten meat, no longer masked behind the door, washed into the room and stung Orson's nose.

He looked at the open door. "Sithyrus," he croaked.

"Welcome, little Dreamshaper," a leathery voice hissed from beyond the doorway. "Welcome to my lair. I've been waiting for you. Won't you ssstep inssside? There'sss sssomeone here jussst *dying* to sssee you."

⌊ THIRTY ⌋

The air felt heavy as Orson looked through the open doorway where Natalie had disappeared. The urge to run was overwhelming, but there was nowhere else to go. Even if there was, he couldn't just abandon his friend. Swallowing his fear, Orson stepped into the next room.

The first thing Orson saw as he entered was the raggedy wooden crib in the middle of the large, cavernous room. There could only be one reason for a crib to be in a place like this. Sarah.

A high roof layered with stalactites pointed down to the floor like giant rocky fingers, creating the illusion of a dozen powerful and treacherous hands reaching down to grab whoever might be foolish enough to come inside. The walls were rough and jagged, lined with dozens of light orbs that barely made a dent in the shadowy stillness. The light of the orbs was nowhere near as brilliant as the flame burning high above the floor in a crescent bowl, hung by a single chain. A trapped breeze rocked the bowl slightly, enough for a tiny dribble of boiling oil to spill over the edge to the floor below. Orson watched as the oil fell and landed precariously close to the rough wooden crib directly below the crescent bowl. The oil sizzled on the hard rock of the floor; the sound made Orson wince.

Behind the crib, Sithyrus flexed its massive jaw, its skin creaking like a broken belt. A small bubble of saliva bubbled on the side of its lip and popped, glopping to the floor. The lizard turned its burning red eyes on Orson and hissed, an evil sound that reminded Orson of a burst, steaming pipe.

"Welcome, boy," it said, its tongue flicking excitedly over scaled lips. Natalie lay in a crumpled heap on the ground only a few feet away from the lizard. A trickle of blood trailed down her forehead.

"Natalie!" Orson called and took a step closer. "Let her go, lizard breath! She's got nothing to do with this!"

"You brought her, boy. She is your ressssponsssibility, not mine." Sithyrus's tail curled around Natalie's unconscious body. The sound of the scaly tail dragging on the floor—like nails on a chalkboard—made the hairs on the back of his neck quiver. "Perhapsss I will ssstart with the little one in the crib. I've been waiting to tassste her."

Sithyrus bent over the crib and turned its pointed snout downwards and flicked its long tongue in a long swipe. Inside the rough wooden structure, Sarah began to cry as the lizard's tongue licked her. The cry that had once irritated Orson to no end brought his heart into his throat.

"Leave her alone, stinkface!"

Sithyrus lifted its head from the crib. "You are brave to insssult me when your friend and sssisssster are only inchesss from my teeth, boy. Move one ssstep closer and you will witnesss what thessse teeth can do to human flesh."

Sithyrus clacked its jaws tauntingly and Orson froze. "Ssso afraid. Are you sure you're the Dreamshaper? You hardly ssseem a threat to me." It leaned over the crib again, growling hungrily.

"No!" Orson cried out, lunging forward a few steps with his hand outstretched. Sithyrus's long snout snapped up from the crib and the lizard fell back a step.

"I told you to ssstay back!" it hissed angrily. "Would you be ssso recklesss with thessse two livesss?"

"I'm not..." Orson started to yell back, when he realized something was wrong. When he had stepped forward, the lizard had actually fallen back for a moment, as though it had been caught off guard by his sudden movement. Why would it do that?

Even the lizard's manner seemed different. It had always been arrogant, for a moment that arrogance had slipped. Sithyrus's beady red eyes flicked back and forth from Orson to Sarah, shifting in a way that made it look nervous. The tip of its tail flapped up and down on the floor, constantly in motion.

Orson frowned. The lizard finally had him where it wanted. Why would it be nervous now? Was it afraid he would escape again?

Sithyrus inadvertently gave him the answer. "Do you really think the feeble training you were given by your ussselesss Queen will help you here? Whatever she taught you, it will not be enough. You may have fooled thossse two idiotsss who caught you wandering the Haunted Mountain before, but I am prepared for you. You won't find me ssso sssimple. Whatever trick you conjured up with them won't help you here."

Fooled them? What trick was it talking about? He hadn't used any tricks to escape capture before. If it hadn't been for Mange, he wouldn't have gotten away last time. Of course, Mange had attacked them so quickly and efficiently that the two Nightmares who had grabbed him hadn't even had a chance to see the dream demon before they were knocked silly. They must have thought Orson had used his power to escape...

Orson's mouth dropped as he realized what was holding the Nightmare lizard back.

It doesn't know how much Aurora has taught me. That had to be the reason Sithyrus was treading so carefully. The lizard wasn't sure how much stronger Orson had become since he'd started training his abilities as a Dreamshaper. Orson knew he wasn't that far into his training, but Sithyrus didn't share that knowledge. All the lizard knew was that Orson had somehow managed to escape capture yet again, leaving two Nightmares unconscious in his wake.

Sithyrus sniffed at the air. A low growl escaped its throat. *It's trying to smell my emotions,* Orson thought. *It wants to see if I'm afraid.* He *was* afraid. Actually, he was terrified beyond belief—denying that would be as honest as trying to convince himself that he could beat Jimmy Scrags in a fist fight—but seeing Sithyrus shifting uncertainly gave him a small boost of confidence. Trying not to show any trace of fear, Orson did the last thing that Sithyrus expected from him. He stepped closer.

"Get away from them, Sithyrus," he spoke slowly, trying to keep his voice from shaking. He hoped the lizard mistook his slow talking for a warning rather than an attempt to control his fear. He took another step and his foot struck a good-sized rock on the floor. "I'm warning you, leave them alone."

Sithyrus reared its ugly head back and looked at Orson in surprise. *Not surprise,* Orson told himself. *Fear. It's afraid of me. I might be able to get us out of here after all.*

"You ssstill don't get it, do you boy?" Sithyrus hissed. Its tongue was flickering erratically. "There isss no essscape for you! You are going to die here. My Massster's planssss *will* come to passs. You cannot ssstop it. The Nightmaresss are too ssstrong for you and your pitiful friendsss, even for your preciousss Queen and her dog. Aurora isss weakened now, and we will crush her easssily."

"She's stopped you before, she'll do it again," Orson retorted flatly. Sithyrus reared its head back and laughed throatily. It sounded forced.

Sithyrus shuffled its feet, nearly stumbling over Natalie's prone form on the floor. It cast a quick, irritated look down at her. Orson took the moment to crouch down quickly and scoop the rock he had kicked with his foot.

"We're going to beat you," Orson said, drawing Sithyrus's attention back away from Natalie. "I'm not running away anymore, Sithyrus. This time, I'm ready for you."

Orson hoped his false bravado wouldn't come back to bite him. He certainly didn't feel ready to take on Sithyrus; nowhere near ready, in fact. But the lizard didn't know that.

Hopefully it would take the bait. If he was going to somehow find a way out of this, he needed to keep the lizard off balance.

Sithyrus spat distastefully. Its tail whipped down precariously close to Natalie's head. "The Dreamlandsss belong to *us* now. There isss nothing you or the ressst of the Dremiansss can do about it! And once we've ssstomped your pathetic resssissstance, and the Machine isss complete, we will feassst on your world, the waking world."

Its eyes flared as it spoke. Grabbing the edge of the crib with its tiny clawed hands, it squeezed so tightly that its scaled knuckles creaked. "We are no longer afraid of the Dreamshaper! How can you keep usss from our victory when you can't even sssave your own sssisssster?"

Orson had taken this too far. With no warning, Sithyrus suddenly plunged its dangerous snout straight down towards the crib. Inside, Sarah shrieked as the open jaws of the giant lizard came at her.

"No!" Orson lunged forward and hurled the rock as hard as he could. His aim was horrible and he watched despairingly as the stone sailed well wide of the giant lizard and bounced uselessly across the floor.

Sithyrus looked up long enough to watch the rock sail past. It sniffed in amusement before dropping its snout again. "A rock?" it hissed gleefully. "You would ssstop me with a rock? I would have hoped for sssomething more."

Orson felt a knot of panic hit him. Sithyrus had called his bluff; Orson didn't know enough about the Dreamshaper power to directly attack the Nightmare. He had tried to stop the lizard with a rock rather than use his magic. Now Sithyrus knew he wasn't much of a threat.

Sithyrus growled happily; any trace of uncertainty was gone now. "You are finished, boy," it hissed triumphantly and Orson knew it was right. He had pushed it too far, and now his opportunity had slipped away. He had just doomed them all. The thought brought a wave of unexpected anger rather than fear. For a moment, he was so distracted by the thought that he had failed that he didn't feel the burst of energy course through his body as he unconsciously let the power of the Dreamshaper come into him. When he felt the sudden rush of energy through his blood, he gasped.

Sithyrus mistook the gasp of surprise for one of fear. As the lizard laughed shrilly, Orson took advantage of the mistake. Using the lesson he had repeated again and again with Aurora, he used his power to lift the badly thrown rock back into the air, sending it with vicious speed at the Nightmare's head. With deadly accuracy, the rock plunged directly into one of Sithyrus's cruel red eyes. It recoiled backwards, roaring in agony and scratching at its damaged eye.

"My eye!" Sithyrus shrieked, stumbling backwards, tripping over Natalie and falling heavily to the floor. "You've ruined my eye!"

Orson lurched forward, trying to get to the crib before Sithyrus had a chance to recover. The Nightmare was quicker. Rising up over the crib, Sithyrus regained its feet and glared at him furiously from its one good eye. The other eye was tightly shut, streaks of blood dripping down from the wrecked skin and mixing with the bubbling drool and foam falling madly from its snarling snout.

"I'LL EAT YOU ALIVE!" Sithyrus screamed, launching itself clear over the crib, high enough for its tail to bang off the fire bowl. A thick stream of searing oil spilled over the side, splashing on the floor only inches from the crib, sizzling as it burned into the ground.

A loose rock on the ground saved Orson's life. As he tried to back up, he stepped down on the rock and slipped, falling to the floor a moment before Sithyrus would have had him. Instead, the Nightmare lizard sailed over his head and landed several feet away.

Something awakened deep inside of Orson, born from

desperation. He could feel it building up, just as he had felt it before, only this time it was stronger than ever before. This was his chance. Sithyrus had missed once; the lizard wouldn't miss again. If he didn't stop this now, he wouldn't be so lucky again.

"Get away from me, Sithyrus," he said, pulling himself to his feet. The snarl on Sithyrus's face grew. Its nostrils flared in anger.

"I'm going to enjoy devouring you, foolish boy," Sithyrus hissed back. "I'm going to pick my teeth with your bonesss when I'm through. I'm going to..."

"You're going to do *nothing*," Orson stopped it. Sithyrus flinched. This was not what the lizard had planned. The boy should be frozen in fear, not standing up to face it.

"You think you can ssstop me? Turn and run, boy, while you have the chance. Not that it will make any differencccce in the end."

"I'm not going to run," Orson retorted. "This has to end. I won't let you hurt my family or friends any more."

Sithyrus snarled. "Come then, let'sss sssettle thisss. Fight me if you dare." Sithyrus leaned back into a stance Orson had seen many times now; the lizard was going to pounce.

"Fight? I don't think so. We're not going to fight. You're going away, Sithyrus, and there's nothing you can do about it."

"What are you talking about, boy? I'm not going..."

"You're going to disappear," Orson said. The room wavered in Orson's vision, fading until he couldn't see anything but Sithyrus. Focusing all of his energy, he directed it towards the Nightmare.

The air around Sithyrus began to shimmer. Sithyrus cried out in anguish and started whipping its head from side to side, lashing out with its tail. Orson was too far away to be struck by anything other than a slight gust of air from the thrashing tail.

"What isss thisss?" Sithyrus hissed as it started rising

slowly into the air. It floated effortlessly, hovering a few feet above the ground, the bulk of its massive weight carried by the mind of a young boy.

"Let me down!" it roared. *"Let me down!"*

"I don't think so," Orson said, his voice sounding distant even to himself. "You tried to hurt us. You tried to *kill us! You tried to kill my sister!"*

"Only to get to you!" Sithyrus protested. "Let me go and they can go free. You have my word!"

"It's too late for that, Sithyrus. Your time's up. You won't hurt anyone ever again." Orson focused his mind on the energy surrounding Sithyrus. He opened himself up, letting more of the magic flow into him. Without fully understanding what he was doing, he created an invisible bubble around the lizard, surrounding Sithyrus as he held it in the air.

"No, stop! *Stop!"* Sithyrus was howling now, but Orson didn't hear it. This lizard—this *Nightmare*—was the cause of all his recent suffering. It had kidnapped Sarah and hurt Natalie. It had tried more than once to kill him. It wanted to destroy them all and wouldn't stop until it had reached its goal. Not unless he stopped it first.

The energy bubble tightened like a draw bag, squeezing fiercely inward. Sithyrus started to shrink into the bag of power, constricting with the bubble as the energy wrap squeezed. The Nightmare had stopped begging now and was shrieking for its life, its raspy voice a high pitched squeal as it struggled hopelessly against the forces binding it. Orson watched as its body contorted to fit inside the inescapable bubble of magic. It was a horrible sight, but Orson was too focused to be shaken. For a moment, Sithyrus's ruined eye popped open, revealing the burst tissue beneath.

Sithyrus let out one last terrible, piteous howl. The room erupted in a flash of blinding light, powerful enough to force Orson to the ground as he shielded his eyes. The flash disappeared as quickly as it had come. Orson opened his eyes.

Sithyrus was gone.

⌐ THIRTY ONE ⌐

For a long moment, the only sound Orson could hear was an annoying ringing in his ears. With great effort, he managed to pull himself to his knees. His vision was blurry; the room around him was awash with dark colours and spots of light. Hanging above his head, something incredibly bright stung his eyes, forcing him to turn away. For a moment he thought he must have broken his glasses and began feeling around the rough ground for them before he remembered he was no longer wearing them.

Orson willed his eyes to work again. Exhausted and hurting, it took a great effort to fix it so he could see clearly again. It worked, but not without a cost—his head felt like it would explode at any moment. Orson tried to ignore the pain and looked towards the crib in the center of the room.

The Nightmare lizard was gone. It seemed too good to be true. Orson wondered if Sithyrus was dead. The only thing that remained were a few splashes of dark blood on the floor, spilled from its ruined eye. Besides the blood, there was no sign that Sithyrus had ever been there at all.

Picking himself off the floor, Orson limped towards the crib. His hurt leg was burning badly now; he hoped the bite from the shadowcat hadn't become infected. Inside the crib, he could hear Sarah softly mewling, no longer crying, almost as though she knew Sithyrus was gone. Her big brother had made the monster go away.

Before Orson reached the crib, however, he saw

something else that made him pause in fear.

Lying behind the crib, Natalie's legs sprawled haphazardly as she lay unmoving on the cold floor. Walking around the crib, he looked down at her with great concern. The blood in her hair had started to turn a sticky purple; it had dried over one of her eyes in a cruel imitation of Sithyrus'ss ruined eye. Her chest wasn't moving.

"Natalie?" he said quietly. He tried to kneel carefully but his leg gave out and he fell awkwardly beside her. Ignoring the pain in his leg—in his whole *body*—he reached out and gave Natalie's shoulder a light shake. She didn't stir. "Natalie, wake up."

He knelt over her, pressing his ear to her lips, hoping to feel even the faintest breeze of air coming from her mouth. There was nothing.

"Natalie," he repeated urgently. "You have to wake up!"

Orson closed his eyes, trying to lure the magic back into himself. Maybe he could use his power to help her somehow. His head started spinning badly. For a moment he thought he felt the faintest spark of the magic but then it was gone, leaving him lightheaded and dizzy. He tried again, but there wasn't even a trace of it the second time. He opened his eyes and shook his head.

"I can't do it," he said to her. He must have overloaded himself in the battle against Sithyrus. Now, all the effort did was make his head hurt. He was somewhat surprised he had even managed to fix his eyes again. That must have taken the last of his strength. If a Nightmare were to stumble on them now, he would be as helpless as Sarah in the crib. "I don't know how to help you, Natalie."

Frustrated, tears threatening the corner of his eyes, Orson stood up and ran a hand through his sweat soaked hair. He couldn't lose Natalie, not like this. She had been his strength throughout everything that had happened. Sarah was safe and Sithyrus was gone, but without Natalie to share in their triumph, it was a hollow victory. Staring down at her prone body, he plunged his hands into his pockets.

His fingers crunched into something dry and flaky. When he pulled his hands free, they were covered in golden flakes.

"The trees," he gasped. "I forgot about the trees!"

Back at the Palace, Lupus told Orson and Natalie about the Delilah trees. Orson forgot that he had grabbed a handful of the tree's golden leaves and stuffed them into his pocket.

Lupus had told them that the leaves of the Delilah trees could be used to make healing potions; that if they were mixed with certain fruit juices the healing properties were quite potent. Orson pulled the rest of the leaves from his pocket. They were ripped and dry, breaking apart easily in his fingers but had not lost their golden ambiance. Orson hoped that meant they had not lost their effectiveness.

Another thought struck him and his stomach bottomed out. What was he going to mix the leaves with?

Looking around the room, he doubted he would find anything in here. The floors and walls were sheer rock, and the slight mildew was not enough to mix a potion from. On the floor beside the crib, he found a tiny bowl that looked like it had held some sort of mushy food—probably what they had been feeding Sarah to keep her quiet. There was only a spoonful of the goopy food left; lifting the bowl to his nose, Orson crinkled away in disgust. It smelled like the muck below the chute in the other room. Even if there had been enough, he didn't think he could have forced *that* into Natalie's mouth. If that's what the Nightmares had fed Sarah...

He didn't have time to worry about that right now. What had Lupus said about using the leaves by themselves? Didn't the wolf mention something about the possibility of the leaves being poisonous if they were used without a mixture?

"Lupus wasn't sure what would happen," he remembered, his voice sounding incredibly loud in the eerie silence of the cavern. Looking down at Natalie, he knew he would have to make a decision quickly.

"Please let this work," he said and leaned over her.

Tilting her head back, he pried her mouth open and began feeding her the handful of crushed leaves, pressing them underneath her tongue to keep her from choking. When her mouth was full, he dropped the rest of the leaves on the floor and cradled her head on his lap. He cleared some of the dried blood from her eye, watching and hoping.

For a long moment, Natalie didn't stir and Orson was afraid the leaves weren't going to work, or—even worse—that he had poisoned her and finished the job Sithyrus had started. "Come on," he whispered, stroking her hair, a single tear streaking dirtily down his cheek. "It has to work."

Natalie twitched in his arms. It was light, but it might as well have been an earthquake to Orson. His jaw clenched tightly, he stared down at her, hoping that the tremor meant something good was happening. Natalie suddenly drew in a dry, gasping breath. Orson let the air out of his lungs in an exaggerated sigh of relief.

Natalie's eyes slowly opened. "Orson?" she croaked in a dry whisper, her voice harsh from the pile of leaves under her tongue. Rolling onto her side, she spat the leaves out onto the floor in a gummy pile. "That's disgusting," she said distastefully. "I'm getting tired of spitting things out."

Then Orson was on her, hugging her so tightly she could barely breathe. "You're okay!" he said gleefully, rocking her back and forth.

"I won't be if you keep shaking me like that," she choked and Orson let go. Running a hand through her hair, she cringed as her fingers brushed the gash on her forehead. "What happened? It feels like somebody hit me on the head with a hockey stick. And why does it taste like I've been eating chalk?"

Orson laughed. "Delilah leaves," he said, reaching out and picking a small piece from her hair. "The ones from the garden at the Palace of Dreams. I had a handful of them in my pocket."

"The healing leaves," Natalie said, sitting up from the floor.

"You were attacked by Sithyrus. I had to use the leaves to save you."

"Did you have to use the whole tree?" Natalie spat again. "Did you feed me the bark as well?" She shook her head. "Sithyrus attacked me? The last thing I remember was that room with the smelly stuff, where I...I..."

"Puked?" Orson helped.

"*Spit*," she frowned darkly at him. "Where I spit."

Orson smiled. "You opened the door and Sithyrus was waiting for us. I think it was hoping I would be the first one through the door, but it got you instead."

Natalie looked around the room. "Where is Sithyrus?"

Orson shrugged. "Gone. Disappeared, I guess would be better."

"Disappeared?" Natalie asked.

"Poof. Gone."

Natalie tugged at a strand of hair as she looked at her friend thoughtfully. "Did you make it disappear?"

"I guess I did." Orson's smile brightened.

Letting go of her hair, Natalie nodded. "Good job," she said simply, but it was enough. Orson thought he might actually be glowing. Despite everything that had happened, he thought this might be the happiest he had felt in months... years, even.

Without warning, Natalie gripped Orson's head in her hands and twisted it so she could see better. Looking into his eyes, her eyebrows drew down in confusion. "Aren't your eyes supposed to be brown?"

Orson looked at her as though she had gone crazy. "Of course they're brown. Are you sure you're okay? Maybe that knock on the head scrambled your brains a little more than we thought."

"They're blue," Natalie said. "And my head is fine, dorkface." She was definitely feeling better.

"They're brown. They've always been brown."

Natalie shook her head. She must still be feeling the effects of Sithyrus's attack. His eyes weren't blue; they'd been brown since the day he was born. Same as his little sister's eyes...

"Sarah!" he gasped and climbed to his feet. All concern over the colour of his eyes vanished instantly. He had been so relieved Natalie had been all right that he had forgotten about the reason they had come here in the first place. Racing to the crib, he ignored the twin throbbing in his leg and head. Grabbing the crib's rim, he looked down at the squirming pink thing tangled in a moldy brown potato sack.

Sarah lay in the crib, staring up at him, her dirty, tear-streaked cheeks glistening in the dim light of the torches. She stared up at him for a long moment, her eyes large and wet. For a moment Orson thought she didn't recognize him until she burst into tears.

"Sarah," he said tenderly and lifted her from the crib. "Sarah, it's okay now. We're gonna take you back home. We're gonna take you back to Mom."

Sarah cried against his shoulder, and Orson loved every moment, every spilled tear. A week ago, he would have done anything to get away from this crying, sopping bundle of diapers and boogers; now he relished every sound, each cry ringing bells of joy in his heart.

"She's okay," he said, turning to show Natalie. Something hot dripped past his face, barely missing him as it splattered to the floor. He looked down at the red-orange spatter of burning oil.

"Orson, *watch out!*" Natalie suddenly screamed. "The bowl is gonna fall!"

He had forgotten all about the bowl hanging directly above the crib. Everything seemed to move in slow motion as Orson looked up just as one of the flaming bowl's chains snapped. The bowl twisted to one side and a glowing orange waterfall poured out over the side, dropped straight towards

Orson and his sister.

Crouching over Sarah to shield her with his body, Orson closed his eyes, waiting for the burning oil to hit. Instead of the oil, something heavy fell over him, covering his back and head. For a moment he thought it must be the bowl, hitting him moments before the oil would wash over them both. The burning never came.

The thing across his back grunted and the sharp smell of sulfur stung his nose. There was a light sizzling sound as the oil poured over whatever was covering him. Holding his breath against the choking smell, he covered his sister's mouth and nose with one hand, holding her tight against his chest with the other.

The sizzling sound stopped and the smell of sulfur became little more than a mild irritation. The weight lifted from Orson's back. He opened his eyes and looked up. Standing over him, a creature with skin so dark it threatened to swallow the light from the room stared down at him. Thick tendrils of steam rose off of its hard, armour plated spikes in twisted coils as the creature watched him through a terrifying mask, its green eyes blazing.

"Mange," Orson croaked before exhaustion sunk its claws deep and the room went black.

⌐ THIRTY TWO ⌐

Orson awoke in a completely different world than the one he remembered. The walls around him were made of smoothly polished marble and the light in the room—though still dim —was comforting rather than creepy. Confused, he tried to sit up and immediately regretted it. His head flared in agonizing pain. With a groan he lay back down.

Something had happened, something bad, and Mange had appeared from nowhere. For a moment Orson could smell the stinging sulfur of burning oil as the dream demon covered him, using his own armoured skin to protect Orson and Sarah from the oil.

Orson pushed the blankets off of his legs and forced himself to sit up. His head was killing him, but for the first time in what felt like months he felt safe. A headache seemed a small price to pay to finally be out of the Haunted Mountain, hopefully for good. He tried rubbing his temples with his fingers, hoping to relieve some of the pressure.

"Can I help with that?" a light voice asked from the doorway. Orson looked out between his fingers as Aurora stepped deeper into the room.

"How long have you been there?" he asked painfully.

"Long enough," she answered, sitting down on the bed beside him. With gentle fingers, she moved Orson's hands away from his face and replaced them with her own. Her hands were cool and the feel of her fingers webbing out on either side of his face sent a pleasant shiver down his spine.

Aurora closed her eyes and Orson felt a small surge of energy pass from her fingers into his head. The energy laced out, humming inside of him and throbbing to the same rhythm as the pulsating pain, gradually taking over until it was all he could feel. The energy disappeared and Orson sighed in disappointment.

"How do you feel now?" she asked and Orson opened his eyes. His headache was gone.

"Better." He touched his face in amazement. "Thanks. You're going to have to teach me how to do that. People seem to get a lot of headaches around me these days."

Aurora laughed and patted him on the shoulder. "Yes, you certainly do seem to give people headaches, Orson Bailey. Including me. That was an incredible risk you took, going to the Haunted Mountain alone. An incredible, *foolish* risk."

Orson shrugged. "I wasn't alone. Natalie was with me."

"Yes, I know. She told me what happened. At least, what she remembered. You had us very worried, Orson."

Orson looked at the Queen with dawning suspicion. "You sent Mange, didn't you?"

"Yes, of course."

"How did you know?"

Aurora smiled slyly. "When Lupus suddenly disappeared in the middle of our meeting, I had a feeling it had something to do with you. As impatient as you were the last time we talked, it was easy to figure what you were up to."

Orson felt his cheeks get hot. So much had happened since he called the wolf into the Haunted Mountain to help them against the shadowcats. Embarrassment quickly turned to regret as he remembered what had happened to Lupus. "Aurora," he said quietly, not able to look her in the face as he told her the news. "We got in trouble in the Haunted Mountain. We stepped into a trap, and I didn't know what else to do, so I called Lupus. He was able to save

Natalie and I, but he..."

"...is just fine," Aurora assured him. Orson looked up at her in astonishment.

"Lupus is okay?"

The Queen smiled and nodded. "Don't worry, he's a resourceful wolf. He escaped with some scratches and bruises, but nothing that won't heal quickly."

"I'm sorry," Orson said and meant it. "I didn't mean for him to get hurt."

Aurora shrugged. "He was just happy to know you were safe."

Orson fell back on the bed. Lupus was okay. The thought brought a tidal wave of relief washing over him. Everyone was okay: Natalie, Sarah and Lupus had all escaped with their lives. Despite the obvious disasters that could have happened, it had all turned out okay.

"You were lucky, Orson," Aurora read his thoughts. "You were all lucky to escape with your lives."

Orson sat back up, the relief quickly fading away. "I'm sorry," he said again. "I didn't want..."

"I was angry at first," Aurora interrupted him, rising from the bed and walking over to the window. "I thought you had learned your lesson after nearly being captured by the Nightmares during your first visit to the Haunted Mountain. When I discovered you had gone again, this time on purpose, I was furious. I couldn't understand how you could be so foolish and risk so many lives. It was incredibly selfish of you."

"Aurora," Orson started but the Queen waved him off.

"When Mange brought you back this time, I started trying to piece together where things had gone wrong. When I first met you, I admit I was worried that we were mistaken. You're so young and impatient, and to place all this pressure upon you...well, I wondered if you would be strong enough to handle it."

Orson looked down at the floor, thinking how he had felt the very same way, how he *still* felt doubts about everything he had learned, despite all he had been through.

Aurora continued. "Then I remembered how I felt when I first discovered I was a Dreamshaper. The doubts, the fear, the anger—I remember it all too well. I had those same impulsive thoughts when I was freshly introduced to this sudden new power that being a Dreamshaper brings. And that's when I realized my mistake."

"Your mistake?"

"Yes, Orson, *my* mistake. Rather than helping you through your fears, I ended up playing into them myself. When I heard you had gone alone to the Haunted Mountains the first time I was afraid, and not just for you. I was afraid for myself, for all of us. When you came back, I was so relieved you were safe that I was ready to lock you in a closet to keep you from hurting yourself. I didn't stop to think that there was more at stake for you than just the Dreamlands."

"Sarah," Orson said.

"Yes, your baby sister. It's hard to stay angry with someone who is only trying to do what they think is necessary to save someone they love."

"How is Sarah? She didn't get burned, did she?"

Aurora smiled brightly. "She's just fine. Not a mark on her. She's lucky to have a brother like you. You saved her life."

"Mange saved her life," Orson said.

"Mange saved you from the fire, but you saved your sister, Orson. She awoke back to the waking world a few hours ago. I'm sure she'll be happy to see you when you finally wake up."

A heavy weight lifted from Orson's heart, but a dozen questions still lingered. "What happened to Sithyrus?" he asked. "What did I do to it?"

"From what I've heard, you made it disappear, much the same as you did with your glasses. Quite the impressive feat, really, especially for someone who has only started his training. It bodes well for the upcoming struggles, I think."

"Will it be back?"

Aurora shrugged. "I don't know. I'm not sure exactly what you did to it, but for the moment it appears we're safe from the lizard."

Another thought struck Orson. "What about the Machine? I never even saw it. Is it still almost finished?"

"I doubt that the Machine is in the Haunted Mountain," Aurora answered. "The Nightmares likely have it hidden somewhere else, not quite so obvious as the Mountain, so that we won't be able to find it. That's one of the things we wanted to discuss at the meeting, and one of the reasons I urged you to wait until we had a chance to discuss what you had heard in your first visit. Even if you had looked for hours after defeating Sithyrus, you probably wouldn't have found any trace of the Machine."

Orson felt sheepish. Even though he had gone into the Haunted Mountain to save Sarah, he had entertained thoughts of destroying the Machine as well, if they'd found it on the way to his sister. "So it's not over, then," he said with a hard sigh.

"No," Aurora shook her head sadly. "It's not over. But by taking out Sithyrus, you've hurt the Nightmares deeply. You did well, Orson. Better than I could have ever envisioned. Now, however, you need to get some rest. You've earned a little time to relax, I think. We'll have time to talk about what happened in more detail later."

Before Aurora could get up, another thought occurred to Orson. "My eyes," he said, feeling just a little silly that he would be thinking about something as insignificant as his eyes with everything else going on around him. "Natalie said my eyes changed colour. Are they really blue?" Aurora smiled and nodded. "They're supposed to be brown. What happened?"

Aurora smiled and pointed to her own blue eyes. "Just another thing we Dreamshapers all have in common," she said simply.

"Will they change back in the waking world?"

"I don't know," Aurora said honestly. "Mine were

already blue before I became the last Dreamshaper. I'm sure you'll find out soon enough when you wake up in your own bed."

Aurora stood up and walked to the door. She started to step out of the room when Orson called out to her. She stopped and turned to face him.

"Is there any hope?"

She looked at him softly. "You've dealt the Nightmares a deep blow, taking away one of their best hunters. If nothing else, you've scared them. They're not holding all the cards anymore."

"Can we win?" Orson swallowed hard. A part of him wanted to believe that he had scared them, but he just couldn't. He had somehow managed to stop Sithyrus, but would that scare the Nightmares or just make them more angry and determined? And if they had gone so far as to kidnap Sarah from him before, what might they do now?

Aurora looked at him, her head tilted curiously. "We just might, Orson. Now that we have our Dreamshaper, we just might."

⌐ THIRTY THREE ⌐

Orson and Mike Spencer stood side by side on the far-left of the gymnasium, watching the other team carefully. Today was Friday, and that meant it was dodgeball day in gym. There were only a handful left on his team, but the other side, led by Jimmy Scrags, wasn't faring any better.

Mike was holding one of the soft red dodgeballs in his hands, looking for an opening to send it hurtling into the other team. Natalie had been knocked out early in the game and was cheering them on loudly. Despite their precarious situation, Orson smiled. It felt good to be cheered on for once. On the other side, Barton was calling out some less than encouraging words. Barton had knocked Natalie from the game early with a vicious throw that caught her by surprise, only to be knocked out in the next instant by Mike Spencer while the bully was still gloating over his victory.

Mike saw his opening and took a shot, whipping the ball right at Frank. The dodgeball caught the bigger boy square in the chest and a cheer rose up from Mike and Orson's team. At the last second, though, Jimmy reached out and snagged the ball before it could touch the floor, saving Frank from elimination. The cheer died down in dramatic disappointment. Jimmy had caught Mike's throw, eliminating Mike from the game. That left Orson without either of his new friends against Jimmy and Frank.

With Jimmy and Frank remaining, Orson didn't like his chances. Both bullies were holding dodgeballs—Jimmy was holding two: one ball in each meaty hand—and looking at Orson like predators eyeing their next victim. Jimmy motioned to Frank to move a few steps to the side, making it harder for Orson to keep an eye on both of them.

With a sudden roar, both bullies attacked Orson, Jimmy aiming for Orson's feet while Frank threw up high. Orson had seen them do this before—he had been the victim of this tactic on many occasions—and was ready for it. Jumping into the air, he leapfrogged Jimmy's ball just as Frank's hit him smack in the shoulder. Reaching awkwardly, he managed to snag Frank's ball in the crook of his elbow, holding onto it tightly as he landed back on the floor. Frank gaped in astonishment as Orson managed to keep control of the ball, knocking the sidekick bully from the game.

Orson smiled as he gripped the ball, almost as shocked as Frank that he had actually caught the throw. He was used to dodging the dodgeballs, not catching them himself. Even Jimmy looked stunned; his cheeks flushed with rage as he watched his thug forced to leave the game by the hands of his worst enemy.

"Lucky catch, Strings," he snarled, brandishing his own ball like a weapon. In Jimmy's hand, Orson supposed it was a weapon.

"What's the matter Jimmy, not used to being alone?" Orson replied, egging Jimmy on. From the sidelines, Natalie and Mike cheered him enthusiastically. Frank and Barton both roared encouragement to their leader. Despite that there were still several members on each team, the rest of the class had fallen into a hush, clearly knowing where the real battle was.

With a raucous war cry, Jimmy stepped forward and launched his ball like a missile, aiming directly for Orson's head. The ball was on course, flying right for Orson's face, ready to do some serious damage on impact. At the last second, Orson dipped to the left and the ball went soaring harmlessly past.

In the same motion, Orson threw his ball as hard as

possible. Jimmy was so busy watching in astonishment as his own throw missed that he didn't react to Orson's throw until it was too late. Orson's ball was leveled straight for Jimmy's chest; at the last moment, Jimmy tried to duck but couldn't get out of the way in time. Instead of hitting the bully in the chest, the ball caught him straight in the nose, surprising Jimmy and sending him sprawling backwards to the floor. The ball bounced lightly on the floor beside the bully and rolled into the feet of another kid.

Jimmy Scrags, the dodgeball king, had just been eliminated. By Orson Bailey.

"No fair," Jimmy said, touching his nose and finding a speckle of blood. Orson's throw had given him a bleeding nose. "He hit me in the face! That doesn't count!"

"You threw for his head first, Jimmy," their teacher scolded. "Besides, you ducked into it. It counts. You're out."

Natalie and Mike screamed in triumph as Jimmy was forced from the game. Orson didn't even feel the ball that hit him in the shoulder, ending his own game. It didn't matter which team won; he had beaten Jimmy Scrags. That was the only victory that mattered. Pumping a fist into the air, knowing he may pay for it somewhere down the road, Orson went to join his friends in celebration on the sidelines.

Dreamshaper

The pleasant morning sun shone warmly through his curtains as Orson lay in his bed, feeling relaxed and recharged for the first time in days. It was Saturday, so there had been no alarm clock to wake him up, and his mother was more than happy to let him sleep a little later. She had her arms full with Sarah, anyway. Ever since Thursday morning, when the hospital had called to tell Mrs. Bailey that Sarah had miraculously woken up, she had poured every bit of love into her mysteriously recovered daughter as she possibly could. For a change, Orson wasn't jealous of his little sister; she had earned all the attention she could get, at least for right now. Later this afternoon, Orson thought he would even read to her from a few of his favorite Sergeant Sharpe comics.

Orson grabbed his glasses from the stand beside his bed and pulled them over his nose, sighing under their unwanted weight but not completely disheartened. He had enjoyed the brief periods of freedom without them in the Dreamlands, but compared to everything else that had happened they hardly seemed worthy of complaint.

Slipping out from his bed covers, Orson stretched his tired muscles, still stiff and sore but in much better shape than they were a few days ago. The aches had started to fade, and underneath the slight discomfort he felt stronger than ever. Dressed only in his favorite Sergeant Sharpe underpants, he walked over to the mirror and looked at the crystal clear reflection.

After Aurora had spoken with him, Orson had found a mirror and discovered that Natalie and the Queen had been right; his eyes had turned blue. Now, however, as he looked into his bedroom mirror in the waking world, they had returned to their normal deep shade of brown. He had rather enjoyed the change—brown was such a boring colour.

Mrs. Bailey had been so shocked and relieved to have Sarah back on Thursday that she had kept Orson home from school, and the three of them spent the entire day together, once the doctors had finished their tests. For the first time that he could remember, Orson had actually felt a little disappointed to be missing school; he was looking forward to talking with Natalie and Mike—Natalie especially. On Friday, yesterday, he had more than made up for the missed day, talking Natalie's ear off at recess as they talked about their adventure in the Haunted Mountain before his unprecedented victory over Jimmy in the dodgeball game. It just may have been the best day of school he had ever had.

Now, as he stretched his arms over his head, Orson

accidentally knocked a piece of paper from the top of his dresser. He knew what was on the paper and hadn't looked at it since returning from the Dreamlands. Sithyrus was gone now, so there was no point in looking at the picture he had drawn. He had been surprised to even find it in the pocket of his pants again; it had a creepy way of turning up unexpectedly. Plucking it off the floor, he decided that he should finally rid himself of it for good.

He pinched the paper between his fingers, preparing to rip it, but stopped. It wouldn't hurt to take one last peek before he destroyed it. A simple reminder of everything he had accomplished in recent weeks. One look, then it would be sent where it belonged, in several pieces at the bottom of his trash bin.

Orson unfolded the paper. It nearly slipped out of his hands as he stared down in disbelief. The page was empty.

The picture he had drawn of Sithyrus had vanished. There wasn't a single marking where the lizard had once been; it was as though the drawing had never been made in the first place.

A cool breeze fluttered through his open window and Orson shivered for a moment. Rather than trashing the empty page, he folded it carefully back up and slid it into the top drawer of his dresser, hiding it under his shirts. As he pushed it deeper underneath his clothes, his fingers brushed against another piece of paper that he had carefully hidden earlier. He pulled out the paper, wondering if the message on this second piece had disappeared as well, but it was still there, a riddle he had yet to figure out. The words *Armed Sherpa* stared up at him from the note and he frowned.

Natalie had asked him once if he had been sure the anagram had meant to say *Armed Sherpa*, but he had brushed it off. It was the only thing he could come up with, and he had tried dozens of possible solutions. Now, as he stared at the words, he wondered if she hadn't been right after all. Today was Saturday, and he nothing but time on his hands, so he decided maybe he would give it one last try.

Carrying the note over to his desk, Orson grabbed a pencil and started reworking the letters. His fingers worked with a mind of their own, moving the pencil smoothly over the paper as though they had been waiting for this opportunity to solve the anagram properly. *Armed* disappeared, replaced by another word that made him gasp lightly: *Dream*.

He didn't need the pencil to figure out what the second word would say. *Sherpa* was not Sherpa at all. He wrote it out anyway and laughed lightly when he discovered that the anagram wasn't supposed to be divided into two words at all. That had been his mistake all along. Underneath the two new words he had created on the paper, he combined them together into one longer, unmistakable word.

Dreamshaper.

Orson laughed again and stared down at the word. He couldn't believe he hadn't thought of it before, though he *had* been fairly busy. He buried the note back in his dresser, beside the empty paper. Opening his bedroom door, he paused and listened. He could hear his mother downstairs in the kitchen, singing happily alongside Sarah's amused giggling and chirping. Listening to them both he smiled, something that was starting to become a little more natural these days.

Maybe, just maybe, everything would be fine after all.

J.W. Crawford

234

Although J.W. Crawford has been following his dream of writing since Junior High School, his underlying passion for writing Young Adult fiction stems from his career as an elementary teacher. Author of two short stories, *Zombiquin* and *Shadow Puppets*, Crawford is proud to debut his first novel with *Dreamshaper* and continue to share his passion for writing and make his first cannonball splash into a pool of talented children's writers.

Raised in the small mountain town of Jasper, Alberta, Canada, Crawford nevertheless continues to be an avid Edmonton Oilers hockey fan.

Fans can reach J.W. Crawford at
JWCDreamshaper@gmail.com

J.W. Crawford

LaVergne, TN USA
28 March 2010

177403LV00004B/6/P